Kate Hewitt

Return
to the
Island

bookouture

Published by Bookouture in 2021

An imprint of Storyfire Ltd.
Carmelite House
50 Victoria Embankment
London EC4Y 0DZ

www.bookouture.com

ISBN: 978-1-80019-229-4
eBook ISBN: 978-1-80019-228-7

Dedicated to my own Ellen, who helped me write this s
and to Caroline, who agreed with me. Love you
Also dedicated to Chris, because he asked—and he's a

CHAPTER ONE

Amherst Island, June 1919

"No matter how you look at it, the numbers don't add up." Sighing, Rose McCafferty rose from the kitchen table and went to fill the kettle.

Ellen Copley sat at the table and gazed at the column of figures her Aunt Rose had been showing her in Dyle's accounting books with their worn cloth covers. She could picture her Uncle Dyle sitting at this very table, the oil lamp casting its comforting, flickering glow, his head bent over the books before he looked up with his ready smile, a flash of humor always lighting his Irish eyes.

But he was gone now and her aunt was right; the farm accounts did not add up. Like so many other small farmers in the desolation of postwar Canada, the outgoings exceeded whatever was going in. The whole world over had been wearied and damaged, and not just by the guns booming in Europe, or the influenza that had ripped across the entire world. Everyone was struggling to make ends meet, or even simply to get them to see each other.

Yet sitting in the cozy kitchen with one of the cats curled up on her lap, the summer sunshine pouring in through the open top half of the kitchen door, the sky outside pale blue and dotted with fleecy clouds, Ellen couldn't quite make herself believe that the McCafferty farm was actually at risk. She certainly didn't *want* to believe it.

It had been three months since she'd stepped off Captain Jonah's little ferry boat and walked through the soft, moonlit darkness all the way to the McCafferty farm. It had been a trip, quite literally, down memory lane, for with each step Ellen had taken, she'd remembered her former life on Amherst Island, this jewel nestled in the ruffled, blue-green waters of Lake Ontario.

She'd recalled how she'd first come to the island, shy and uncertain, nearly thirteen years old, adrift in the world with her father in New Mexico and her Aunt Ruth and Uncle Hamish back in Vermont seeming happy enough to see the back of her.

How she'd blossomed under her Aunt Rose's gentle care and Uncle Dyle's infectious good humor, surrounded by her boisterous cousins, who had become as good as siblings to her. How she'd made so many good friends—two brothers Jed and Lucas Lyman at the top of that list, along with Louisa Hopper, who had accompanied her one summer to Amherst Island, admittedly to Ellen's displeasure, and was now Jed's wife.

Things had changed in the fifteen years since she'd first come to Amherst Island, a shy girl growing in confidence, gaining affection. The war had changed them all. It had left its painful, often invisible mark on nearly every islander's life in one way or another. Gone were so many of the young boys Ellen had been at school with—some forever, others changed indelibly by the war.

She hated seeing the haggard looks of grief and despair on so many young men's faces, men who had been but carefree farm boys a short time ago, but who now could not forget the horrors of war—horrors they'd seen, endured, and in some cases committed. Horrors Ellen knew herself, at least in some part, having experienced them while serving as a nurse in France.

The worst, though, was the blankness she often saw on her cousin Peter's face, as if he were indifferent to everything around him, a visitor in his own house, and one who would be leaving shortly, while Ellen herself finally felt as if she'd come home.

Three months ago, when she'd arrived at the McCaffertys' door, Aunt Rose had swept her up into a hug before bursting into tears. She'd held her apron to her face, dabbing her eyes and trying to laugh.

"Oh Ellen, what a welcome! I am sorry. It's just I'm so very, very glad to see you. It's been so long. Too long. And I thought… I feared…" Rose shook her head, not wanting to put that terrible fear into words. She'd dropped her apron, her eyes still filled with tears even as she gave Ellen the most wonderful smile. "I really am so glad. It's been so long, with all your years in Glasgow."

For the three years before the war had started and Ellen had enlisted as a nurse, she'd been studying at the prestigious Glasgow School of Art, a life that now seemed like the most distant of memories.

Back then, before the war, she'd been looking forward to a future as a lecturer in drawing. A future that had glittered with promise: she'd had an exhibition at one of Glasgow's best art galleries, and she'd also had a fiancé, or almost. All of it was long gone now, nothing more than memories and regret.

"I always wanted to come back," Ellen had told her aunt. "I always meant to, and I'm here now, Aunt Rose."

"So you are," Aunt Rose had murmured, and hugged her again tightly. "So you are."

The truth was, though, that Ellen had not entirely thought through her return to the island; it had been an instinctive decision, borne from her heart rather than her head. Amherst Island was where she belonged, more than Glasgow, more than Seaton, where her Uncle Hamish lived, and more than with her father, who was still working the rail yards out in New Mexico. The island was her heart's home, the place where she felt most herself, most comfortable and most alive. Coming here after the ravages and heartache of war had felt not only right, but absolutely necessary.

Within just a few days, Ellen had realized there was no question about whether she would stay on the island, at least not in her own mind. Although she could have gone back to Glasgow, where she still had friends and a house of her own, despite it being the country of her birth, it had never been home the way the island was, with its tree-shaded lanes and gentle hills, surrounded by the shimmering blue-green waters of Lake Ontario.

Aunt Rose had made up the bed in the little room at the back of the house that had always been hers and Ellen had settled into farming life almost—*almost*—as if she'd never left. Seven years on and she felt older, wearier, wiser, and so very glad to be home.

She'd soon learned that the farm had struggled in the last year, since her Uncle Dyle had taken ill. He'd left fields fallow, and with Peter fighting in France, the crops had withered or rotted where they lay. Rose had done her best to keep things going, but it was too much for one woman even with the help of her children, now mostly grown and away from home. Caroline, or Caro as she'd always been called, was twenty-two and while she had stayed and helped with the farm work, Sarah, now twenty-one, had gone to Gananoque on the mainland to be a schoolteacher. At nineteen Gracie was on scholarship at Queen's, determined to become a modern career woman and Andrew, the youngest at sixteen, went to high school in Kingston but wanted to leave school and help at home. Rose had forbidden it, determined that all her children would get an education and have opportunities, especially in these troubling times.

Between Ellen, Rose, Caro, and Peter, they had just about managed to keep things afloat, the crops planted in May before Ellen had arrived. But wheat prices had fallen and the money they received for the milk they sent to the cheese factory in

Emerald, on the far side of the island, was not enough to keep them clothed and fed.

"I don't know what to do," Rose said now as she poured them both cups of tea from the big brown pot. "Part of me thinks I should just sell up, buy some little place in Stella or even on the mainland, but I hate the thought of leaving the home that Dyle and I made together. We came here twenty-five years ago now, Ellen, with nothing but hope in our hearts and a few worn coins clanking together in Dyle's pocket. And, in truth, I don't know if anyone would buy such a poky place as this. Dyle managed to eke a living out of it, but..." She shrugged helplessly, sorrow and worry clouding her faded blue eyes. "These are hard times for everyone now."

"I know," Ellen answered quietly. The newspapers were full of the discontent that had seized Canada, along with much of the world. Workers' strikes, food still rationed, and no jobs to be had for the returning soldiers, often embittered as well as weary. It was the same hard story everywhere, with no solace to be found.

"What do you think I should do, Ellen?" Rose asked as she joined her at the table and poured milk into both their teacups.

"Oh Aunt Rose, I wish I knew." Ellen smiled tiredly. She knew her aunt sorely missed the guidance of her husband Dyle, and Peter, as eldest son and now twenty-three years old, was not yet fulfilling his filial duty and interesting himself in the farm—or in anything. But that was something neither of them liked to talk about. As Rose would say, with a brave smile, "Peter's only been back from France for a few months. It's early days; he'll come back to himself, once he's settled in." She always said this with brittle determination though, and never in her son's hearing.

Soon after she had arrived back on Amherst Island, Ellen had offered Aunt Rose her own modest savings, given to her by her almost-fiancé Henry McAvoy upon his death seven years ago, with the sinking of the *Titanic*, although no one, not even Aunt

Rose, knew about that sorrowful chapter in her history. Ellen had never had a chance to accept his proposal, as he'd made it before sailing. She'd promised to give her answer upon his return, but he never had returned and so her acceptance had remained unspoken.

The relationship had been so fragile, so secret, even from his disapproving parents, that Ellen had never felt comfortable telling anyone the truth. Sometimes she wondered what the truth even was. Had she loved Henry, or could she simply have learned to love him, in time? Now she would never know.

She'd bought a small house in Glasgow with the money he had left her and invested what little was left. Her old friend Ruby and her brother Dougie lived in that little house, dear friends whom Ellen still missed, even as she remained determined to stay on the island, at least until the situation with the farm was stable. In any case, Rose had done as Ellen had expected and stoutly refused her offer.

"I'm not going to take your money to keep this farm afloat, Ellen. You'll need it yourself one day."

"This farm is my home," Ellen had insisted. "I want you to take it, Aunt Rose. For my sake as much as yours. I can't think of a better way to spend it."

But her aunt would not be moved. "There has to be some other way," she'd stated firmly. "I won't be taking the inheritance of my niece, especially when you're as good as my own daughter. Not for this. Not for anything. It wouldn't be right."

Despite her aunt's protestations, Ellen had tried to help where she could, using her own money to buy a few treats and trinkets for Caro, and sending parcels of cake and lemonade to Gracie and Andrew in Kingston. But such small gestures did nothing to help the greater issue of the McCaffertys' failing livelihood.

"What about selling off only some of the farm's acreage?" Ellen suggested hesitantly as she took a sip of tea. "Just a few acres, to tide you over until the harvest? We aren't able to farm all the land this summer as it is…" Several fields lay fallow because Rose hadn't had the manpower to plant them all. Neighbors had helped when they could, but everyone was struggling.

"Oh Ellen, I've already thought about selling some of the back pasture." Rose took a sip of tea, her face drawn in weary lines. "As much as I hate the thought of breaking this place up, it might be the only answer. *If* someone will buy those acres. I don't know if anyone on the island will. I'm not the only one thinking of selling, you know."

"What about Mr. Lyman?" The Lymans' farm adjoined the McCaffertys', and John Lyman worked the land with his older son Jed, who had returned from the war damaged in both spirit and body; he'd lost an arm in the evacuation of Villiers-Cotterets, the field hospital where Ellen had been serving as a nurse. Since his return to the island a few months ago, he'd retreated into himself, and become more taciturn than ever, much to her dismay.

Always a man of quiet reserve, Ellen feared he'd become positively surly in the wake of his own tragedies, understandable yet no less concerning. During the war, he and his wife Louisa had become estranged, and she'd moved back to Vermont when Jed had enlisted, returning only when he'd come back wounded near the end of the war. Then, right on the eve of the Armistice, they'd lost little Thomas—their first and only child—to the terrible influenza. It was a great deal of sorrow for them both to bear, and after the funeral here on the island Louisa had returned to her parents in Seaton. Although still married, they did not live as husband and wife, and Ellen wondered if they ever would again.

She had only seen Jed a handful of times since she'd come back to the island, while his brother Lucas she hadn't seen at all. After he'd been demobbed he'd gone straight to Toronto and back to his old life as a junior lawyer at a successful practice, although he'd written her several letters since she'd returned.

Thinking of the two Lyman men always made Ellen feel tangled up inside; once she'd believed herself in love with Jed, but years ago he'd married Louisa instead. As for Lucas… he'd always been a dear friend, but when he'd declared his own romantic intentions towards her during their days in Kingston, an unhappy awkwardness had sprung up between them that even four years of war hadn't quite erased. The last time she'd seen him, while nursing in France, he'd as good as declared his intentions again, and Ellen had not known how to respond… or even how to feel about it.

"Do you think John would want more land?" Rose asked with a dubious shake of her head, taking Ellen out of her troubled reminiscences.

"He's got some hired men helping him, and I've heard he's talked about acquiring more livestock. He might want the pasture for the cattle." More and more, it looked as if the future for farming might be in livestock rather than dairy or wheat, but the farms on the island were too small to have the hundreds, or even thousands, of cattle required to be truly prosperous.

Ellen had read in the newspaper about the huge cattle farms out west, in Alberta. Thousands and thousands of cattle, and acres and acres of empty grassland for them to roam. It was a good life if you had the means, but it wasn't the way things were done on Amherst Island, where islanders had been farming their smallholdings for nearly a century.

"I suppose there's no harm asking Mr. Lyman at least, is there?" she asked, trying to inject a note of pragmatic cheerfulness into her voice.

Rose sighed. "I'd hate him to buy it out of pity."

"I don't think he would." Ellen smiled wryly. "Times are too hard for that."

"Yes, that's true." Rose straightened and gave one brisk nod as she did her best to banish her worries. "You're right, we could talk to him, at least. And then we'd have to see the man Dyle dealt with at the bank in Kingston. He'll help arrange things, I'm sure, so it's all above board and proper."

"Yes…"

Rose bit her lip. "Would you… would you mind going, Ellen? I don't think I can face it. The bank… all those papers and bills… " Rose smiled in apology and Ellen reached over to squeeze her hand, conscious of how much her aunt had coped with in the long years she'd been gone—widowed, her oldest son going to war, two daughters having left to find their own fortunes, and now a failing farm she was trying so desperately to keep going.

"Of course I'll go, Aunt Rose," she said as they sat in the pool of afternoon sunshine, their hands still clasped. "I'll do whatever I can to help you… and the farm."

CHAPTER TWO

Later that day, as the sun was starting to sink towards the tranquil surface of Lake Ontario, Ellen walked the familiar path between the McCafferty and Lyman farms. The leaves on the birch and maple trees that served as an informal border between the two properties were bright and green, and everything felt fresh with the promise of early summer, the air sweet with the smell of wild strawberries. Black flies buzzed around Ellen's head and she swatted them away as she walked by the pond, its waters still in the oncoming twilight, the last of the sunlight burnishing its placid surface like a golden mirror.

How strange and yet how right it felt to be back on the island, walking this familiar and beloved path. The view had changed little over the course of the years, but Ellen knew she was no longer the shy yet carefree young girl who had once skipped across the path, a sketchbook under her arm, intent on an afternoon's drawing.

In truth, she hadn't picked up a pencil or paintbrush in years and, more depressingly, she hadn't even wanted to. Her friend and mentor from her Glasgow days, Norah Neilson Gray, had been inspired by their time serving as nurses for wounded French soldiers at Royaumont Abbey, and had written Ellen a letter describing the painting she was working on, a portrait of a Belgian refugee, that she hoped would be exhibited.

Ellen had felt no such inspiration when she'd been nursing. It had been all she could do simply to survive the days, each one holding its own horror and challenge as the wounded had poured into the hospital and the sky had been lit orange from the shelling. And now that she was back on the island, she wanted only to forget the memories that still plagued her nights and haunted her dreams—skies orange from shelling, the crack and boom of guns, the men who came into the abbey hospital with sightless eyes and shocked faces, missing limbs and torn-open stomachs… No, there was nothing from those years that she wished to capture on canvas, or sketch with a pencil. Nothing at all.

Even here, in the place she loved more than any other, with the sun's final rays glinting off the pond in a shimmer of gold, the leaves on the trees as jewel-bright as the feathers of a peacock, she felt nothing but a weary sort of satisfaction at being back where she'd been happiest. Once, her fingers would have been practically itching to clasp a bit of charcoal, but not now. Now she simply wanted to be. Perhaps in time the urge to draw or paint would return. But she was too busy with the concerns of the farm to worry much about it now, or even care about the lack of desire she felt in herself. After all she'd seen in France, art seemed like a luxury, even a frivolity, that neither she, nor anyone else, could afford.

A dog barked as Ellen approached the Lyman farmhouse, the first stars coming out in a violet, twilit sky, and then fell silent as he recognized Ellen. The old beagle trotted up to her and lowered his head for a pat, his drooping ears nearly touching the ground, and she caressed its silky head before mounting the weathered porch steps.

She hesitated, her hand at the door, part of her deeply reluctant to knock and disturb Jed. Things had become so strained between them, any remnant of their old friendship feeling like a distant memory in light of all that had happened over the years—Jed and Louisa's marriage, as well as the war with all its injury, grief, and loss. Yet they had to move forward somehow, into whatever future they could fashion. Taking a deep breath, Ellen knocked on the back door.

Jed answered after a few moments, looking tired and careworn. He wore his shirtsleeve pinned neatly up to his shoulder, the other one rolled up his strong left forearm. He nodded a curt hello to Ellen.

"May I come in, Jed?" Ellen asked and he stepped aside with a gruff apology.

"We don't get many visitors these days. Coffee?"

"Yes, please."

Jed had become adept at doing things with a single left hand, and now he poured Ellen a coffee from the tin pot keeping warm on the range. Ellen knew better than to ask to help; her years in France had taught her that those with amputations needed to manage on their own, for their own dignity and wellbeing. Helping would hurt him more, and in any case Jed had never been one for being mollycoddled.

"How are things here?" Ellen asked, trying for a friendly, casual tone, as she sipped from her mug.

Jed shrugged, bracing one hip against the range. "Same as everywhere else, I suppose. We do all right, but it's not easy."

"No." Ellen sipped her coffee as she eyed Jed covertly. Lines ran from his nose to his mouth, lines that she didn't think had been there a year ago, when she'd seen him in France. Jed's return to the island had been difficult, thanks to his injury, but also to his absent wife Louisa and the loss of his son Thomas. Louisa Lyman had left the island when Jed went to war, returning only for a few months when he'd come back wounded. After Thomas' death she'd returned to Seaton once more and seemed to have no intention of coming back to her husband.

But Ellen knew better than to ask Jed about Louisa. Their own past was too tangled and fraught to speak easily of those days—although Jed had never made a declaration of love or even affection, there had been both an ease and expectation between them that once had filled Ellen with hope.

Once, and only once, had he mentioned the words they should have had, and Ellen had cut him off before more could be said. It had been too late anyway; he'd already pledged himself to Louisa. But more than one lonely evening had passed with her wondering just what those words might have been.

"You and your father seem to be doing all right," she said as she took a sip of coffee, banishing futile thoughts of what-if from her mind. "I saw your fields as I walked by the pond—the corn's already coming up nicely."

Jed merely gave a grunt in reply, and sipped his coffee. Ellen gazed at him with a growing sense of despair. Jed had never had the ease of conversation like Lucas, but there had been a familiarity between them that would have once made a conversation like this one a simple pleasure. Instead, now it felt like so much hard work, Ellen decided to do away with pleasantries.

"Aunt Rose is thinking of selling some land," she said bluntly. "The farm's too big for her to manage now with Dyle gone, and the truth is we need the money. I thought you should get first refusal, since your land borders the McCaffertys', and I heard your father was thinking of taking on more livestock, so I thought he could use some extra pasture—"

Jed shook his head, the movement definitive enough that Ellen fell silent, feeling chastised. "We can barely manage what we have." He gestured to his shoulder, the missing limb. "You think I can manage more?"

Ellen heard the bitterness in his voice and saw the anger snapping in his gray eyes, and her heart twisted in sympathy. "I thought your father was thinking of hiring more men."

"We can't afford more men."

"The price of beef is going to rise, so they say—"

"We can't buy your aunt's land, Ellen." Jed's voice was curt and Ellen felt rebuked.

"I understand," she said quietly.

Jed dumped his coffee in the big stone sink, the mug rattling in the bottom. He turned back to Ellen, a challenge in his eyes as well as a dismissal. He wanted her to leave.

"I'm sorry for asking," she said, and Jed just shrugged.

Ellen hesitated, wanting to say something more, wanting to reach him, but everything about him—his expression, the tension in his body, the anger in his eyes—made her too apprehensive to say anything else. She tried not to feel stung by his overt unfriendliness.

She rose from her chair, even though she hadn't finished her drink. "Thank you for the coffee," she said quietly, putting the mug in the sink with Jed's.

At the door, she turned back, again wanting to say something, but it was all too clear that Jed was simply waiting for her to leave.

"Goodbye, then," she said.

Jed didn't reply.

Dusk had fallen as she headed back towards the McCafferty farm, skirting the pond that was now a dark oval, brushed by moonlight, weary in both body and spirit. Shadows gathered under the trees and the sky had darkened from gold to violet to indigo, the stars twinkling so high above like promises no one could keep.

Ellen drew a deep breath, breathing in the island she so loved—the sharp tang of cedar and pine, the sun-warmed scent of berries and daisies that lingered on into the evening, the honest, earthy smells of animal and dirt. In the twilit distance, a cow lowed, a soft, mournful sound. Ellen let her breath out in a disconsolate sigh.

She had no solution for Aunt Rose, but far worse was the realization that she may have lost Jed's friendship forever. Of course, she'd lost it long ago, when he'd married Louisa. But even though there had been a certain proper and respectful distance between them upon his marriage, she'd still counted him as a friend, a good one. Someone who understood her, who loved her, in his own, quiet way. Now he seemed more like a stranger, and a hostile one at that.

He was cutting everyone off, retreating further and further into himself, because of the losses he'd experienced in life, and she had no idea what she could do about it, if anything.

Back at the McCafferty farm, Rose had already gone to bed. Ellen came in quietly, the old floorboards creaking as she tiptoed across the kitchen floor, feeling her way in the moonlit darkness.

"You needn't be so quiet." The voice, coming from the kitchen table, was disembodied in the darkness.

"Oh!" Ellen pressed her hand to her chest. "Peter," she said, as she blinked and began to make out her cousin's shape sitting at the kitchen table. "What are you doing here in the dark? It's getting late—"

"No point in wasting precious oil," Peter answered with a shrug, his voice flat. "And, in any case, I couldn't sleep."

"I could make you some hot milk," Ellen suggested. "Sometimes that helps."

"Nothing helps, Ellen." Peter sounded so bleak and yet so matter-of-fact that Ellen's heart ached. Where was the little boy who used to run up and down the stairs, whooping and pretending he was an Indian, armed with a wooden spoon?

"Oh, Peter." She moved to the icebox where the leftover milk from that morning was keeping cool with the last of the melting ice. "Let me make you some, anyway. It can't hurt." She felt a desperate need to do something—she couldn't help Jed, but perhaps she could help Peter.

Her cousin didn't answer as Ellen stirred up the coals in the range and poured some milk in a pan to heat. The kitchen was quiet and dark, the only sounds the embers settling in the grate and the gentle hiss of the milk warming in the pan. Outside, a whippoorwill gave its familiar, lonely call.

Peter shifted in his chair, his face unreadable in the darkness. "Do you get nightmares, Ellen?" he asked and she stiffened in surprise, one hand still stretched up for one of the mugs hanging on hooks above the sink.

"Sometimes," she said, turning slowly to face him. "Sometimes, especially about the mad rush in 1918, and the evacuation from Villiers-Cotterets, back to Royaumont. I can still hear the whistling of the shells, and feel the earth shake when they landed." Peter nodded, and Ellen asked cautiously, "What about you? Do you get nightmares, Peter? Is that why you can't sleep?"

In the three months since she'd been back on the island, Peter had never spoken about his three years of military service. He'd hardly spoken at all since his return. He would busy himself with farm work, some days working until he was wrung out and exhausted, other days leaving a job half-done, only to wander off and return after dark, refusing to answer any questions, seeming as if he were existing in another place, a different universe.

Rose had tried everything, from leaving him alone to demanding he talk to her, all attempts to bring the light of the living back into Peter's eyes. None of it had worked; Peter sat and ate with them, moved about the house and farm, but it was as if the person inhabiting the young, vital body wasn't there anymore. He had gone somewhere else, and no one knew where.

"I don't get nightmares," Peter told her as he leaned back in his chair, angling his head so the moonlight caught his cheekbone, and Ellen could see how closed his expression was. "Not if I stay awake."

"Oh, Peter…" Sympathy and apprehension tangled inside her. Too many young men, young men who'd once had hope and a future, had the same blankness inside that Peter did. She'd seen it at Royaumont, and she saw it here on the island. The trouble was, no one knew what to do about it.

"Don't feel sorry for me," he told her sharply. "I couldn't stand that, Ellen. I only mentioned it to you because I thought you might be a little bit the same. You know what it was like out there, at least a little."

"A little," Ellen agreed. But serving as a nurse on the Front had been far safer and easier than serving as a soldier. She'd dodged shells and taken cover from the bombing, but she'd never had to hold a gun, much less shoot it. "Perhaps you should talk to Jed, or one of the other boys who came home…" Sadly there were only a handful of them.

"Oh, Ellen." Peter shook his head and gave a weary, cynical laugh. "The last thing any of us want to do is talk about it. Do you think we'd like to gather together like a group of old women with their knitting, and chat about the old days?" His voice was hard and flat. "It's hard enough to forget as it is."

"If you can't forget, then perhaps talking would help." Ellen took the pan of milk off the hob and poured it into a mug. But when she offered it to Peter, he shook his head and rose from the table.

"No, thank you. I don't actually want help to sleep." In the darkness, she could not make out his expression, and she watched with both sorrow and alarm as he headed for the kitchen door. "I think I'll walk."

"It's dark, Peter, at least take a light—"

"There's a moon." They both glanced at the rising, full moon, queen of a tranquil sky, bathing the farmyard in lambent silver. "Lovely, isn't it?" Peter remarked. "No need to be afraid of it now."

It wasn't until he'd gone outside with the quiet creak of the door that Ellen realized what he meant, how a full moon on the battlefield had made it easy for German snipers to pick soldiers off. She shivered despite the balmy night air, the peaceful silence of a summer's evening, because the remark made her realize afresh how haunted Peter was by the war. How all the veterans must be. Would they ever recover? Or would the whole world live in thrall to those four desperate, dreadful years?

She drank the milk herself, alone in the dark of the kitchen, and then headed upstairs to bed. She doubted tonight was the first time Peter had gone walking out in the darkness, and she knew she simply had to trust that he would make his way back safely.

Caro peeked her head out of her bedroom as Ellen came down the hall. "Did you only just get back from the Lymans', Ellen?"

"A little while ago." Rose had told Caro and Peter her plans to sell some of the farm land at suppertime, and neither of them had protested. It was clear to everyone that something had to be done, and Ellen had left for the Lymans' farm as soon as the dishes were cleared.

"And what did he say?" Caro asked. She stepped into the hallway, barefoot and in her nightgown, one golden-brown plait lying over her shoulder, her forehead creased with worry. She was twenty-two years old, but she looked as if she carried the weight of the world on her young shoulders, often working from dawn to dusk to keep the farm going.

"Jed's not interested," Ellen admitted. "Wouldn't entertain the notion for a moment. Things are hard over there too, it seems, in more ways than one." She sighed, shaking her head. "Will any of the men who came back ever be themselves again, do you think?"

"I hope so, in time." Caro wrapped her arms around herself. "In time, surely," she repeated, as if to convince herself. "It's early days yet. That's what Mother keeps saying about Peter."

Ellen met Caro's worried gaze in silent acknowledgment of Peter's troubles. "Yes, in time," she agreed, although she felt far from convinced. But time was the only thing they had, the only thing they could pin their hopes on. "I'm going to Kingston tomorrow, to talk to the man at the bank. It won't be a very pleasant chore, but Kingston is always nice to visit. Why don't you come along?" She smiled, hoping to lift Caro's troubled spirits. "Fancy a day gadding about town? We could say hello to Gracie and Andrew, as well."

"I would, but I doubt you'll be doing much gadding," Caro replied wryly. "Gracie and Andrew will be home in a few weeks, and in any case, there's too much work to be done here. I can't miss a whole day out."

Ellen laid a hand on her arm. "You work so hard, Caro. Everyone does."

"And you work the hardest, Ellen. It seems as if you're always weeding the garden, or working the mangle."

"I'm glad to help." She far preferred being busy than left alone with her thoughts, wondering what her future held, or if it really could be on her beloved island.

"And Mother is glad you're back. I am, too. It helps, to have the company." She hesitated, her eyebrows drawing together. "You won't... you won't go away again?"

"And where would I go?" Ellen answered with a soft laugh.

"Back to Glasgow. You have a house there, don't you? And that art school would want you back, I'm sure. Mother showed us the bit in the paper about your exhibition years ago now, but still. You could have that all back again."

"Did she?" Ellen shook her head wryly. "I didn't know she'd even seen the article."

"Your landlady sent it. She was terribly proud of you, and we were too, of course."

"Dear Norah." Ellen smiled and then sighed. "It all seems a long time ago now. Another life."

"So you don't have a hankering to go back to Glasgow, live a glamorous city life as a lady artist?" Caro spoke teasingly, but even in the darkness of the hallway, Ellen saw the real worry in her eyes.

"Not a bit, Caro," she said firmly. "When I came back here, I was coming home. I felt it, deep in my bones. I enjoyed my days in Glasgow, but even though I was born there, it never felt like home the way Amherst Island has. I'm staying here for as long as you'll have me."

"You know how long that is," Caro answered, drawing her into a quick hug. "Forever, or at least until you marry and have your own family."

"I hardly see that happening," Ellen answered with a rueful laugh. "I'm twenty-eight years old, most certainly on the shelf."

"And I'm already twenty-two," Caro acknowledged. "And not many men left to marry, at that. But who knows what the future may bring? We both can hope." Caro did not sound particularly optimistic.

"Yes, of course," Ellen said firmly. "Especially for you. You're a young woman yet, Caro. I'm sure the men will be lining up to dance with you at the barn dance next Saturday."

Caro's lips twisted wryly. "The few men that are left, and even those that are don't seem to want to dance. But I'll be there, kicking up my heels, don't you worry!"

Ellen smiled and said goodnight before going to her own bedroom. Caro's determined pragmatism had helped to lift her own flagging spirits.

She'd meant what she'd said about staying, yet as she readied for bed she thought of her life back in Glasgow, the life she could have had, first as Henry McAvoy's wife, before he'd drowned when the *Titanic* had sunk, and then as a lecturer at the Glasgow School of Art, living in her cozy little house with her friends Ruby and Dougie, holding exhibitions at the Society of Lady Artists in Blythewood Square, taking tea at Miss Cranston's Tea Rooms. It all seemed so pleasant now as she faced the struggles of the farm, of Peter's blank face, of Jed's unfriendliness.

She sat by the window, letting the cool night air sweep over her. She could smell the damp soil of June and the freshness of the lake water, hear the distant call of the whippoorwill, and she closed her eyes, letting the island's smells and sounds seep into her, imbuing her with strength.

No matter all she had once hoped for and lost, this was home and always would be.

CHAPTER THREE

The next morning, Ellen took Captain Jonah's little boat to Ogdensburg, and then the train to Kingston. She wondered, as she watched the surface of the lake ruffle up into whitecaps, how long Jonah would be offering his rather ramshackle ferry service. There was talk, now that there were over fifty motorcars on the island, of having a "proper" ferry service to Kingston, with the ability to transport cars. The days of driving them over the ice, with half the island waiting and marveling at such a miracle on the far shore, were nearly over. Enterprise and industry were coming even to this loved yet forgotten corner of the earth, a prospect which brought Ellen both excitement and a little tinge of sorrow, as change always did.

In Kingston, Ellen breathed in the city sights and smells, from the clanging of the tram cars down Division Street to the chiming of the bells of Queen's University. It had been eight years since she'd last been in the bustling city, when she'd been a young nursing student at Kingston General Hospital, determined to make a name for herself.

She'd ended up leaving the program after just one year, when she'd become ill with typhoid, and then she'd met dear Henry on a train to Chicago to visit her father, and the course of her life had been changed yet again. He'd seen her sketching and invited her to submit a portfolio to the Glasgow School of Art; she'd done so, and just a few months later she'd traveled to Glasgow to take up her place.

Now Ellen headed for the smart office building of Kingston's trademark limestone and the offices of the McCaffertys' bank, hoping to secure a different kind of future for the McCaffertys—and herself.

"Of course we can put up some of the land for sale," the man who handled the McCaffertys' affairs said after he'd gone through the paperwork.

Ellen sat on a hard chair in front of his desk, clutching her reticule tightly as people bustled all around the big limestone building, its vaulted ceiling and marble floor giving it an air of wealth and security that was sadly lacking in so many other parts of Canada.

"But I am afraid, Miss Copley, that the price of land is deflated these days. Quite deflated." He spread his hands helplessly. "So many are selling, you see, and it is likely only another islander would want the land you're offering, as it's not a sizeable enough parcel to attract mainland buyers."

"We offered it to our nearest neighbors already," Ellen confessed. "But they have trouble enough managing their own patch."

"That's the story the country over. Not enough able-bodied men to work the land, and yet not enough jobs for the wounded soldiers who have returned and need to work. It is a sorry conundrum indeed." He shook his head, seemingly truly regretful, even though he looked comfortable enough in his three-piece suit, a gold pocket watch gleaming at his waist.

"Indeed it is," Ellen answered. "But considering our debts, which are substantial, I believe we have little choice but to sell at least some of the acreage and hope that it might attract interest."

"And if it doesn't?" the man asked as he raised his eyebrows in polite but determined inquiry. "Will Mrs. McCafferty consider selling the entire property? Because, while the price would be lower than it would have been before the war, an entire smallholding, with the farmhouse included, would attract considerably more interest."

Ellen's chest tightened at the thought of selling the McCafferty farm. To lose it forever, the only place she could really call home... and what of Rose, and all the McCaffertys? They'd all been born in the front bedroom, they'd lived and loved and lost in those dear rooms.

How many times had she walked up the maple-shaded lane as the sun had slanted between the green, leafy boughs and the weathered white clapboard of the farmhouse with its green-roofed porch had come into view? She could not bear the thought of losing it, and she didn't think any of the McCaffertys could, either.

"Let us hope that it does not come to such desperate circumstances as those," she replied stiffly. "In the meantime, let us put the agreed acreage up for sale and see what interest it brings."

"I shall see to the paperwork," he promised, and Ellen made to leave, feeling more discouraged than before. She'd been hoping to return to the island with good news, but it seemed that was difficult to find anywhere these days.

She was walking down Division Street, wondering if she should find somewhere to have a modest luncheon before going for tea with Gracie and Andrew, when she heard someone calling to her from behind.

"Ellen! Ellen Copley, fancy seeing you here!"

Ellen turned around, a smile splitting her face when she saw who was coming towards her, eating up the pavement with his long, eager strides. "Lucas! What are you doing in Kingston?"

"Had some business to attend to, a client of mine who is a professor at Queen's. I'm here for a few days, and I thought I'd come to the island afterward." He stood in front of her, looking much the same as she'd last seen him in France a year ago now. His sandy brown hair was gray at the temples, but his blue eyes were as friendly as ever, his smile as sincere, his expression one of genuine warmth and affection.

"It's been a long time since you've been back on the island," Ellen said, trying to keep a slight note of accusation out of her voice. She didn't understand why Lucas had stayed away, especially when it was clear that Jed and his father were struggling so much. Still, it wasn't her place to speak of it. She smiled and added lightly, "I've been there three months and haven't seen neither hide nor hair of you."

"I've been busy, I'm afraid," Lucas replied, his eyes shadowing briefly. "Getting things sorted at the office. Everything's in a terrible muddle after the war, so many men coming back to claim jobs, so many estates left in disarray." He made a face. "And so many men not coming back at all. But I'm going to travel on to the island tomorrow. What about you? You haven't mentioned in your letters whether you're going back to Glasgow or not."

"I'm not planning to," Ellen answered.

"Not even for the art school?" Lucas asked with a frown, and then he took her by the arm and drew her away from the bustling crowds on the pavement. "We can't conduct a conversation out here on the street. Have you had lunch?"

"I was just thinking about finding somewhere," Ellen admitted.

"Let me treat you, then," Lucas said, and before she could demur, he was drawing her away from the street and towards a restaurant on Princess Street with white linen tablecloths and waiters who were more smartly dressed than she was.

"This is far too elegant for the likes of me," Ellen protested as a waiter placed a heavy napkin in her lap and Lucas proffered a menu.

"You underestimate yourself," he answered easily. "It's so good to see you, Ellen. And, by the sounds of things on the island, you deserve a little treat."

Ellen sighed and opened her menu. "I wish I could give all the McCaffertys a treat," she said and scanned the offerings.

Crab Cocktail, Chicken à la Reine, Leg of Mutton with Creamed Cauliflower… Her mouth watered. Rose's meals were solid, homegrown fare, and delicious at that, but she hadn't eaten in a restaurant since she'd come to Amherst Island.

"Has it been very hard?" Lucas asked quietly and she closed the menu.

"Hard enough." Briefly she told him about the possibility of selling the land, as well as the need to do it. "But it's not just that," she continued after a moment. "I feel as if the war will never end. I know it has, of course," she said hastily, "but the effects go on and on. Peter…" She stopped, remembering her cousin's bleak look in the dark kitchen and Lucas frowned.

"Peter?"

"He's suffering," Ellen said quietly. "Nightmares and restlessness. Sometimes he just stares into space…"

"The thousand-yard stare?" Lucas surmised and she drew back, startled.

"Shell shock?" Despite Peter's moods and silences, she had not considered such an unwelcome possibility. "Oh no, surely not as bad as that—"

"I'm sorry. I shouldn't have suggested it."

And yet Peter did exhibit some of the classic signs of shell shock. Ellen had certainly seen enough during her time nursing at Royaumont, although it had taken years to admit it was a distinct diagnosis. But Peter, dear Peter, suffering from that dreadful condition? It would be so much easier if he was just having a hard time, as so many other ex-servicemen were, settling back into civilian life.

"Let's talk of more pleasant things," Lucas suggested. "Such as what to eat. Our waiter is eyeing us expectantly. Have you decided what you'd like? I insist you order all three courses."

"I couldn't—" Ellen protested and Lucas shook his head, all mock severity.

"You must. I will be put out, otherwise."

Ellen pursed her lips, torn between a deep, yearning pleasure at the thought of abandoning all her cares for an hour or two and simply enjoying such a fine meal, and a niggling irritation that Lucas could afford three-course dinners in elegant restaurants while his family struggled to keep their farm afloat. Did he not care about island life any longer?

They ordered their food, and as the waiter left, she asked one of the questions that had been burning in her heart since she'd first come back to Jasper Lane. "Why haven't you come back to the island, Lucas?"

"I told you," he answered. "I've been busy."

"It must be busy indeed, not to be able to see your own family."

The easy smile left Lucas's face and he looked away. "Are you cross with me?" he said after a moment, his voice deliberately light.

"Not cross. That sounds like a child's response."

"Disappointed, then!" He held his hand to his heart as if she'd dealt him a mortal blow, still keeping his tone light and even laughing. "That's far worse. How shall I survive under the frowning eye of Ellen Copley's displeasure?"

Ellen couldn't help but smile at Lucas's obvious theatrics, but she could tell he was avoiding taking the topic seriously—or giving her a straight answer, and she decided to drop it for now. "I shall look forward to seeing you there shortly," she said. "Will you be staying for the barn dance at the Hewitsons on Saturday night?"

"I wouldn't miss it for the world. Will you save me a dance?"

"Maybe," Ellen teased. "If you're lucky!"

"I hope I am," Lucas answered, and for a second, no more, his gaze rested on hers in an unnervingly meaningful way. The days of Lucas insisting he loved her were long past, Ellen knew. They'd been so young, only nineteen, when Lucas had, in his first year at Queen's, told Ellen he'd fallen in love with her. He'd said so again, more or less, in France, but Ellen had chosen to dismiss that declaration as a product of war and all the uncertainty it had brought. Certainly since then Lucas had said nothing of any deeper feelings.

And as much as she loved Lucas, Ellen had believed it hadn't been in that way, and she'd told him so. The truth was, back in Kingston and even a little bit in France, she'd still been in love with Jed, a heartache that had gone on for years until she'd finally forced herself to move on. Now when she thought of Jed's surly rebuff yesterday, Ellen wondered how they'd ever truly been close. It seemed like a lifetime ago and, she reflected sadly, in truth it was.

"So tell me why you aren't returning to Glasgow," Lucas said as their first course arrived and they both dug into their crab cocktails. "I thought you'd take up your position at the art school. Weren't they keeping it for you? And you had a house, as I recall…"

"I still have a house, and my friends are living in it," Ellen answered. Wistfully, she thought of Ruby and Dougie and the jolly times the three of them had together, gathered around the kitchen table as the nights drew in.

"So what is keeping you from returning? It sounds as if your life is there now, Ellen, not on the island."

Ellen took a bite of crab, trying not to let Lucas's well-meaning remark sting. "It may seem like that from afar," she agreed slowly, "but it didn't inside." She tapped her chest lightly. "Besides, I don't know that I could be a lecturer at the School of Art when I have not put pencil to paper in years."

"Haven't you?" Lucas looked dismayed by the news; he'd always been a staunch supporter of her artistic ambitions, such as they'd been.

"No, not since before the war. I simply couldn't."

He nodded slowly in understanding. Although Lucas had been in intelligence for much of the war rather than on the front lines like Jed, he'd seen his fair share of the horrors too, Ellen knew.

"But the war is over now," he said after a moment. "And you have always been inspired by the island."

"Which is partly why I returned," Ellen explained with a smile.

"Have you drawn anything since you've been back?" he asked.

She shook her head. "No, not yet. I've been kept busy helping with the farm and the never-ending chores that need to be done. I haven't had a moment even to think about drawing."

"That's a pity—"

"It is what it is." Ellen heard the hard note entering her voice and she knew Lucas did too. Spending hours drawing and daydreaming seemed like an offensive luxury now, an insult to the McCaffertys and how hard they worked. Couldn't Lucas see that?

"Well, I won't bang on about it," Lucas told her with a laugh, reading her mood correctly. "It's only I know what talent you have, Ellen, and I know how much it means to you. But if you're not intending to return to Glasgow, I for one can't help but be pleased. I'm glad you're back on the island, for my sake, if not your own."

"Even though you hardly come back yourself?" Ellen couldn't keep from asking, and Lucas smiled and shook his head.

"Not that again, Ellen. I have duties in Toronto that keep from me from the island."

"I know, but—"

"I promise you, I shall be back tomorrow," Lucas assured her. "And dance with you on Saturday night!"

Ellen smiled at that, glad that her friendship with Lucas at least remained untarnished. As for Jed… well, there was no real reason to think overmuch about Jed. And yet she couldn't stop herself from asking Lucas a little while later as they had their dessert, "Will Louisa return to the island, do you think?"

Lucas's face fell as he took a forkful of chocolate cake and reduced it to crumbs with the tines of his fork. "I don't rightly know," he answered after a moment. "And I don't believe Jed does either."

"But surely now the war's over and he's back…"

"Things were bad between them, Ellen," Lucas said quietly. "Really bad. I don't know that anyone can just walk back into a marriage after all that."

"But what else can Louisa do?" Thoughts of scandal and divorce flitted through her mind. Surely Louisa would not take it as far as that?

"Stay where she is, and have Jed stay where he is, and let them live their lives separately," Lucas answered with a shrug. "I'm sure there's more than one married couple who agreed to the same, after the war. Nobody's the same."

"You don't seem too changed," Ellen remarked, more to lighten the mood than anything else.

"I was luckier than some. Most, even. I never went over the top the way Jed and so many poor fellows had to. I did most of my work away from the Front."

"But you were in danger, too."

Lucas shrugged again. "It wasn't the same," he said, and Ellen noted the shadows that had entered his eyes. Did Lucas feel as if his military service wasn't as laudable as his brother's? She knew he'd been doing something hush-hush for the British government, but what, he'd never been able to say. Was it some sort of guilt that kept him away from the island, feeling he hadn't fought in the trenches the way all the other island boys had, Jed included? She knew not to ask, not now, at least.

"Well, I must thank you indeed for this lovely luncheon," she said brightly. "I can't remember the last time I ate so well! And I'm meant to be taking Andrew and Gracie out for tea, but I'm afraid I won't eat a bite."

"I'm sorry to have spoiled it for you," Lucas answered, his eyes crinkling in a smile.

"I'm not," Ellen returned with a laugh. "But I should take my leave, as they will be waiting for me."

Gallantly, Lucas rose from the table. "I'll see you out, and then return to settle the bill."

"You've been so kind, Lucas."

Briefly, he touched her hand with his own. "It has been my pleasure, Ellen, but I think you know that."

She fought an urge to slide her gaze away from his own warm one as she gathered her gloves and reticule. Surely she was imagining that note of quiet yearning in Lucas's voice. The days when he'd cared for her in that way were long gone.

"I shall see you at the barn dance," Lucas promised her as they bid farewell on the street. He pressed her hand once more, and Ellen smiled at him.

"I look forward to it," she assured him, and as she walked down the street, she felt Lucas's gaze on her all the way until she'd turned the corner.

CHAPTER FOUR

The night of the Hewitsons' barn dance was balmy and clear, with a slight breeze blowing off the bright waters of Lake Ontario lending a freshness to the air.

Ellen put on her best pink silk dress, with the dropped waist that had become fashionable recently, the hem barely skimming her ankles. It looked shocking somehow, here on the island, where everyone was still wearing fashions from before the war, shirtwaists and skirts that brushed the ground, but in Glasgow or even Kingston, Ellen knew she would have fitted right in.

"You look like you've stepped out of the pages of that *Vogue* magazine," Caro told her with smiling envy as she ran her hands down the sides of her own well-worn dress, one whose hem she'd mended and collar replaced several times over.

"I can't imagine myself in one of those magazines," Ellen told her. She'd only seen the upscale magazine with its many fashion pages a few times, but she was quite sure she looked nothing like the sleek, sophisticated women featured in it. "Perhaps I should have my hair bobbed or shingled," she mused as she tucked a few stray wisps up with pins. "So many women are doing it now. I saw women with hair barely past their ears when I was in Kingston." Like Caro, she'd put her near waist-length hair up in its usual boring bun.

"Oh no, your hair is glorious," Caro protested. "That color—it's a cross between a chestnut and a sunset. If only you could wear it down!"

"Now that would be scandalous," Ellen teased and grabbed her matching wrap. Even though the evening was warm, when the sun went down, the temperature dropped so it was pleasantly cool. "But thank you for the compliment."

The dance was in full swing when she, Caro, Rose, and Peter arrived by wagon. Ellen had thought Peter wouldn't attend; he hated crowds now and didn't even like going to church anymore, sometimes leaving before the service was over, but he'd been sitting in the kitchen in his best Sunday suit when Ellen and Caro had come downstairs, his hands resting on his knees.

"Don't you look handsome, Peter," Rose had exclaimed, her face flushed with pleasure at seeing her son taking part and looking it as well, but Peter had just given her a blank, almost indifferent look, and her face fell although she said nothing more.

"I think we've all scrubbed up rather nicely," Caro had put in cheerfully, and Rose gave her a quick smile of gratitude before they'd all started towards the Hewitsons, with Peter driving the wagon.

Now, as she surveyed the swept barnyard that served as a dance floor, Ellen couldn't keep from humming under her breath as the makeshift band struck up another tune and couples took to the dirt floor. Within minutes, Henry Spearson, Johnny from Ellen's year's little brother, had whirled Caro away, and Ellen tried not to mind feeling a bit like a wallflower. She was twenty-eight years old, after all, and certainly past the first blush of youth. Perhaps no one would ask her to dance tonight.

Instinctively, without even realizing she was doing so, she scanned the barnyard for Jed, but he was nowhere to be seen. Perhaps he hadn't even come. Either way, Ellen doubted he would be willing to dance, with her or anyone else.

She was still looking for him, even though she knew that he wasn't there, when she felt a tap on her shoulder and she turned around to see Lucas smiling expectantly at her.

"You promised a dance," he reminded her, and she nodded her happy assent.

"So I did, and I'm pleased you remembered!"

Lucas took her in his arms and they started around the dance floor as couples whirled around them. It felt nice to dance again, freeing somehow, the cares slipping away from her shoulders every time they spun around.

Lucas gave her an appraising, serious look. "You look lovely, Ellen."

"You've cleaned up quite nicely yourself," Ellen answered lightly. Lucas's hair was brushed back with pomade and he wore a city suit with a celluloid collar that put the local boys' homespun trousers and shirts to shame.

"Thank you very much indeed," Lucas replied with a grin, before his considering look turned serious. "Have you come to any conclusions about the farm?"

Ellen shook her head. "I'm afraid not. We're going to put the pasture on the market, but the manager at the bank didn't sound terribly optimistic." Her stomach knotted as she thought of the potential consequences. "I don't know what we'll do if Aunt Rose loses the farm. She's spoken about moving to Stella or even off island, but I can't imagine her anywhere but here." She sighed dispiritedly. "I wish she'd let me help."

"As generous an idea as that is, your money would only go so far, Ellen," Lucas told her gently. "Your aunt needs a sustainable solution. An ongoing source of income, not just an injection of cash."

"You sound like a lawyer," Ellen teased, although with the faintest touch of irritation. Lucas seemed to be more sensible than sympathetic, and his distance from the island, emotional as well as physical, still possessed the power to hurt her. "Besides, where are we meant to get an ongoing source of income? With the prices the way they are—"

"Actually, I have an idea." Lucas whirled her around again as Ellen stared at him blankly.

"You have an idea?" she repeated. She had no idea what plan Lucas could come up with to save the farm, but judging from the slight yet confident smile curving his lips, he seemed quite certain about it. A flicker of curiosity as well as doubt rippled through her. What on earth could Lucas be thinking of?

"I do," he confirmed as his smile widened. "But I'm not going to explain it to you while we are dancing."

"Then when—"

"After." He whirled her around again, faster this time, and laughing now, Ellen let herself be carried by the tune until the song ended and the couples began to disperse.

With one hand on her elbow, Lucas bore Ellen away from the barnyard, and towards a flat limestone ledge that jutted out into the lake's waters, now touched by the gold of the setting sun. It was such a perfect, tranquil moment—the lake still and smooth, the sky wide and open.

Ellen settled on the stone, spreading her skirt out, as she tilted her face to the last of the setting sun.

"That's better," Lucas said as he sat next to her, fanning his face. "It was hot over there."

Ellen lowered her head as she turned to give him a serious look. "Lucas... what did you mean, you had an idea? Aunt Rose and I have thought of everything, from making only cheese to getting rid of all the livestock." The McCafferty farm, like so many other smallholdings on the island, had a bit of everything, but only a little. They could never compete with the huge beef or dairy farms springing up out west. "Nothing comes close to helping make ends meet."

"Ah, but I'm not talking about using the land to farm," Lucas said with a twinkle, "although I think you would need to have some farming element, in order to keep your customers feeling as if they were getting the real experience."

Ellen shook her head slowly. "Customers? What on earth are you going on about?"

"Or perhaps I should say guests." The smile he gave her was wry, his blue eyes glinting with humor.

"Now I'm really confused." She gave an uncertain laugh, and Lucas leaned forward, earnest now, the teasing twinkle in his eye replaced by a gleam of determination.

"Ellen, I hate the idea of you not using your talents," he said, and took her hands in his. "You are an artist, and you were going to be a teacher of art. Why not do those things here? Use the abilities and talents God gave you?"

"Here? *How?*" Ellen stared at him in disbelief, fighting a prickle of annoyance that even now, when things were so desperate for the McCaffertys, he was going on about her art. She tried to pull her hands from his, but Lucas held on, smiling faintly as he noted her resistance.

"Don't get het up—let me tell you. You could run a guest house where you offer art lessons. I know you're struggling, but so many society women are restless and bored. The rich haven't suffered in the war, from it, in the same way. Their businesses are booming and they're looking for amusement. I see it in Toronto, and I know it's happening all over. Boston, New York, Chicago… Why not offer a holiday for people like that, with more money than sense, more time than work? You could arrange different lessons in sketching and painting, have trips to vantage points on the island, meals in the farmhouse, even a little help on the farm if they wanted to. I think society women would find it amusing to turn their hand to a bit of work—shelling a pea or collecting an egg. They would love the novelty."

"I don't want to *amuse* people," Ellen exclaimed, and this time she did pull her hands from Lucas's. She felt strange and shivery, as if he'd suggested something unreasonable, outrageous, even insulting. "And I certainly don't want to offer up our life here as some sort of commodity or—or entertainment!"

"Even if it saved Jasper Lane?" Lucas countered quietly.

"It wouldn't."

"You don't know that."

She shook her head, unsure why she suddenly felt so angry. "Do you actually think running some sort of holiday service would pay our bills?" She meant to sound incredulous and scathing, but she heard a faint note of hope in her voice, and she realized that was why she was angry. How could Lucas give her a slender thread of hope, when it so clearly led to nowhere? No one would pay for a holiday in a ramshackle farmhouse, to be given art lessons by a has-been painter, who herself hadn't drawn anything in years. She shook her head, annoyed at herself now for dreaming about it even for a second. "It's impossible."

"To believe a thing impossible is to make it so," Lucas quoted. "I heard people say that in France. Why don't you want to believe it could work?"

"Because I don't want to get my hopes up," Ellen replied shortly. "Or Aunt Rose's, for that matter."

"But what if you got your hopes up and they were realized?" Lucas leaned forward, his gaze, as it swept over her face, seeming far too knowing. "What are you so afraid of, Ellen?"

Of trying and failing. Of not being good enough.

Ellen swallowed as she looked out at the lake. "Everything, I suppose," she said after a moment. "I don't want to give my heart to something only for it to fail." She'd done that before, too many times, and while this professional enterprise wasn't the same as a failed romance, it was still dangerous, and Ellen felt too battered to try again. Perhaps that was really why she'd come back to the island—because it was safe.

Lucas regarded her thoughtfully, a look of sorrowful understanding in his eyes.

Ellen looked away, knowing he saw too much. He always had, ever since they'd been children. He'd understood and encouraged her drawing far more than Jed or anyone else ever had; he'd seen how much it had meant to her. She still held those childhood conversations dear, even as she reminded herself that that was all they had been.

"Better to give your heart away than to hold onto it," he said quietly. "Don't you think?"

"In some cases, yes," Ellen answered as she turned back to meet his compassionate gaze. "But in this case, Lucas, I simply don't think it could work. How would we even begin?"

"You could place an advertisement in the city newspapers. It could be as simple as that. You've got the space—the farmhouse has seven or eight bedrooms, at least."

"Seven," Ellen admitted reluctantly. "But they're not of hotel quality—"

"People wouldn't be looking for hotel quality. Yes, you might have to smarten things up a bit, and you'd need to share a room with Caro, but I wager you could offer four guest rooms for the whole summer season—charge fifteen dollars a week."

"*Fifteen dollars*," Ellen repeated wonderingly. "Surely not!"

"With meals and art lessons provided? Some people would be willing to be pay twenty."

"Per *room*?"

Lucas nodded, and Ellen laughed out loud.

"Eighty dollars a week all summer long," she mused out loud, already imagining the farm bustling and prosperous, with a hired man or two to help with the fields, the barn roof replaced, a new tractor... "It seems far too good to be true."

"Admittedly, you may not be booked up the entire summer..." Lucas warned her.

"Even half that would be more than enough..." She sighed and shook her head. For a second, she'd let her dreams run wild, but now she was returning to reality with a thud. "I just can't see how it would work."

"And so you won't even try?" Lucas's voice was gentle.

Ellen looked away; darkness was slipping over the lake like a cloak, and from the barnyard, she could hear the merry strains of the fiddle, a sudden burst of feminine laughter. "You always had more faith in me than I had in myself," she admitted in a low voice.

"And it has always been warranted." Lucas touched her cheek, a butterfly brush of his fingers. "At least think about it, Ellen. For my sake if not your own." He gave her a fathomless, lingering look, and wordlessly she nodded. Lucas rose from the rock where they'd been sitting, extending his hand down to her.

"One more dance?" he suggested with a smile and she agreed, her head and heart both whirling from everything Lucas had suggested, and the dreams she couldn't yet bring herself to believe in.

CHAPTER FIVE

In the week since the Hewitsons' barn dance, Ellen had done her best to dismiss Lucas's idea of offering art holidays, mainly because she told herself, over and over, that it just *couldn't* work. They lived on a poor farm, in a ramshackle farmhouse. There were rotten floorboards on the porch and mice in the kitchen, despite their Malkin's best efforts. The ceiling in one of the bedrooms leaked, and the sofa in the front parlor was threadbare. No one would want to stay there. No one would *pay* to stay there, and pay enough to keep the McCaffertys provided for. Certainly not wealthy city people who were used to the finer things in life.

She was almost angry with Lucas for suggesting such a thing, for naming amounts and for giving her that treacherous kernel of hope. *What if…* what if there *was* a way for her to keep the McCaffertys in their home, and she could stay as well…

That little kernel wasn't enough to voice the idea to Rose or Caro or anyone; in fact, she felt humiliated just by the thought. How could she propose to the McCaffertys that she keep them afloat by offering art classes? It was arrogant in the extreme, as well as foolish. And so she went about her days, helping in the kitchen and the garden, picking wild strawberries for jam and darning socks, doing all she could to keep things going.

"There's been no word from the bank," Rose told her one evening after supper, when Ellen was helping her wash dishes. Peter had gone outside to see to the animals, and Caro was taking a berry pie to Iris Wilson, a war widow with three little ones who was struggling along with everyone else on the island and had recently come down with a bad summer cold. "No one's interested in buying that back pasture, and I don't think anyone ever will be. In truth, I'm not surprised. It's all big farms out West now, with a thousand dairy cows or more. We simply haven't got enough to manage." Rose managed a smile, although Ellen could see the lines of strain from her nose to her mouth, the look of despair in her faded blue eyes.

"If you did sell the farm," Ellen asked slowly, hating even to bring up the question, "where would you go? Somewhere in Stella?" She could not imagine them all displaced, scattered across the country.

And where would *she* go? Back to Glasgow? It seemed the most practical possibility, and yet she resisted it. The island was her home. It was the McCaffertys' home as well. They had to find a way to stay, somehow.

Rose sighed as she slowly wiped a plate dry. "I don't rightly know, to tell the truth. A place in Stella would be an expense, still. I suppose I could throw myself on my brother, your Uncle Hamish's charity, although he has his own struggles now, poor man."

Ellen nodded slowly in sorrowful agreement. When she'd first arrived in America, she'd lived with her Uncle Hamish and Aunt Ruth in the small town of Seaton, Vermont, where they'd run the general store. Ruth had died years ago, and Hamish had sold the store when it had been overtaken by the glossy promises of the Sears Roebuck catalogue. Now he lived in a set of rooms above Seaton's new drugstore, and worked the counter part-time, even though he was past sixty years of age. He seemed happy enough, although Ellen knew he still missed Aunt Ruth terribly. She could not imagine Aunt Rose sharing his small living quarters, or keeping house for him.

"And if you didn't go to Uncle Hamish?" she asked.

Rose sighed. "Perhaps to Gananoque, where Sarah is, although she only has a room in a boarding house. No one's got much space to spare anymore, have they?" she said with a sad smile. "Nothing is the same as it was." Rose paused as she gazed out the kitchen window at the golden evening. "Life was hard enough, goodness knows, before the war, but I'd go back to those days in a heartbeat sometimes."

"So would I," Ellen agreed quietly. The war had shaped everyone, molded them in hard and heartfelt ways. It had left gaping holes in the very fabric of island life and it was impossible to knit it back together; the only way forward was to make something new from the tattered remnants. But what? And how?

Again Ellen thought of Lucas's outlandish idea. She hadn't mentioned it to anyone because she didn't want to offer false hope, which she knew from bitter experience was worse than none. But if there *was* a way… If she could help to save the farm and keep Aunt Rose and her cousins safe in their home… Surely she couldn't let her own fear and doubt keep her from at least suggesting it. If Rose thought it was a mad idea, then she'd drop it at once. But surely her aunt deserved to know about the possibility, at least.

Ellen took a deep breath. "Lucas Lyman mentioned something to me," she said as they finished the dishes and Rose put the kettle on the stove. Ellen hung the damp dish towel over the railing on the cooking range. "An idea about the farm. It sounds mad, I think, and it probably is, but I felt I should at least mention it to you, just in case…"

The hope that leapt into Rose's eyes and animated her face made Ellen's heart sink. What if it all came to nothing? Which it probably would. She still couldn't believe that anyone, never mind wealthy society ladies, would want to spend their vacations at Jasper Lane.

"Lucas did?" Rose said as she got the teapot down and began to make tea. "He's such a fancy man in Toronto these days. His father is so proud of him, I know."

"Yes, although I imagine Mr. Lyman could use Lucas's help back on the farm," Ellen said with a bit more acerbity than she'd meant to reveal.

Rose raised her eyebrows. "I think Lucas is most useful right where he is. But what idea did he have about our farm? I can't even imagine."

"It really does sound mad," Ellen warned her aunt. She felt embarrassed to mention the art holidays, the presumption that she had enough skill to offer them. She hadn't picked up a paintbrush or pencil in years, and still had no real desire to do so. How could she possibly teach others?

"I don't mind mad," Rose answered. "At this point, I'd happily welcome any idea. The madder, the better!" She sat down at the table and Ellen joined, the teapot between them.

The kitchen was quiet and peaceful, the view of rolling fields to the placid, glittering surface of Lake Ontario making Ellen think, for one wild second, that city tourists *would* want to come here. It was certainly the loveliest place she'd ever been, the only place where she felt as if the very land seeped into her bones and became a part of her.

"Are you going to tell me, then?" Rose asked with a smile as she poured them both cups of tea.

Ellen took hers with a murmured thanks, taking a sip as she steeled herself for what lay ahead. "Well… Lucas had the idea of offering holidays here to city folks. Art holidays, actually." She let out an embarrassed laugh as she felt herself start to blush. "We could—well, I could—teach people to draw and paint, things like that, but also give them a little taste of helping on a farm. No mucking out stalls, of course, or any of the hard or dirty work. Just feeding a few chickens, picking a few berries, simply things city folk might enjoy, make them feel useful…" She trailed off, embarrassed by her suggestion. When she'd said it out loud, she realized how ridiculous it all sounded. What city folk wanted to feed chickens?

Rose was staring at her, a look of rapt incredulity on her face, her teacup stalled halfway to her lips.

Ellen smiled uneasily. "It is mad, isn't it? I knew it was. I shouldn't have even mentioned it…"

"No, no, I think it sounds brilliant. Art holidays! I would so love for you to use your talent, Ellen." Rose paused, frowning as she sipped her tea. "But I have no idea what city people want these days. The farthest I've gone in years is Kingston."

"Lucas seems to think the good matrons of Toronto would love to rusticate here, but, of course, we wouldn't know unless we tried. And trying would be a risk," Ellen continued hurriedly, feeling compelled to point out all the dangers and downsides of the foolhardy plan. "We'd most likely have to spend some money to smarten the place up a bit…"

Rose looked around the kitchen in all of its shabby comfort and laughed. "Of course we would. And advertising and art supplies too, I suppose. Would we advertise in the newspapers?"

"I'll pay for those," Ellen said firmly. Rose opened her mouth to protest, but Ellen cut her off with a firm shake of her head. "Please, Aunt Rose. I insist. You won't let me help in other ways, but this would benefit me as well. You must let me. If I'm to share in any profit or benefit, then I shall share in the cost, as well."

"You sound quite convincing," Rose answered with a wry laugh. "And so I'll agree." She paused, her expression turning both serious and wistful. "Do you think we can manage it, Ellen? Really?"

Belatedly, Ellen realized she'd been talking as if it was all about to become a reality, as if all they needed was a lick of fresh paint and a paragraph in the back of the *Toronto Daily Star*. Her heart lurched and then suddenly skipped a beat in excitement. What if that *was* all they needed, more or less? Could they actually do this…? Was she mad for thinking—hoping—that they could? Rose was clearly looking to her for an answer.

"Manage what?" Caro asked as she came into the kitchen, swatting her hand in front of her face. "Ugh, the black flies are terrible tonight. I nearly got eaten alive walking through the woods to the Wilsons." She washed her hands at the sink and then turned to look at them both, eyebrows raised. "You both look like Malkin after he's got at the cream. Guilty and proud and just a little bit sick. What's going on?"

Rose let out a little laugh as she went to fetch a cup for Caro. "Ellen has come up with the most amazing idea—"

"It's Lucas's idea," Ellen protested, not wanting to take the credit, especially if Caro thought the idea was absurd. She was just beginning to hope it might actually be possible. "I just told it to Aunt Rose. And I'm not sure it will even work."

"An idea?" Caro folded her arms, managing to look both wary and hopeful. "What is it, then?"

"Art holidays!" Rose exclaimed, and then proceeded to tell Caro Lucas's plans, while her daughter's eyebrows drew closer and closer together in a skeptical frown. She clearly was not caught up in the fancy of it the way Rose was.

"You think rich city people would pay to board here?" she asked, her voice full of doubt. "Louisa didn't think much of it, back in the day, and I can't imagine any Toronto ladies would feel differently."

"That's true." And Louisa, Ellen realized with an unpleasant plunging sensation in her middle, was most likely the kind of customer they would be trying to attract—a wealthy, bored woman, looking to be entertained and amused. Caro was right—back in the day, Louisa had turned her nose up at the farmhouse, and indeed the whole island, even though she'd ended up marrying an islander. She'd gone now, left Jed and the farmhouse and the life they'd built together, and Ellen didn't know if she'd ever be back.

"It sounds like a nice idea," Caro continued kindly but firmly, "but I can't imagine we'd ever gain enough guests to pay our way. And they'd want all sorts of silly luxuries—breakfast in bed and champagne and caviar, no doubt. They'd expect a hotel, and they'd get a farm."

"Breakfast in bed we could do," Rose said, her smile faltering, and Ellen could see she'd already lost her enthusiasm, her shoulders slumping and her mouth turning down. "But perhaps you're right, Caro. We are a shabby lot..." Rose fought for a smile and Ellen's heart ached.

She couldn't bring herself to say anything encouraging; it felt cruel. She'd been right all along, she thought with a pang. It *had* been a mad idea. The farmhouse and their simple life there weren't smart enough to cater to city tourists and all of their fussy wants. Why had Lucas put the dream in her heart, and why, oh why, had she mentioned it to Rose?

"Never mind," Ellen said as bracingly as she could. "It was just an idea. We can think of something else."

To which neither Caro nor Rose replied, for they knew as well as Ellen that there was nothing to say.

That evening, Ellen wrote Lucas. She sat at the little desk in the window of her bedroom overlooking the copse of birches that separated the Lymans' property from the McCaffertys'. If she craned her neck, she could just make out the Lymans' farmhouse; she hadn't seen Jed once since she'd asked him about buying the pasture and he'd turned her down flat.

Ellen sighed, knowing she could hardly blame Jed for refusing, although his surly manner had stung. She wondered if he would even care that the McCaffertys might be leaving the island; he seemed not to care about much these days.

She spent a good hour composing the short letter to Lucas, to inform him they would not be turning the McCafferty farmhouse into some sort of ludicrous McCafferty inn. It was hard not to let an accusing note color her words, because in truth she was annoyed, and even angry, with Lucas for giving her the idea in the first place. It was an unfair sentiment, Ellen knew, and yet she felt it all the same. Vain hope was a terrible thing, and yet that is what she'd dared to have, when she had allowed Lucas to kindle her dreams.

Thank you for thinking of us, she finished writing, *but if selling the farm comes to pass, as indeed it seems likely to, then it is most sensible for Aunt Rose to move to Seaton or Gananoque, and I suppose I shall return to Glasgow.*

She put her pen down and pressed her fingertips to her eyes. To go back again after only a few months on the island… it felt unbearable. Impossible, even. Yet what other choice did she have? She could not throw herself on her Uncle Hamish's mercy along with all of the McCaffertys, nor would she want to. At least she had somewhere to go, a house waiting for her, with her friends Ruby and Dougie living there. They'd be surprised to see her, but they'd welcome her, Ellen knew, and she would have a home, even a happy one, to live in. She could surely not complain, for others had it so much worse.

The lecturing role at the Glasgow School of Art she'd been offered had no doubt been filled by now, but Ellen would have enough to get by for a little while, at least. Perhaps she could offer art tuition to schoolgirls, similar to what she'd have done here, but across the sea, in a whole other world. She could find her way, and yet none of it appealed in the least.

She sent the letter the next day, her heart heavy as she handed it over at the store in Stella, for the post that traveled by ferry. Rose had told her that morning that she intended to put the farm up for sale; her eyes had been sad, her smile wry as she'd looked helplessly at Ellen.

"I really don't think there's anything else to do. I can't manage the farm on my own, and I won't sacrifice my children's livelihoods to keep this place going. Even if Peter and Andrew both worked the land as much as they would, we'd barely eke out a living. Times are just too hard."

"I wish there was another way," Ellen had cried, and Rose had nodded in sympathy.

"So do I, Ellen. So do I."

Despite her aunt's resolution, Ellen couldn't bring herself to start making arrangements for her own travel yet; she still hoped for some eleventh-hour rescue, although from what quarter it would come, she could not say. In any case, it would be some weeks, or perhaps even months, before Rose was able to finalize the plans for herself and the family, and Ellen certainly wouldn't leave before then.

There would be enough to arrange, with all the children to be thought of; Caro had decided to find a position as a school-teacher—there was a post opening in Napanee—and Peter, still seeming utterly indifferent to all possibilities, would stay with Rose for the meantime, wherever she went. Andrew would continue at Glebe, Gracie at Queen's, and Sarah at Gananoque.

"There's no rush, really," Rose had said tiredly, trying to seem both practical and brave. "It will be some months before the farm sells, I should think, although I'd rather be settled before winter."

Ellen wrote to make an appointment with the bank for the next week that she dreaded keeping. Rose had agreed to go with her, to sign the papers that would allow Jasper Lane to be put up for sale. It all felt so very final, and yet they'd all come to the conclusion, Caro and Peter as well, that there was nothing else they could do.

"Better to sell the farm now, before it gets into even more disrepair," Caro had said with brave pragmatism. "Perhaps we'll get a good offer."

And if they didn't? Ellen dreaded to think, even as the possibility brought a treacherous flicker of relief.

For now, at least, she and Rose could both enjoy the sunshine as they sat on the front porch, shelling the summer's first crop of peas. Caro had gone to the Wilsons again; Iris was still poorly and the children needed care.

"I shall miss this place," Rose said with a sigh as she sat in a rocking chair on the porch, a bowl of peas in her lap. "I know I shouldn't complain, as so many others are facing the same." She ran her thumbnail along the seam of a pod and dropped the bright green peas neatly into the bowl. "At least Sarah shall be all right. She'll keep her teaching post, and Gracie will stay at Queen's. Thank goodness she received that scholarship." Rose's concerned gaze moved towards the barn, where Peter was working. "It's Peter I worry for the most," she said in a low voice. "At least here he has the farm to occupy him. I'd say a town like Gananoque might be better for him, especially if he could find a proper job, but there aren't that many going these days, and, in truth, I don't know if he'd be hired anyway, or if he'd be able to keep at it."

"I know." Ellen worried about Peter too. He was so silent and distant, as if he'd tucked a large part of himself away and even he wasn't able to find it again. The upheaval of losing the farm and having to move would surely not help at all, and she hated to think of him spending his days sitting in a chair, simply waiting for the hours to pass, with nothing useful to do.

Rose squinted as she looked down Jasper Lane, the trees arching overhead casting it into shadow. "Good heavens, isn't that Bert Sanders on his old bicycle?"

Ellen looked down the lane, suppressing a smile at the sight of the rather corpulent Bert wobbling along the dirt road on a rusty bicycle. "I believe it is. What do you suppose he wants?"

"He runs the telegraph office, although people don't use it nearly as much as they used to now everyone's getting a telephone."

Rose shook her head, smiling. "Such newfangled notions! I can't see us having one anytime soon." She glanced at the house with fond sorrow. "Do you suppose the new owners might put one in?"

"Let's not think of that yet, Aunt Rose." Ellen glanced again at Bert, wobbling ever closer. "Do you think we have a telegram?" Gone were the days when a telegram meant only bad news, a son or sweetheart, a brother or friend missing in action, presumed dead, or worse. Far worse. Even so, Ellen couldn't keep her heart from fluttering in fear. Who could be needing to reach them so urgently?

"Hello, Mrs. McCafferty, Miss Copley." Bert, huffing and puffing, came to a stop in front of the porch, the bicycle wobbling so much Ellen feared he would fall right off, into the dirt. "I have a telegram for Miss Copley, from Toronto."

"The only person I know in Toronto is Lucas," Ellen said, surprised. "But why on earth would he send me a telegram?"

Rose's smile held a hint of hope as well as a good dose of curiosity. "There's only one way to find out."

Feeling an unsettling mixture of unease and excitement, Ellen took the telegram from Bert, who, with his thumbs hooked into his suspenders, clearly had no compunction about remaining to hear what it said, and would no doubt have the news spread over Stella before the sun was down.

Ellen unfolded the telegram, her anxious gaze scanning the typewritten missive. "I suspected you would tell me it wouldn't work. Stop," she read out loud. She glanced nervously at Rose, who gave her an encouraging if uncertain smile. "So I took the liberty of making arrangements myself. Stop."

"Arrangements…" Rose held one hand to her heart, her eyes wide as the implications of what Lucas was communicating began to become clear.

"The first…" Ellen continued and then stopped, hardly able to believe what she was reading.

"Ellen," Rose implored as she twisted her hands in her apron, pea pods falling and scattering on the weathered boards of the porch. "What does it say? The first what?"

"Yes," Bert chimed in, leaning forward so he could hear the rest. "The first what?"

Ellen looked up at Rose, her mouth curving in a trembling smile as she read the rest of the telegram, her voice filled with disbelief. "The first guests arrive Friday."

CHAPTER SIX

The next three days were a flurry of activity and excitement as they all prepared for the guests Lucas had arranged—the wife of one of the partners in his law firm and her two sisters, coming for a week's holiday and art lessons.

"I don't know what he was thinking," Caro complained, although her eyes were sparkling, as she put endless sheets through the mangle. "Three days to set the house to rights! You don't even have any art supplies. And what about the state of the front parlor?"

"We'll find a way," Ellen said, determined to make this work now that it was actually happening. Although at times it felt as if there were a thousand obstacles in their way, at least there was possibility. *Hope.* She was grateful to Lucas, even if part of her was exasperated with his seeming high-handedness. What if they weren't ready in time? What if, thanks to the rush, it was all a disaster?

"I'm just grateful dear Lucas is giving us a chance," Rose said as she tilted her head upwards to survey Peter repairing the roof tiles. "It's given us all a new energy, even him." She nodded towards Peter. "At least I think it has."

"I think so too," Ellen assured her aunt. Although Peter hadn't seemed particularly enthusiastic about welcoming guests, he'd set to his ever-increasing list of tasks with a dogged determination that was better than his usual malaise of indifference. "And when Gracie, Sarah, and Andrew all arrive home, we'll have lots of helpers."

"But fewer rooms." Rose sighed, shaking her head. "If I let myself dwell on it all too long, I wonder how on earth any of this can work."

Ellen laid a comforting hand on her aunt's arm. "Let's just focus on this first visit," she said. "And hopefully the rest will take care of itself."

Although, in her experience, little took care of itself.

Still, there was plenty to be getting on with—in addition to the roof repairs, they needed to fix the rotten boards in the porch, paint the second bedroom, and plant flowers in the empty beds in the front garden. Then there was the food to get in; Rose had planned elaborate menus that would have her in the kitchen most of the day until Caro convinced her that good, plain country food was what such ladies would be expecting.

"If they wanted Oysters Rockefeller, they should have gone to New York!" she'd declared, making Rose smile.

"I wasn't going to make oysters. But Chicken à la King might do nicely. I saw the recipe in *Woman's Home Companion*."

It was agreed Ellen would travel to Kingston to put in an order with the grocer's and also to buy some art supplies for her lessons, a prospect which filled her with both excitement and trepidation. Could she really teach society ladies how to draw and paint? At the moment she didn't even know where to begin.

Right now, however, she needed to help Caro with all the sheets to be pushed through the mangle, hard and heavy work. They were both red-faced and sweaty by the end of it, with the sodden, dripping sheets still needing to be hung out on the line.

Caro paused in their exertions to give Ellen a frank and anxious look. "What if it's all a disaster, Ellen? I know Lucas means well, but he's dropped us right in it, whether he meant to or not. These fancy Toronto women might turn their noses up at all of us!"

"They might," Ellen agreed. In her darker moments, she thought it likely. Even with new roof tiles and a fresh coat of paint, the farmhouse looked weathered and worn. Lovable, yes, but definitely shabby, and a far cry from the fancy hotels such women would be used to. "But if they do," she continued with as much optimism as she could muster, "we're only back where we started. We haven't lost anything, not really. Not as much as we will lose, if we don't try."

Caro nodded soberly. "I don't want to leave the island," she confessed quietly. "And I know my mother doesn't, either. I can't stand the thought of her heart breaking yet again."

They shared a look full of sorrow and understanding, before Caro turned back to the sheets and Ellen went to dust the three front bedrooms they'd decided would be for guests. Peter would take the box room off the kitchen, and Caro would share with Rose. When Andrew, Gracie, and Sarah came home, they would be squeezed even more, but still with space for three guest bedrooms.

Back in the house, Ellen paused in the front hallway as she surveyed the rooms she was so familiar with, yet was now trying to see with fresh eyes. The brass runner on the stairs was well worn, the Turkish pattern of vines and flowers faded to pale obscurity. The photograph on the wall of Rose and Dyle's wedding day—both of them looking so young and so serious—was faded too, to a pale brown tint.

Ellen took a step towards the front parlor, with its overstuffed settee of stiff horsehair, the two faded armchairs flanking the fireplace, the cabbage rose wallpaper that was peeling at one high corner. She'd spent so many happy days in the room—birthday celebrations, and Christmases with everyone gathered around the tree perched precariously by the window, cozy winter nights tucked up with a book or a game of checkers, spring evenings with the windows thrown open to the balmy breezes rolling off the lake.

She loved this room and all the precious memories it held, but would sniffy society ladies from Toronto feel the same? They didn't have any memories to cherish; what if all they saw was the stuffing coming out of the sofa cushion, or the sun-faded streaks on the curtains?

Well, Ellen resolved, if they did, then so be it. She still wanted to try, and try as hard as she could. Selling Jasper Lane felt like defeat, a surrender none of them wanted. She'd certainly faced more trying circumstances than these in her life—the death of her mother when she was only a child; her father haring off to New Mexico when she wasn't much older; Aunt Ruth and Uncle's Hamish's hard welcome... all of it had made her long for a home, a true home, and this was it. She would do her best to hold onto it.

Turning from the room with a determined step, Ellen headed upstairs.

Although there was much work to do, there was no denying that Lucas's telegram had put a spring in everyone's step, a sparkle in their eyes, even if they were all anxious for the plan to succeed—and desperately afraid that it wouldn't. Even Peter had started to lose a little bit of the dazed, distant look in his eyes as he finished repairing the roof, fixing the porch boards, and even painting the wagon a smart new cream. Ellen just hoped, after all the effort they'd put into sprucing the farmhouse up, it wouldn't be in vain.

Two days before their guests were due to arrive, Ellen took the train into Kingston and visited an art shop near the university, breathing in the old, familiar smells of oil and turpentine, paint and charcoal. She walked slowly among the aisles, picking up a tube of oil paint and running her fingers through the bristles of a brush.

Trepidation and yearning rolled through her... It had been so long—so very long since she'd even considered drawing anything at all, and yet now she was to instruct others. The thought was incredibly daunting, and yet thrilling too.

"May I help you?" the young woman behind the counter asked politely. "Is there something you need?"

Ellen let out a tremulous laugh. She'd left all her art supplies in Glasgow, so she had nothing, not even a set of pencils. "Yes," she told the woman with a wavering smile. "There is quite a lot I need, actually."

Back at Jasper Lane, Ellen deposited her paper-wrapped parcels in her bedroom and then set off to walk the property, looking for appropriate and appealing places to paint or sketch, half wondering yet again just what she was doing. Yes, she'd once been something of an artist, even if the notion seemed laughable now, with aspirations to exhibit and sell paintings. Now she felt like a fraud, a farm girl with a paintbrush clutched in one fist. She'd tried to explain something of that to Caro, but the younger woman had simply shaken her head with impatience.

"Ellen, you went to a fancy art school and you had your exhibition written up in the newspaper. Who else around here is more qualified to let a few old biddies dabble with pencils or pots of paints?"

"I suppose," Ellen had said, but she still doubted herself, not that Caro could really understand.

Now, as she walked the path along the pond where she'd once sat so many times and taken pencil to paper, she wondered if it would be too damp and mossy for the ladies. She'd always been happy to curl up on the flat rock that jutted out over the pond, or lean against the base of the huge maple whose leafy branches stretched out over the water. But she could not see ladies from Toronto doing the same.

If they brought chairs, perhaps… Peter could accompany them in the wagon, and Caro could bring tea and muffins to make it all seem a bit more amenable.

"What are you doing here?"

Startled, Ellen whirled around, one hand pressed to her chest. Jed stood by the gate to the Lymans' field, a silhouette in the oncoming twilight.

"Jed! You scared me."

"I saw you from afar and thought you might be a tramp," Jed stated rather flatly. "I heard from Captain Jonah that they're coming to the island now. Ex-soldiers with nowhere to go."

"Have pity on them, surely," Ellen returned gently. "Poor men having endured so much."

"Some of them have been known to be violent."

"Not here on the island," Ellen protested. "I haven't heard any such thing."

Jed merely shrugged, and she took a step towards him.

"How are you, Jed?" she asked quietly. "Really?"

In the oncoming darkness, she couldn't make out his expression. He stood very still, his left hand resting on the gate, his other arm an empty sleeve pinned to his overall.

"I'm fine."

"You don't seem—"

"Heard you're getting gussied up for some city visitors," he remarked rather flatly.

"Yes, it was Lucas's idea. Did he tell you? I don't know whether it will keep us afloat, but we've got to try." Ellen smiled, but she sensed Jed didn't return it, even though she could hardly see his face.

He merely nodded once, and then turned back to the Lyman farm without another word.

Ellen watched him go, sorrow rushing through her in a wave of poignant memory. Jed... dear Jed... even before she'd fallen in love with him, they'd been friends. Such good friends. She recalled twilit evenings talking in the barn, or playing games of tag among the trees by the pond, their leaves russet and scarlet under a crystalline sky. Where had it all gone? And would they ever be able to get it back? As Ellen watched Jed disappear into the gathering shadows, she feared the answers to those questions more than ever.

CHAPTER SEVEN

The day before their three guests were to arrive, Rose brought down three patchwork quilts from the attic that she'd stitched as a young bride.

"They're a bit musty, but if we aired them out, I thought they might do," she said nervously. "I'd almost forgotten about them, to tell you the truth. Are they too old-fashioned and fusty?"

"Oh, no, not at all, Aunt Rose, they're gorgeous," Ellen exclaimed as she examined the intricate needlework and faded although still lovely colors.

"I know they're hardly the latest style…"

"They're exactly what we need," Ellen declared firmly. "It's this kind of homely touch that these city types want, isn't it?" She didn't wait for Rose's reply as she continued, "I love these quilts, and our guests will too. I'm sure of it."

"They are beautiful, Mam," Caro added as she fingered the rose pattern on one. "I never learned to stitch like this."

"Well, why would you, when you can buy one made by a machine from the Sears Roebuck catalogue?" Rose sighed as she shook one of the quilts out. "Sometimes I feel as if I'm a hundred years old. It's meant to be dry tonight—why don't we hang them up now?"

That evening, after another full day's work, Ellen, Caro, and Rose all sat slumped around the kitchen table, exhausted by the nonstop scrubbing and cleaning.

"I don't think I've ever seen the house this clean," Caro remarked with a tired laugh. "Do you suppose they'll notice?"

"They'd notice if it wasn't tidy," Rose replied practically. "But there's no point worrying about it either way now." Their three lady guests were due tomorrow on the four o'clock train to Kingston. It was far past the time for last-minute doubts or panic to set in.

"I wonder what they'll be like," Caro mused. "I must confess, I'm picturing them to be snooty and la-di-da like Louisa."

"Caro," Rose said in gentle reproof. "Louisa came to appreciate our island ways."

"Did she?" Caro's voice was laced with incredulity. "Not that I could see. She high-tailed it to Kingston and them back to the States just as soon as she could. She wasn't much of a friend to Ellen back in the day, either, as I recall."

Rose gave her oldest daughter a stern look. "She had her fair share of sorrows, Caro."

"As have we all," Caro returned, fiery as ever. "I know you want to be kind and forgiving, Mam, but Louisa treated Jed poorly. Very poorly indeed."

"We weren't talking about Jed, but about our guests arriving tomorrow," Rose replied. "And you don't know all that goes on in a marriage, Caro. It is not for us to gossip or judge."

Caro flushed at this rebuke and Ellen gave her a sympathetic look while staying quiet. She did not know her own feelings entirely on the subject of Jed and Louisa's marriage, and in any case, she had no desire to say any of them out loud.

Rose heaved a sigh as she rose from the table. "I suppose we should all get to bed. It's going to be a long day tomorrow." She cast a worried glance towards the barn, where the light from a lantern was just visible. Peter had been out there most of the evening, as he often was, simply, Ellen suspected, for the privacy.

Caro put a hand on her mother's shoulder. "He'll come in when he comes in," she said quietly and Rose gave a trembling smile.

"Yes, it's just I'm afraid when that will be."

Ellen had the feeling her aunt was talking about more than Peter coming in from the barn.

At half past four the next afternoon, Ellen and Caro stood on the front porch while Rose bustled nervously inside, all of them waiting for Peter to come back from the ferry with their first guests, Viola Gardener and her two sisters. He'd been in good spirits as he'd gone out, whistling while he hitched up the horses. Ellen had smiled to see it.

Lucas hadn't given any detail in his telegram, or the letter that had followed, filled with encouragement for them all but very little information about their guests beyond that he knew the wife of his employer socially, but only a little.

Would they be kind and understanding, or sniffily disapproving? Or what if they were only coming at all because Lucas had begged for a favor? The possibility brought a flush of humiliation to Ellen's cheeks. She knew they were desperate, but she still didn't want charity, and she didn't think Aunt Rose or any of the McCaffertys did, either. What if that's all this was?

Her distant gaze focused on the golden-green pasture stretching to the horizon, the sun shining benevolently over it—and then it sharpened on the broken fence between the McCafferty property and the Lymans'.

"Oh, no."

"What is it?" Rose poked her head through the kitchen doorway, instantly alert. She'd been in a flutter all morning, dusting things that had already been dusted not once but two or three times. When Ellen had come downstairs just after dawn, thinking she had risen early, both Caro and Rose had already been up and about, smiling guiltily and admitting they couldn't sleep.

"It's fine," Ellen assured Rose as she hurried off the porch. Maddie, their dairy cow, had broken the fence several times over the last few months; she seemed intent on getting into the Lymans' vegetable patch and eating all of their pea shoots.

"Oh, no, is it Maddie again?" Rose asked anxiously and Ellen waved her away before lifting up her skirts to avoid the mud puddles in the barnyard; it had rained last night after all, and the quilts were damp and still airing on the line, yet another worry added to the ones Rose already had.

"Don't worry, I'll get her," she called as she grabbed a length of rope and went in search of the errant cow. Of course this would happen just as they were expecting their new guests! If Peter hadn't been fetching them from the ferry, he would have done it, but Ellen knew the job now fell to her. She could hardly ask Rose to go tramping through the fields, and Caro needed to be there to support her. If all went well, she could have Maddie in the barn and be back at the house to tidy herself before the wagon came up the lane.

Ellen sighed and then squared her shoulders, determined to bring back their recalcitrant bovine.

The fields between the Lyman and McCafferty properties were wet and muddy from last night's rain, and Ellen grimaced as her best boots, worn for the ladies' arrival, were soon slicked with the stuff, the hem of her Sunday dress coated in brown. She was going to look a complete fright when she returned—hardly what three society ladies would want to see!

"*Maddie,*" she hissed when she caught sight of the cow, smack in the middle of the Lymans' vegetable patch, blissfully pulling up and chewing their prize shoots. Ellen dreaded to think what Jed or his father would say when they saw the damage. "Come here, you dratted cow!"

Moving as gingerly as she could through the Lymans' vegetable garden, she reached Maddie and then slipped the rope around her thick neck, breathing a sigh of relief when the silly cow didn't resist. Now to get her back home, and as quickly as possible.

"Come on, Maddie." Ellen pulled the rope, but the cow didn't budge, a pea shoot dangling from the corner of her mouth as she chewed with placid determination. "Come *on*," Ellen urged, a bit desperately now.

Maddie let out a resistant moo. Ellen felt like screaming or stamping her foot or both. How could this be happening now?

"Move, you absurd animal!" she cried, only to hear the slap of the Lymans' screen door open and shut, and then the heavy tread of a man's boots.

"Need some help there, Ellen?" Jed asked dryly.

"I wouldn't mind, actually." Ellen turned to look at him; Jed stood on the porch in his shirtsleeves and suspenders, his expression unreadable and not particularly friendly. "I'm sorry about your peas. We've had an early crop already, so I'll bring some over later."

He shrugged one shoulder as he came down from the porch. "Doesn't much matter, I suppose. We haven't got a woman to manage the garden, in any case, and much of it has run to weeds, as you can see. Maddie is welcome to those. No one else will be pulling them out."

There could be no denying the weary bitterness in Jed's tone, and with Caro's words from last night still ringing in Ellen's ears, she found herself asking, her eyes on Maddie as she didn't dare look at Jed, "Is… is Louisa going to come back, do you think?"

Jed was silent, and Ellen felt the tension thrumming through him. "Doesn't look like it, does it?" he finally answered shortly. "Now, let's get this cow home before the stupid beast ruins the rest of my garden." He yanked on the rope and, sensing a stronger master, Maddie trotted obediently after him.

Ellen walked next to Jed, one hand on Maddie's now-docile head as she snuck glances at the boy she'd once counted as a friend, the man she'd once loved. His expression was both obdurate and grim, his eyes shadowed with a pain Ellen knew he would never express. Her heart ached for him, and yet he remained utterly unreachable. Would he always remain so?

"Jed," she said as they approached the fence where Maddie had broken through. "Why don't you come to supper one night? Rose would love—"

"I'm busy enough as it is," Jed cut her off, his tone brusque. "Now you'd best get this fence mended before Maddie comes through it again."

Ellen sighed, swallowing her disappointment at his curt rebuff. "Yes, of course, I'll make sure Peter sees to it today. I'm sorry about Maddie." She stood there, her skirts and boots muddy, her heart still sore, longing to say something that would reach Jed, to jostle him out of the gray fog he seemed to be determined to immerse himself in. Then she heard the McCaffertys' wagon rumbling up Jasper Lane, and her heart lurched for an entirely different reason. "Our guests…"

"Don't want to keep them waiting," Jed said, his mouth twisting. "Especially since Lucas arranged it so they'll save your farm."

Without waiting for a reply, he dropped Maddie's rope and turned to walk back the way he came. Ellen watched him go, wondering at the new bitterness she'd heard in his voice. Was Lucas doing nothing to help his own family's farm, even as he put himself out for the McCaffertys?

She didn't have time to dwell on it then, however; three well-turned-out ladies in wide skirts, cinched waists and elegant hats were emerging from the McCaffertys' buckboard, looking slightly harried from the bumpy ride but interested, at least, in going inside the farmhouse.

Taking a deep breath, Ellen hurried across the field towards them.

By the time she arrived at the house, their guests had been ushered into the front hallway and were staring around in what Ellen feared was bemusement. She thought she'd been looking at the McCaffertys' farmhouse through critical eyes, but in that moment she realized afresh how shabby and secondhand everything was—even the glass jar of daisies on the table by the door looked too homely, picked that morning, already dropping petals.

"Welcome to Jasper Lane," Caro said with a wide smile, a determined glitter lighting her hazel eyes. "We hope you'll be happy here. We'll show you your rooms and give you an opportunity to refresh yourselves before afternoon tea, and then Miss Copley, lately from the Glasgow School of Art, will be leading your art lessons!"

At least one of the women, with her hair swept up in a graying bouffant under a wide-brimmed hat, made an appropriate noise of approval, while the older sister with iron-gray hair scraped back into a bun and a face as sour as a lemon looked distinctly unimpressed. The third lady, who looked about ten years younger than the others, had a dreamy and rather vacant expression and seemed not to have heard, but Ellen blushed all the same. Caro had made her sound grander than she was, especially considering she had three inches of mud on the hem of her dress, and her boots were still caked in the stuff.

While Caro showed the three women to their rooms, Ellen hurried upstairs to change her dress and boots, and then hare back downstairs to help Rose with the tea things.

"Do you think it's going well?" she whispered to Rose as they arranged fresh scones on a plate.

"I don't know," Rose admitted. She looked flushed and excited, her hands twisted in her apron. "It seems to be, although did you see that one with the enormous ostrich feather in her hat? She turned her nose up a bit, I think, and I can't really blame her." Rose looked around anxiously. "Everything is a bit worn, isn't it?

The runner in the hall is nearly threadbare. I didn't notice until now, when Mrs. Gardener nearly tripped over it."

"It doesn't matter," Ellen said firmly. "Who cares about a runner?" Yet silently she vowed to get it replaced before the next lot of guests came—*if* they came. Perhaps they never would.

Soon, the women were coming back downstairs, and Caro led them to the front parlor, chatting easily about island life and the interesting sights they might see there.

"The views from the South Shore are quite the best—I'm sure you'll want to paint or sketch from that vantage point. And there have been known to be fossils found on the beach."

"It all sounds fascinating," the older woman with the elegant updo, who had earlier introduced herself as Viola Gardener, assured her in a carrying voice, and Ellen and Rose exchanged quick, relieved smiles.

Afternoon tea was mostly a success, with Viola, the woman with the bouffant hair, exclaiming over Rose's fresh scones—her aunt, Ellen thought proudly, had always had a light hand with pastry dough. Even Edith, the older sister who continued to look so sour, had managed to put away two.

When they'd finished their tea, all three women were determined to go for a stroll, sketchbooks in hand, leaving Ellen no choice but to accompany them. She hadn't planned on giving an art lesson the day they arrived, assuming the women would take the rest of the afternoon to rest and refresh themselves, but she agreed with alacrity when they all looked at her expectantly.

"Of course, if you wish to sketch now, I can take you to a pretty spot on the property," she said hurriedly. "Although I thought you would wish to rest before dinner…"

Patience, the youngest of the three, smiled warmly at her, but Edith gave a deliberate sniff.

"I should think we want to get our money's worth."

"Oh, Edith, enough about money," Viola said with a laugh. "Didn't you hear Miss McCafferty say that Miss Copley has taught at the Glasgow School of Art? I've read about that renowned institution in the papers. We consider ourselves fortunate indeed to be under your tutelage, Miss Copley."

"Oh, well…" Ellen blushed and trailed off uncertainly. Although she'd been offered a teaching position at the school, she'd never actually taken it up and she couldn't help but feel she was there under false pretenses, not that she intended on illuminating any of the ladies to the truth of her situation. "You'll need sturdy boots and a hat," she told them, and Patience, who was a bit dreamy and silly, looked surprised.

"A hat? But it's already nearly six o'clock. The sun won't be high for much longer."

"Not for the sun," Ellen said apologetically. "But for the black flies. I'm afraid they can be quite a nuisance at this time of year."

"Flies…!" Edith exclaimed, but Viola just laughed.

"We are in the country, my dears. What did you expect? Now, let us get ready at once. I, for one, am quite looking forward to having a little adventure, and before supper, as well!"

Within just a few minutes, Ellen was leading the three ladies outside, each with a sketchbook under her arm. It was a lovely evening, with shreds of golden cloud racing across the horizon, and a breeze off the lake fortunately keeping the worst of the flies away.

Ellen had already decided to take them to a tall maple tree on top of a hill beyond the cow pasture, as it had the best and highest view of the south shore from all the property.

Unfortunately, as it meant walking through the cow pasture, Ellen had to warn the ladies not to step in the cowpats, something Edith found distasteful in the extreme.

"We are in the country, Edith," Viola reminded her. "Once again, I ask, what did you expect?"

"Not to tramp through a field like a farm laborer," Edith shot back, and Ellen's heart sank. As kind as Viola seemed, her older sister's sharp, disapproving manner seemed likely to make the trip a failure. She certainly didn't sound as if she was going to recommend Jasper Lane to her friends and acquaintances back in Toronto.

Ellen tried to keep her spirits up and her manner cheerful as they left the cow pasture behind and started up the hill, with Edith and Patience both huffing and puffing dramatically, although Viola was able to match Ellen's less-than-brisk pace.

"You mustn't mind Edith," she told Ellen with a smile. "She complains about everything. She takes pleasure in it. It doesn't mean she isn't enjoying herself. In fact, I suspect that the more she complains, the more she enjoys herself. But that is just a theory."

"I'm afraid she has some cause to complain," Ellen replied ruefully. "You must know that you are our first guests—we are not at all experienced hoteliers."

"And nor would I expect you to be. But—oh!" Viola stopped as they crested the hill, one hand pressed to her generous bosom as she took in the view from the top.

In truth, it was a wondrous thing to behold, and certainly to draw. Everything brimmed with green life, the fields stretching onto a powder-blue sky, sunlight glinting off the aquamarine surface of the lake in the distance, making it shimmer. Looking at it all made Ellen's heart feel as if it could burst—she didn't want to leave this wonderful place. She didn't want any of the McCaffertys to leave it. If only this holiday were a success! If she could win over Patience, and Edith too…

"How absolutely lovely." Viola gave her one of her warm smiles before starting over. "I barely know where to begin in drawing it! Come, Edith, Patience. Have you ever seen something so magnificent?"

"I believe the views in Tuscany were better," Edith replied sourly, and Ellen choked back a laugh. Tuscany…!

"Yes, but we are in our very own Canada," Viola returned patiently. "And it is as lovely as Tuscany, if not even more so. Come and admit it, Edith!"

"It is pretty enough," Edith allowed, and Viola shot Ellen a knowing, triumphant smile.

"I knew you would think so," she said, and settled on a patch of soft grass, her sketchbook on her lap.

The other two women followed suit, and Ellen breathed a sigh of relief as they all opened their sketchbooks—until each one turned to her with an expectant look on her face, Edith's beadily so.

"What shall we draw?" Viola asked simply, pencil poised, and Ellen stared at her blankly.

"Why, the—the view, I suppose," she stammered. It seemed obvious to her, and yet the three sisters were looking as if they needed to be told what to do in every particular.

"Yes, but where should we begin?" Viola asked. "With the lake or the tree or the grass right in front of me? I am afraid we are terrible amateurs, Miss Copley. We will need complete instruction."

"Ah, yes, of course." Like donning an old dress and finding it still fit, Ellen began to bend herself to the shape of her role. "It is best to begin with the largest shapes and outlines, and then add detail as you go along. Broad strokes to start, to get the spirit of the thing, and then fill it in."

Taking Viola's pencil between her fingers, she drew a few quick strokes to give shape to the trees on the horizon, and something in her came to life. She'd forgotten how a pencil felt between her fingers, how the lines seemed to spring from both her heart and hand.

"Like this—do you see?"

"Oh, you are a magician!" Viola exclaimed, and Edith and Patience both scrambled over to examine her work, while Ellen flushed and insisted she was nothing of the sort, even as she longed to take back the pencil and sketch some more herself. It had been a long time since she'd felt that deep-seated craving.

"It's not bad," Edith said with another one of her sniffs, and Patience set to drawing the large maple on top of the hill, with the clumsy, simple lines of a child.

Soon, Ellen was hurrying from lady to lady, encouraging and instructing as best as she could.

"Miss Copley, I'm having trouble with the shape of this tree," Patience called. "Could you help?"

Patience, Ellen had seen immediately, was a lamentable artist, but she tried to help as much as she could. Edith drew with severe, stark lines and no subtlety, which was about what Ellen would have expected, and Viola took great enjoyment in drawing all over the page, although Ellen would not recognize it as the view from the hill.

"Why does the tree look so big in comparison to the lake?" Viola asked as she proffered her drawing to Ellen, who studied it thoughtfully for a moment. Viola was certainly the most spirited and friendliest of the sisters, a woman in her late forties with deep lines by her sharp blue eyes and a quick, ready smile.

"I believe it's a matter of perspective," she murmured, and with a few quick pencil strokes, she showed Viola how to draw the tree in relation to the sky and lake.

"Oh, but you are clever!" Viola exclaimed. "Isn't she, Edith?"

"I wouldn't know," Edith replied sourly. She wasn't drawing any longer, merely sitting looking stern with her sketchbook on her knees.

"Don't mind her," Viola whispered. "She's just annoyed she's having a lovely time."

Ellen smothered a laugh at that assessment. Edith certainly did not appear as if she were having a lovely time. "I shall take that into account," she whispered back with a grateful smile.

Viola sat back to study her appraisingly, making Ellen want to squirm under the older woman's seemingly knowing gaze. "I've been wondering what kind of woman had captured Mr. Lyman's interest so thoroughly."

"What!" Ellen stared at her, shocked and appalled by the obvious insinuation. "Oh no, I am afraid you have misunderstood. It's not like that between Mr. Lyman and me at all…"

"Isn't it? Lucas Lyman had been most concerned on your behalf. He has seemed most insistent that we would find this to be a pleasant place."

"And I hope you do find it so," Ellen answered a bit stiffly. She had a sudden, horrible feeling that the only reason Viola Gardener had come at all was to satisfy her curiosity about Lucas's alleged love interest. And while Lucas might have felt that way about her once, Ellen was quite sure he didn't any longer, not after all these years.

"Oh my dear, I assure you we do." Viola laughed and patted Ellen's arm. "Please, don't look so affronted. Is there any help for a middle-aged matron's curiosity? We are here because we are enjoying ourselves." She threw her sister a humorous look. "Even Edith."

Ellen's thoughts were still in a turmoil as they walked back to the farmhouse under a setting sun for the evening meal Caro and Rose had been hard at work preparing. Could it be that Viola Gardener and her sisters had merely come to have a look at the woman the handsome junior partner of her husband's law firm recommended? If so, Ellen doubted whether they would have any more bookings. There were precious few people in the world who needed to have their curiosity satisfied on that score.

Her insides tightened with anxiety at the possibility that this might have all been for nothing, a mere lark on Viola Gardener's part. As for her sisters, Ellen could not see them recommending Jasper Lane to anyone, no matter Viola's insistence that Edith really was enjoying herself.

The only hope, Ellen realized, was to convince Viola to abandon her curiosity and actually truly enjoy the holiday, recommend it to friends. She seemed an amicable woman, so surely that was a possibility?

Fortunately, supper went well, with all three sisters perking up considerably when they viewed Rose and Caro's impressive spread—Chicken à la King, followed by an apple and pear crumble with fresh cream from Maddie that morning.

After the meal, they retired to the front parlor to enjoy some quiet, and Peter laid a fire, as a chill had come over the fields with the setting of the sun.

Ellen retreated to the kitchen with Caro and Rose, all of them breathing large, gusty sighs of relief before they started on the washing up.

"Only six more days to go," Caro whispered, which for some reason sent both Ellen and Rose into a fit of giggles.

"Ssh, they'll hear us," Rose hissed as she wiped tears of laughter from her eyes. "I don't even know why I'm laughing—I think I'm just so plum tired."

"Miss Edith has the face of a prune," Caro said, dropping her voice even lower. "But she had two helpings of dessert."

"She's one that will always be hard to please," Rose acknowledged. "But Viola seems so very nice. Oh, I hope the rest of the week goes by without too many trials. I fear it's going to feel like a very long week."

It was after ten o'clock before the women retired for the night, and Ellen was looking forward to seeing her own bed. She was bone-weary, aching in every muscle and sinew as she settled under the covers, a high crescent of moon sending an arc of silver light across the floor. Tomorrow she'd take the ladies to the south shore, where they could paint the lake in watercolors. She wondered how Patience would handle a paintbrush. Edith, she felt sure, would find something to complain about.

Perhaps she would do a bit of painting herself. She flexed her fingers, remembering the pleasure she'd felt at sketching again, like exercising an old, forgotten muscle. Maybe she'd even get out her old sketchbooks again...

It felt as if Ellen had only just dropped off to sleep when she was being shaken awake, and Caro's face was pressed close to hers.

"What..." Ellen began on a gasp, only to have Caro shush her.

"Don't wake Mam, or our guests."

"I won't." Ellen sat up, pushing her heavy braid over her shoulder as she blinked sleep out of her eyes.

Caro perched on the edge of the bed, her expression drawn and serious.

"Caro, what is it?"

"It's Peter," Caro whispered starkly, her hands knotted in her lap. "He's missing, Ellen."

CHAPTER EIGHT

"Missing?" Ellen rose from her bed, her heart starting to thump. "What do you mean, missing?"

"He's not in his bed. He's not even in the house," Caro explained, looking more and more anxious with every passing second. "I couldn't sleep and so I went downstairs. The back door is wide open, and his boots are gone." In the moonlit room, Caro's face was pale and grim, fear flashing in her hazel eyes. "I don't know where he is, Ellen, but we need to find him."

"And we will." Ellen swallowed hard. She hadn't mentioned Peter's nocturnal wanderings to anyone, because she'd thought they were harmless. He'd always come back to the house before too long. But as she and Caro stared at each other, she heard the grandfather clock in the hall chime three somber notes. He had never been out that late before.

With a pang of guilt, Ellen realized she hadn't paid too much attention to Peter since the arrival of their guests. He'd been quiet at supper, even for him, and he'd gone off immediately afterward. She didn't think Caro or Rose had given him much thought, either; they'd all been wrapped up in Viola Gardener and her sisters. What if something had happened to him?

"Ellen," Caro urged, reaching for her arm. "What shall we do?"

"We'll look for him." Ellen hurried to dress, her finger flying over the buttons. "Let's not tell your mother just yet. She'd only worry, and he might be close by. Perhaps he fell asleep in the barn. You know how he goes out there sometimes, just to get away?"

"Yes…" Caro nodded, a new hope lighting her eyes. If only it could be that simple… and yet Ellen already feared that it wasn't.

She grabbed a shawl and stuck her bare feet into boots before quietly heading downstairs and then outside to the still, moonlit night, with Caro following behind her. The sky was clear and scattered with stars, the only sound the gentle whoosh of the breeze, and the occasional distant cry of a fox.

Ellen walked across the barnyard, peaceful in the darkness, and slipped into the animal- and hay-scented yard. The animals rustled in their displeasure at being disturbed, and it only took a few moments of slipping among the stalls to realize Peter wasn't there.

"Well?" Caro demanded as Ellen came out of the barn. She shook her head. "Where else could he be? Why would he walk out so late at night?"

"He's gone out before," Ellen admitted. "I've been downstairs when he's come in."

Caro pressed her lips together. "I didn't realize…"

"I'm sorry, I should have told you. We both know Peter has been troubled, but I wasn't truly worried… it was never this late." Ellen trailed off, feeling wretched. Why hadn't she mentioned Peter's late-night walks to Caro or Rose? Surely they deserved to know.

She supposed it was because she felt a certain empathy for Peter's restlessness, in a way she knew her cousin and aunt couldn't. They hadn't been in France. They hadn't lain under a fiery sky, listening to the shelling, waiting for the thud. They didn't understand how hard it could be to remember that life wasn't like that any longer, or even that it once had.

Caro squared her shoulders, a determined set to her chin. "We just need to find him, then. Surely he won't have gone too far. I'll check the rest of the outbuildings, and you can go towards the wood."

Ellen took a deep breath as she scanned the darkened fields, gentle pastures stretching to the wood of birches and maples that separated their property from the Lymans'. An owl called softly in the night, the only sound in the stillness. Where on earth could Peter be?

While Caro headed to the chicken coop and milking parlor, Ellen took a lantern and then started off through the fields. It felt strange to be out alone in the darkness, the sky wide and black above her, the grass alive with the rustlings of field mice and who knew what else.

Ellen lifted her lantern and swung it an arc as she called out as loud as she dared. "Peter! Peter, where are you?"

There was no reply.

Still she walked on, through the gently rolling fields and towards the wood whose darkness seemed impenetrable under a sliver of moon, the whisper of grass against her nightdress as the damp chill in the air penetrated through her thin wrap.

How long had Peter been out here? What if he'd been hurt? She dreaded to think of him lying somewhere in the wood or lost in a field, bleeding, insensible, or worse.

"Peter…" she called again, a ragged edge to her voice. "Peter, it's Ellen, where are you?"

Ellen spent an hour going through the wood; the sky was starting to lighten to a dank gray, the wood turning into recognizable shapes of trees and rocks, as she finally turned back towards Jasper Lane.

Caro was waiting on the porch as she came through the fields, both worried and weary.

"You didn't find him?" Caro called out, and Ellen shook her head. "What should we do?" Caro asked as she pulled her shawl more tightly around her shoulders. "Should we wake Mam?"

"Not yet…" Ellen bit her lip. She hated to think of how worried Rose would be. "Perhaps we should tell someone else, though."

"But who?" Caro sounded despairing. "Peter's old friends from school are gone—either dead or moved away. He has no one now."

"What about Jed?" Ellen asked quietly.

Caro stared at her. "Jed…"

"He's a veteran, too."

"Yes, and he's even more sullen than Peter is," Caro returned with some heat, frustration now taking the place of fear. "He's so unfriendly these days and he doesn't want to help anyone, not even himself."

"Perhaps, but at heart he's always been one to help others. You know that, Caro. You've seen it yourself." She just hoped it was still true.

"I know the war has changed everyone, Jed included." Caro squinted towards the wood as if she could make Peter out among the trees, her shoulders slumping when she saw no one. "Peter's not anywhere. We could spend the whole night tramping these woods looking for him, and then what good would we be for our guests tomorrow? Let's go back to the house and hope he finds his way back eventually."

Ellen stared at her in alarmed dismay. "But what if he's hurt? He could be out there suffering, Caro. Shouldn't we let someone know?"

Caro gave her a quelling look, one that Ellen had never been the subject of before. "Peter has his pride, Ellen. The last thing he'd want is the whole island up in arms about him, trawling the woods and lanes, thinking he's lost his senses, or worse."

"No, I suppose not," Ellen said slowly, but she still felt deeply uneasy by Caro's decision as they headed back to the farmhouse, the sky now a pale, pearly gray, the horizon pink with the approach of dawn.

"There's no point going back to sleep, I suppose," Caro said with a sigh as they climbed the weathered steps to the front porch. "The animals will need seeing to, especially without Peter here."

"Yes, I suppose." Ellen put away the lantern and opened the screen door to the kitchen, stopping in surprise at the sight that greeted her.

"*Peter...!*"

He sat at the kitchen table, his expression dazed and unfocused, mud smudged on his face and his boots, inexplicably, clutched in his lap.

Ellen ran towards him, stopping before she reached him as she registered the blank look on his face.

"Peter, we've been looking for you everywhere," she said softly. "Where have you been?"

"I was on patrol," he said, as if it were obvious, and Ellen gaped at him.

Caro came in through the door, stopping as suddenly as she had. "Peter..."

"No man's land," Peter explained without looking at either of them. "Made it all the way to the trenches, but I couldn't see anything in the dark. A Jerry came round the corner and I shot him."

Ellen felt a cold, creeping dread steal through her at his flat tone, his unfocused gaze. And why was he holding his boots? "Peter, are you remembering something from the war?" she asked gently. "It must have been very terrible."

"Ran for cover in a shell crater full of mud. There were bodies in there... old ones." A shudder ran through him and he clutched his boots more tightly. "Felt as if they were drowning me, but I managed to get out. I took my boots off when I got back." He gestured to the boots in his lap. "Trench foot is a nasty business, you know. Can't let your feet get wet."

Ellen made no reply, her mind spinning. Peter didn't seem as if he were remembering a night from months or even years ago. He seemed as if he were reliving it now. He hadn't looked at either her or Caro once since they'd come into the kitchen.

Ellen glanced at Caro, whose face was pale, one hand at her throat.

"Peter…" Caro spoke with authority although she looked shaken. "Listen to me. You've had a bad night of it, to be sure, but you need to go to sleep now. You're off duty and your commanding officer insists you get some rest. You'll have another patrol tomorrow, and you need to be prepared."

Ellen struggled not to gape at Caro; why on earth was she participating in this fantasy? In all her years at Royaumont, the doctors had never suggested such a thing. They had always striven to reassure soldiers caught in the midst of their nightmares, to comfort them and remind them of their reality—that they were safe and well.

Before she could say anything, however, Peter blinked, his expression becoming a little more focused, although he didn't turn to look at Caro. "How do you know Captain Smythe?" Before Caro could come up with an answer, he shook his head slowly, gazing around the kitchen in confusion. "Where am I?"

"You're home, Peter," Ellen said, her voice trembling. "You're safe on Jasper Lane. You're *home.*"

Both women held their breaths as Peter absorbed this news. Ellen wondered if he would get angry with them, if he was still in this haunted dream world of terrible memories. But he rose slowly and stiffly from his chair.

"I need some sleep," he said, and walked from the room, still holding his boots.

In the ensuing silence, Caro and Ellen stood there, both of them reeling from the terrible, surreal exchange.

"We can't talk about this now," Caro said finally. "He's safe in bed, that's all that matters. Later, we'll decide what to do, who to tell. Right now we need to get started with the day."

Numbly, Ellen nodded and went to get dressed properly before she helped Caro with the morning chores.

After such a tumultuous start, the rest of the morning went smoothly enough, although Ellen was aching with tiredness and still reeling from Peter's strange episode.

Viola, Patience, and Edith all happily ate the breakfast that Rose and Caro cooked, Edith taking triple helpings of porridge so back in the kitchen Caro muttered that there wouldn't be any for Peter when he came downstairs.

"Is Peter still sleeping?" Rose exclaimed in surprise, and Ellen and Caro exchanged looks.

"He seemed tired," Caro said evasively.

"But he always gets up at dawn, to milk the cows," Rose said, frowning. "And the pair of you look like Gracie and Andrew did when they'd dipped their fingers in the cooling jam. What's going on? Has something happened?"

"Peter's fine, Mam," Caro said. "He's asleep in bed."

"Yes, but why?" A rare anger flashed in Rose's eyes as she gazed sternly at her daughter. "Don't coddle me, Caro, and don't keep the truth from me, either. What's going on?"

"Peter was wandering in the night," Ellen said quietly.

Caro flashed her an angry look that surprised her with its ferocity.

"Wandering…" Rose looked between them both. "What do you mean?"

"He was having a stroll, Mam, nothing more. He couldn't sleep. It's common enough with ex-soldiers." Caro gave Ellen another quelling look that she understood plainly enough. Her cousin didn't want her telling Rose about Peter's odd episode.

"I feel as if I haven't got to the bottom of this," Rose said as she went to slice more bread for toast. "But I will eventually, I promise you."

Ellen tried to meet Caro's eyes, but the younger woman refused to look at her as she went back into the dining room to see to their guests. Fighting a deepening unease, Ellen went upstairs to gather her art supplies together for the morning's lesson.

By the time their guests had finished breakfast, Peter had come downstairs and, after a cup of coffee and some porridge, was ready to drive the ladies and Ellen to a vantage point by the Bay of Quinte Reach.

He made no mention of the events of last night, which wouldn't have surprised Ellen, except neither did he seem embarrassed or defensive about his actions. She had a terrible feeling he didn't remember them, but she said nothing of it to either him or Caro, who had seemed determined to avoid her.

It was a lovely day, the sky cornflower blue with fleecy white clouds that matched the surface of the lake, ruffled with whitecaps. Ellen did her best to put her worries to one side as she focused on the art lesson at hand—painting the lake in watercolors.

The three women arranged themselves at various comfortable spots on the bluff and Ellen walked between them, offering advice and encouragement.

Despite the sunshine and the beauty of the day, she could not relax into the moment and enjoy the women's attempts, amateurish as they undoubtedly were, at capturing the beautiful view. Her stomach seethed with her nerves and she kept going over that odd conversation with Peter, remembering the queer, dazed look in his eyes, the way he'd spoken in a monotone…

She hated to admit it, even in the anguished privacy of her own thoughts, but she feared that Peter was indeed afflicted with the terrible shell shock—the dreaded "thousand-yard stare" and all it encompassed. She needed to talk to Caro again, she decided. Her cousin had seemed quite touchy that morning, as if she didn't want Ellen to interfere, and yet she'd looked to her for advice before. Surely she would wish to hear Ellen's thoughts on the matter, especially considering that she, of all of them, had the most experience with shell-shocked soldiers? Perhaps between them they could decide on an appropriate course of action.

"Oh, Miss Copley," Patience called in a girlish trill, despite the fact that she had to be at least fifty. "What do you think of my maple tree? These are maples trees, aren't they?"

"Actually, they're hickory," Ellen said, summoning a smile as she went forward to inspect Patience's rather simplistic drawing. "This is lovely, but I do think it would benefit from a bit more depth…"

At noon, Peter returned with the wagon and took the women back to Jasper Lane for a cold luncheon. Thankfully, they all chose to rest in the afternoon, giving Ellen a few hours to catch up on the sleep she missed the night before, although she felt so worried about Peter that she thought she wouldn't sleep.

She'd only just managed to drop off into an uneasy doze before she was woken by Rose knocking on the door; Viola and her sisters wished to have help with their still lifes in the parlor, which they'd started last night.

The rest of the day passed in a rush of chores and tasks, with Ellen feeling as if she were constantly scurrying to and fro, between Rose and the rest of the family and their three guests, who, as pleasant as at least two of them could be, still seemed to have endless demands, whether it was cups of tea, "something to nibble on," or hot bath water at an inconvenient time of day.

By evening, Ellen felt ready to drop, and she hadn't had a chance to speak to Caro about Peter. She hadn't even seen Peter since lunchtime, and she had no idea what sort of frame of mind he was in now.

After supper, Ellen tidied up with Rose while their three guests relaxed in the parlor. Caro had gone to see Iris Wilson again, and bring her and her three little ones something to eat.

"Truth be told, Ellen, I'll be glad when these ladies have gone," Rose whispered. "They've been lovely, but it's hard work, looking after three ladies like this. They do like things a certain way, even Viola, and she's the nicest of the bunch."

"It is challenging," Ellen agreed. At supper, Edith had asked for a different dessert than the shortcake with strawberries that Rose had made, and of course there wasn't any. Rose had been mortified, and Ellen had felt like giving the persnickety Edith a good shake. She'd opened a jar of preserves instead and served it with some shortbread biscuits, and Rose had given her a grateful look. "But it will be well worth it, I hope," she said now to Rose with an encouraging smile.

"Yes…" Rose smiled back tiredly. "Do you think there'll be any more bookings?"

"I couldn't say, Aunt Rose. Hopefully our three lady guests will go back and tell all their friends about us." Ellen didn't mention her fears that they'd only come out of curiosity and nothing more. Rose had enough to worry about, and it seemed arrogant to think these women had come all this way simply to find out about her and her relationship to Lucas.

As Rose went into the parlor to see to their guests' comfort, Ellen stepped out to the front porch and breathed in the cool evening air. Golden light spread like syrup over the horizon, and pale lavender clouds drifted by like shreds of silk. If she strained her ears, she could hear the lap of the lake waters against the rocky shore, a sound that had lulled her to sleep many a night. It was a perfect, tranquil scene, and yet Ellen still felt uneasy.

Peter had joined them for supper, saying little, and had then headed out to the barn afterwards. A normal enough thing for him to do, but tonight it made Ellen afraid. With a moment's quiet, she decided it was as good a time as any to speak to him. Steeling herself, Ellen stepped off the porch and went in search of him.

Peter was in with the cows, settling them in their stalls after they'd been driven into the barn. Ellen stepped inside the barn, breathing in the pungent yet comforting scents of hay and animal.

"Peter," she said gently, and he looked up, hazel eyes narrowing as if he already knew what she was about.

"Do you need something, Ellen?"

"Just to talk to you."

"Oh?" Peter's tone was not encouraging. "I have work to do here."

"I know, I can help if you like."

"Muck in with the cows?" he asked with a shake of his head, before he folded his arms. "Well, then? What is it?"

Ellen took a quick, steadying breath as she tried to pitch her voice friendly and casual. "Do you... do you remember last night, Peter?"

He frowned, his eyes narrowing. "What do you mean?"

"You went walking in the night—"

"I often do, when I can't sleep. What of it?"

"It's just, it seemed different last night. It was later, quite a bit later..." She trailed off, feeling as if she were fumbling in the dark as much as she had last night, stumbling through fields with only a lantern for light.

"What of it?" Peter repeated, sounding aggressive now. Ellen wasn't sure if he was reacting angrily because he remembered what he'd done—or he didn't. "It hardly seems worth your mentioning it, especially when you have so many other things to do, with those ladies in there." He nodded meaningfully towards the house.

"It's just… you had mud on your face," Ellen explained in a fumbled rush. "You'd taken off your boots and you were holding them in your lap."

Peter's jaw tightened as anger flickered in his eyes. Ellen realized that despite her so-called experience, she'd handled this all wrong. She'd damaged his pride, just as Caro had said, and made him feel humiliated.

"Do you remember what you were doing?" she asked gently.

Peter stared at her for a long moment, that anger still in his eyes, his jaw bunched. "I don't know what you're talking about," he said finally.

"Peter, last night you were talking as if—as if it was still wartime!" Ellen pressed, feeling the need to explain why she was concerned. "You mentioned Captain Smythe and trench foot and falling into a crater made by a shell—" He flinched, and she took a step towards him, one hand held out. "Do you not remember? It was—"

"I don't," Peter cut her off, his voice flat and final. "I don't know what you're talking about."

He walked out of the barn without looking at her once, leaving Ellen standing there with the cows.

Caro had just come back from the Wilsons as Ellen came into the kitchen. She gave Ellen a sharp, questioning look, and Ellen shook her head. She didn't want to tell Caro about her conversation with Peter now, especially as she realized she feared her cousin wouldn't appreciate her having spoken to him without her permission.

"How is Iris Wilson?" she asked instead.

"Not very well, I'm afraid. She's taken poorly with a bad summer cold that just won't shift and the little ones need so much care. The oldest is only eight, poor mite, and they're all just about half-starved." Caro sighed. "It's as heartbreaking a scene as you could ever imagine. I don't know what will happen if she doesn't start getting better."

"That's terrible." For a moment, Ellen was distracted from her own worries. "What more can we do?"

"I left her with enough food in the house for several days and the children settled. I'll go back tomorrow and see if she's any worse, and make sure they're managing. The oldest is good with the little ones, at least."

"There seems no end to people's difficulties these days," Ellen said with a troubled frown. "When will it get better, Caro?"

"I don't know." Caro nodded towards the parlor. "How are our guests?"

"Enjoying themselves, I think. At least, they're not asking for anything at the moment." Ellen sank into a chair at the kitchen table with a little sigh of relief. "I hope they'll occupy themselves for the rest of the evening. Aunt Rose could certainly use the rest."

"That pinch-faced one had some gall, asking for a second pudding!" Caro said in a low voice. "What does she think we are? A restaurant in Toronto, with a menu to boot?"

"I don't know if she thought about it at all. But they're only here for a few more days."

"Yes." Caro tidied her hair, bending to peer in the small, cracked mirror above the washbasin. "Well, I'll check on them, at any rate. You look ready to drop."

"I'm not. But, Caro…" Ellen lowered her voice. She knew she couldn't hide her conversation with Peter from Caro for very long, as tempting as it was to do just that. There had always been honesty between them, and yet this morning Caro had seemed so sharp and cold. Ellen hoped that, in her tiredness, she had just been imagining it. "I spoke to Peter a few moments ago, in the barn."

Caro stiffened. "Oh?" she said, sounding, for a moment, remarkably like her brother.

"Yes, I asked him about last night, and he said he didn't know what I was talking about."

Caro sighed impatiently, her eyes snapping with anger just as they had that morning. "Of course he would. He's *proud,* Ellen. He wouldn't want to admit it. You never should have talked to him, especially without speaking to me first."

Stung, Ellen tried to form an even-tempered reply. "But I was worried…"

"And I'm worried as well," Caro fired back. "But there's nothing we can do about it, is there? Besides keep an eye on him."

"I'm not sure that's true," Ellen protested.

Caro's gaze narrowed. "What do you mean?"

"If Peter…" Ellen took a deep breath. "If he has shell shock—"

"He does not have shell shock!" Caro lowered her voice as she cast a concerned, furious look towards the parlor. "He's just troubled, Ellen, the same as every soldier that managed to come home from France. Surely you, as a nurse, know how that is?"

"Yes, of course I do." Ellen hesitated, knowing she needed to tread gently. "But, Caro, Peter thought it was wartime—"

"He was dreaming. Or maybe just remembering. He knew he was in the kitchen sure enough."

"Only after you acted as if he were still on the Front. Why did you talk to him as if it was still wartime—"

"I just wanted to get him back to bed! He came to soon enough. It doesn't have to mean anything, Ellen." Caro's eyes flashed. "Just because you were in France you think you know more than I do, but you don't."

This was such a blatantly unfair remark that Ellen did not know how to respond to it. "You know I have Peter's best interests at heart, don't you?" she asked.

Caro straightened her cuffs and apron and shot Ellen a shockingly scornful look. "Do you?" she asked. "He's not your brother, after all." She walked out of the room, leaving Ellen feeling even worse than before. She'd never fallen out with Caro, not even when they were young girls, prone to quarrel.

Her cousin's icy demeanor and seeming determination to remind Ellen that she wasn't a McCafferty hurt more than Ellen wanted to let it. Jasper Lane was her home. The McCaffertys were her family. She couldn't bear for it to change now.

CHAPTER NINE

Ellen and Caro kept a silent truce for the next few days, as they managed their guests, with Caro and Rose doing the cooking and cleaning and Ellen taking the three sisters to various points around the island to sketch and paint.

Although Patience, Viola, and Edith were all mediocre artists at best, Ellen discovered she enjoyed thinking about design and form again, and even the feel of a stick of charcoal between her fingers was a welcome relief, a kind of homecoming she hadn't expected. It made her ache to open up her own sketchbook and look through drawings from years ago, perhaps even create new ones, something she'd wondered whether she would ever do again.

In the current circumstances, however, she was kept busy enough encouraging the three ladies in their artistic ambitions.

By the time Viola Gardener and her sisters were on their way back to the mainland, Ellen, Rose, and Caro were exhausted, relieved, and excited all at once.

"That eases the burden, certainly," Rose said as she carefully put the money received from the sisters for their food and board in an old flour tin kept on a high shelf in the kitchen; she'd never held with banks.

"Do you think we'll get more bookings?" Caro asked. It was the question they'd all been asking themselves, and Ellen had no answers.

"I suppose we can only wait and see," she said, although she certainly hoped they did. Although the last few weeks had had their challenges, Ellen knew this was the only way forward to save the farm.

"Gracie, Sarah and Andrew will be returning home next week," Rose said, her forehead furrowing. "We'll be pinched for space if we do get many more."

"Gracie and Sarah can share the little bedroom," Caro said, and Rose looked at her, startled.

"But that's Ellen's bedroom! It always has been."

"I don't mind," Ellen said quickly. "I'll sleep wherever, honestly, Aunt Rose." She felt a flush come to her face at the way Caro had broached the subject, as if where she slept was of no consequence.

"I don't know…"

"I'm already sharing with you," Caro pointed out. "Ellen could share as well."

Rose gave her daughter a troubled look, but Ellen jumped in again with alacrity. "Of course I can. I can make up a bed on the floor of the back bedroom, and Gracie and Sarah can take the bed. It's no bother."

"We can't have you sleeping on the floor," Rose protested, and then sighed. "In any case, it's most likely not even going to be a concern. We have to get the bookings first."

It was early evening, the day still warm and golden, and with everything quiet at Jasper Lane, Ellen decided to walk across to the Lymans' farm. She was still smarting from Caro's comments, and she was also still worried about Peter. Although he hadn't had another episode since they'd found him in the kitchen, she felt he'd been more quiet and distant than usual.

Whenever Ellen looked concerned, Caro had shot her a warning look, a silent command not to say anything. That hurt too—since she'd arrived at Jasper Lane as a tangle-haired twelve-year-old, Ellen had felt embraced and loved by the McCaffertys. She'd always felt part of the family, unquestioningly and unreservedly, and now, for the first time, it seemed as if Caro was making the point that she wasn't. It wasn't Ellen's place to interfere, or even to worry about Peter. If Caro had her way, it seemed she wouldn't even have a place to sleep!

And yet Ellen couldn't help but both worry and interfere, for Peter's sake—and so she found herself climbing the steps to the Lymans' front porch, looking for Jed.

"Ellen." He greeted her at the door as unsmiling as ever, his shirt pinned neatly across his shoulder, his other arm well-muscled, his hand covered with nicks and scars from his work in farm and field.

"May I come in, Jed?" Ellen asked, and after a second's pause he stepped aside.

The kitchen bore evidence of being home to two bachelors, with dirty dishes piled up by the large stone sink and dust or grime on most surfaces.

Jed noticed her looking around and gave a slight, challenging grimace. "I wasn't expecting guests."

"I know." Ellen tried to smile. She hated how hostile Jed seemed, as unreachable as Peter, but in a completely different way. "Jed, I wanted to talk to you about Peter."

"Peter?" Jed frowned. "What have I to do with him?"

"What do you have to do with him?" Ellen repeated incredulously, amazed even now at how dismissive he seemed. "He's your neighbor, and a childhood friend, and a fellow soldier. Surely that is more than enough?"

Jed's jaw tightened and he didn't answer.

Ellen sighed. "I don't want to fight with you."

"Then don't."

She shook her head, realizing that any remarks she made about Jed's attitude should be saved for another day; her first concern right now was Peter. "I came here to ask for your help and advice. Because no matter how you seem to—to hate me now, I know we were friends once and I know you care about the McCaffertys almost as much as I do."

Jed turned away, taking the dented kettle from on top of the range and filling it with water. "I don't hate you," he said in a low voice, his back to her.

"Oh." Ellen managed a strained laugh, although she felt far from happy. All her old relationships had begun to feel fraught, or even as if they were failing.. "That's a relief, I suppose."

"But I don't know what I can do for Peter. I didn't see him even once during the war. I don't know what he's been through, and in any case he's nearly ten years younger than me. We've never been close friends."

Ellen sighed. "I don't know what you can do, either. But I'm worried about him, and you're the only person I could think of to talk to. You've been through what he has, Jed. You know what it was like, on the Front."

Jed turned around, his face impassive as he folded his good arm across his waist. "So why are you worried about him, then?"

"Because… because I think he might be suffering from shell shock." She hated even saying it; it made it feel more real.

Jed's expression didn't change; if anything, he looked even less impressed than before. "Every boy or man I know who fought in the war has scars, Ellen. Nightmares, or the shakes, or both. It doesn't mean he's got shell shock."

"A few nights ago he went wandering—"

"A man likes to have a little space."

"I know that, Jed, but when we found him…" Ellen took a steadying breath, trying to curb her impatience. "He was acting as if it was still wartime. Talking about patrols and no man's land and trench foot like it was all happening right there and then. And he wouldn't look at either Caro or me, it was as if we didn't exist in that moment. As if he was somewhere else entirely…"

The kettle started to whistle and Jed turned away. Ellen suppressed a stab of frustration. No one seemed as worried about Peter as she was. No one seemed to *want* to worry about him. Perhaps she was overreacting, but she still remembered the boy who had careened down the stairs with a wooden spoon brandished like a tomahawk. A boy who had so much irrepressible energy and cheer, whose boisterous laughter had echoed through the rooms of the McCafferty farmhouse, whose eyes had sparkled as he'd detailed all his madcap adventures. Where had that boy gone? And was there any way she could help to get him back?

"Caro refuses to talk about it," Ellen said quietly. "She more or less told me to mind my own business."

"Then maybe you should."

Ellen drew a sharp, hurt breath. She should have expected no less from Jed, considering how surly he'd been, but she hadn't. "After all these years, am I to be treated as an off-islander?" she asked, the words scraping her throat.

Jed turned and gave her a level look. "You were gone a long time."

"So were you." Hurt flashed through her, pang after pang. No one was on her side, it seemed. Leaving all those years ago for Glasgow and then France had severed something; the ties she'd always believed would bind her to this beloved place had been well and truly cut.

It didn't matter that both the McCaffertys and Lymans, as well as a host of other islanders, had encouraged her to follow her dreams, or that Jed, Lucas, Peter, and a handful of other island boys had joined up as soon as they could. Lots of people had been gone from the island, but she felt alone in her off-islander status, which got trotted out when it was convenient and no one wanted her interfering.

"Jed, I'm trying to help," she stated, a throb of urgency in her voice. "I'm serious about Peter. Something's wrong. Caro might not want to admit it, but if you could just talk to him. See for yourself…"

Jed made coffee, the process taking twice as long on account of his one arm. Ellen waited, her fists clenched, hope and hurt and frustration all warring within her. How had it all come to this?

"And if he is suffering as you say?" Jed asked at last. "Then what? What am I supposed to do?"

"I'm not asking you to do anything besides talk to him and help me decide if he really is shell-shocked. After that we could take him to a doctor. There are hospitals that specialize in treatment for men like Peter."

"They cost money. A lot of money." Jed handed her a cup of coffee, his expression less hostile now, although no less sullen. "Money the McCaffertys don't have."

"I have it," Ellen said quietly.

Jed cocked his head, surprise flaring in his gray-green eyes. "You do?"

"I… I have an inheritance." She bit her lip, realizing she'd never spoken to Jed about Henry McAvoy. "From my late fiancé."

His eyes widened as his impassive gaze scanned her face once more. "You had a fiancé? No one ever said."

"No one has ever known. It was before the war, in Glasgow." She swallowed hard. "It wasn't actually official. He'd asked me to marry him, and I was going to accept when he returned from a trip to America. He died on the *Titanic*."

"I'm sorry," Jed said quietly, the words sincere.

Ellen nodded jerkily. Henry McAvoy's death still hurt after all these years, but it was a dull pain. Their romance had been brief, tender and sweet, but little more than a spark too swiftly extinguished. "I would happily use that money for Peter," she said.

"If the McCaffertys accepted it."

"They have to! If Peter's health, his very life, is at stake…"

Jed shrugged, seeming indifferent even now as he took a sip of coffee.

Ellen bit down on her frustration. What would it take to reach this man? "Won't you please help him, Jed?"

"I'm not a doctor, Ellen. Far from it."

"I know, but you spent four years at the Front. You know what a man suffering from shell shock looks like. More than I do, perhaps, since men in such a state weren't often treated at a hospital. If you really do think that's what it is…" Ellen took a deep breath. "You could tell Caro and Rose and the rest of the McCaffertys. Perhaps they'll listen to you, a proper islander, more than they would me." She couldn't keep the bitterness from her voice.

"Oh, Ellen." Jed shook his head, his features softening with sadness. "The McCaffertys love you, you know. They always have. This thing with Peter isn't about you not being family."

"What is it, then?" Ellen asked, hurt vibrating in her voice. Caro's coolness had affected her more than she wanted to admit to Jed or even to herself.

"Fear," Jed said simply. "They know the truth and so they're afraid to look at it too closely. I know what that's like." He looked away, the set of his face grim, and Ellen's heart gave a painful little twist.

"Do you mean… do you mean because of the war, or… because of Louisa?" she asked quietly.

Ellen held her breath, waiting for Jed to answer. After what felt like an endless moment, he gave a terse nod. "We were troubled long before she left me," he said in a low voice. "Even before the war started."

"But it must have been made worse by Thomas' death," Ellen said softly.

"Don't," Jed said. "Don't let's talk about that." He put down his coffee cup and briefly, so briefly, put his hand on top of hers. "I'll do what you say. I'll talk to Peter."

CHAPTER TEN

Three days after Ellen's conversation with Jed, Gracie, Sarah, and Andrew all came home, and Ellen put her worries about Peter aside to enjoy the celebrations. Rose cooked one of the chickens and made a chocolate cake and it was lovely to have the house full of love and laughter again, the way it had been when Ellen had been a shy, lonely child, welcomed into the bosom of this rambunctious family, finally feeling as if she belonged somewhere.

Since she'd stopped trying to talk about Peter, Caro had softened towards her, although Ellen still sensed a reserve from her cousin that she knew hadn't been there before. She just hoped Jed was right and it was fear rather than lack of affection that was motivating Caro's coolness.

Sarah, Gracie, and Andrew had all greeted her with exuberant hugs at least. She'd seen them all several times since her arrival back on the island, but no one would have guessed it from the enthusiasm with which they greeted her now. Their warm embraces were a balm to Ellen's battered soul, as was the laughter and conversation that flew across the kitchen table the evening of their arrival, as everyone finished their dessert and Rose put on the kettle.

"Don't go putting on airs," Andrew warned Gracie as he leaned back in his chair, plates scattered with chocolate crumbs in front of everyone. "Now that you're a university girl."

"Airs? Me?" Gracie raised her eyebrows, her blue eyes sparkling with humor and audacity. She'd always been whip-smart and sassy, and now that she was nearly grown-up, Ellen could see what a beauty she'd become, with her black curls and bright eyes, just like Dyle's. She'd have half the men at Queen's setting their caps for her, Ellen was sure.

"And what about you, Sarah?" Ellen asked. "Are you enjoying teaching at Gananoque?"

"Oh, yes." Sarah smiled, the opposite of her younger sister, with her soft cloud of brown hair and hazel eyes, her quiet, shy ways. "Yes, I love teaching, although there are a few boys in my classroom who'd like to get the better of me. They put a frog in my desk drawer on the very first day, but they'd forgotten I was a country girl."

Ellen laughed. "I'm sure you put them in their places."

"I did," Sarah assured her, her smile widening. "Never worry about that! I may be quiet, but I know when to use my voice."

"Will you stay at Gananoque?" Ellen asked.

"They've offered me a two-year contract, and I've accepted. That is if…" She glanced inquiringly at Rose, who was spooning tea leaves into the big brown pot.

"Don't ask me what the fate of this farm is, love, because I'm sure I don't know. If we get more bookings, we might just be able to hold onto this place. Especially with Ellen being such a marvel! Mrs. Viola Gardener was singing her praises the whole week long."

"She wasn't," Ellen protested, blushing. Viola had been complimentary, but she felt embarrassed by how Rose seemed to attribute the week's success solely to her. They'd all worked hard.

"These women wouldn't be coming if they didn't have a proper lady artist to show them how to sketch and draw," Rose said seriously. "None of this would be possible without you."

"And it might not again," Caro interjected. "We haven't had another booking yet."

Ellen glanced at her and saw the way her lips were pursed. Was Caro envious, she wondered, feeling that Rose was giving her more attention or praise? Was that part of the reason she'd been so prickly? Or was it really just about Peter?

Ellen looked back at Peter, who had seemed more lighthearted since his siblings' arrival, leaning his chair back on its legs and smiling faintly as both girls regaled him with stories of their adventures as independent young women. Ellen experienced a pang of bittersweet memory—once, she'd been like them, full of excitement and anticipation for what lay ahead, and all the possibilities that had been open to her. It had been a long time since she'd felt like that. The war, along with too much loss and grief, had put paid to such carefree notions.

"Washed up at twenty-eight," she muttered ruefully as she dumped the dirty dishwater outside after supper. She supposed it wasn't that old, even if it felt like it. Most women her age were married with several children by now, but Ellen doubted she ever would be, especially with the dearth of eligible men since the war. There certainly wasn't anyone on the island she could think of that way.

She straightened, putting her hands on the small of her back to ease the crick that had formed there, smiling wryly as she considered her predicament—an old maid before she was thirty, living in a ramshackle farmhouse, with not a soul about she could even dream about in that way. Well, she supposed there were worse places to be.

It was a tranquil summer's evening, dragonflies humming in the air, the setting sun turning everything to gold. Peter and Andrew were out in the barn seeing to the animals, and Ellen had shooed Gracie and Sarah from the kitchen, insisting they put their feet up with Aunt Rose in the parlor while she saw to the washing up. Caro had set off for the Wilsons again, intending to stay the night if needed.

"I keep thinking about those poor children," she'd told Rose while Ellen had filled the sink with soapy water. "All alone, with just their ill mam, and they haven't much money, let me tell you. They're as good as dressed in rags."

"Why don't you bring them some of your old dresses?" Rose had suggested. "You could cut them down and sew them to size. I'll help."

"That's a lovely idea," Caro had said, brightening. "They could certainly use a few more things."

"I can help too," Ellen had offered with an uncertain smile, and Caro's gaze had skated over her.

"You've never been much good with a needle," she'd said, not unkindly, and Ellen did her best not to feel hurt. It was true enough, anyway.

Caro had left soon after with her things for the Wilson children, and with everyone in the parlor, Ellen now looked forward to a few quiet moments in the kitchen. The last few days had been happy but fraught with work and care, and she was glad simply to be, watching the sun set over the lake and putting the kitchen to rights.

Whatever Caro was feeling, she told herself, it would blow over. They'd all been under such pressure these last few weeks, with the fear of losing the farm looming over their heads, and then the demands of their guests taking all their time. Never mind that it had been three days since Viola Gardener and her sister had left; Caro would come round. And if she didn't, Ellen decided, then she would talk to her. They'd always been close. She did not want to lose that precious connection now, simply from want of trying to hold onto it.

The washing finished and the kitchen tidied, Ellen went into the parlor, pausing in the doorway to view the scene with a deep-seated contentment. Gracie was curled up one end of the shabby horsehair sofa that had been in the room since Ellen had first arrived, over fifteen years ago, and Sarah was sitting on the other, an open book forgotten in her lap. Rose, as ever, was darning something, but she seemed to have forgotten that as well, for her needles lay in her lap and her face was alight with laughter. Andrew was sprawled in a chair by the fire, Peter was sitting on the piano stool, his long fingers playing a few discordant notes as he listened—the piano hadn't been tuned in years. Her family, she thought, and she didn't care whether she was an off-islander or not. This was her family.

"Oh Ellen, come join us," Rose entreated with a laugh as she beckoned to her with one hand. "Gracie has just been regaling us with the most amazing stories from university. She and her college chums have been daring each other to do the most ridiculous things—wrapping each other in bandages, for a start!"

"We had to have *some* fun," Gracie protested, laughing, "when they turned Grant Hall into a military hospital and had us all rolling bandages! Although the matron *was* cross. But the bandages were perfectly fine—we didn't harm anything or anyone, I promise."

"I'm sure, I'm sure," Ellen answered as she took a seat on the sofa next to Sarah. "It all sounds like a wonderful time." She smiled at Peter, who smiled back faintly and played a few more notes.

It was so pleasant sitting there, listening to Gracie's self-important chatter as she tossed her black curls, dark eyes sparkling defiantly, so like Dyle. Ellen wondered if she'd ever possessed such passion. She didn't think she had, even during her Glasgow days, when she'd been determined to pursue her art. She sighed and tucked her legs up under her on the sofa. Goodness, but she was feeling old tonight.

Sarah suddenly leaned forward to place a hand on Ellen's, her eyes warm with affection. "Oh, Ellen, it's so good to have you back with us, just like old days. Just like the way it's supposed to be."

Ellen looked at her in surprise, a smile spreading slowly over her face as she took in Sarah's warmhearted sincerity. "It's good to be back."

And it was. Sitting there in the cozy room, with laughter in the air, Ellen could almost forget Caro's harsh words.

"Ah, Gracie," Peter said dryly, "you shall have all the Queen's boys eating out of your hand before you finish your freshman year."

"I hope so," Gracie returned with another toss of her curls, and Peter laughed.

Ellen heartened to hear the sound. Perhaps she had been over-reacting about the funny turn he'd taken. He seemed perfectly at ease and happy now, if only a little remote, and as Ellen sat back in her chair, she wanted to let the worries and cares that had been near to tormenting her these last few days slip away, like pearls off a string. She wanted simply to enjoy these lovely moments, because she knew they came all too rarely, and they were so very precious.

The next morning, Ellen woke early to dazzling sunlight and headed down to the kitchen to get the day's work started. Rose had been looking tired lately, and she hoped her aunt might have a rest while she got breakfast on, and saw to the morning chores.

The air was fresh and cool at this time of day, although with the promise of heat later. It would be a good drying day, Ellen thought, with the breeze coming off the lake. Perhaps she would do the sheets on her bed, and her Sunday dress as well, whose hem was still caked in mud.

Indeed, the morning passed in a pleasant round of chores, with Gracie and Sarah stumbling down, but Ellen insisting they sit down and relax. She was happy enough to bustle about, making breakfast, collecting the eggs, and putting the bed sheets into soak, stopping only when she saw Bert on his trusty bicycle, waving another telegram.

Rose, who had been sitting at the kitchen table with Sarah, the cat in her lap as she sipped a cup of tea, gave Ellen a glance that was filled with both anxiety and hope. "Do you think…"

"There's only one way to find out," Ellen said cheerfully, and, wiping her hand on her apron, she went to the front door.

Bert handed her the telegram from Toronto, craning his neck to try to read it. "Do you think it's more of those fancy people of yours, Ellen?" he asked.

"They're not mine, and I'm afraid I have no idea, Bert, but thank you for the telegram," Ellen said crisply, and put it in her apron pocket. She had no intention of Bert hearing another telegram read out and then passing their business to everyone on the island yet again.

"Have a good day, then," he said rather sadly, and then wobbled off on his bicycle.

"Poor Bert," Sarah said with a smile as Ellen came back into the kitchen. "I think he lives vicariously through all the telegrams, not that many come to the island. What does it say, Ellen?"

"I don't know, because I haven't opened it," Ellen replied, laughing as she took it out of her pocket.

"Read it, Ellen, do," Rose implored, and Gracie nodded, curious now, too.

"Do you think it's another booking?"

Ellen opened the telegram and scanned the few lines. "It isn't another booking," she said, looking up with an incredulous smile, almost wanting to laugh out loud. "It's three."

"Three!"

"Goodness gracious!"

"Oh, my." Rose pressed a hand to her chest. "I never expected... How will we manage?"

"Gracie and Sarah will go into the back bedroom, just as we said," Ellen explained practically. "And I can sleep on the floor—"

"On the floor! Ellen, you mustn't!"

"No, you can have the box room," Peter said as he came into the kitchen from the barn, having overheard some of the news.

"And Andrew and I can make up some beds in the hayloft. That's most sensible."

"You can't spend the winter in the hayloft," Rose protested.

"And so we won't. It's midsummer, and neither of us will mind," Peter replied.

"Speak for yourself," Andrew returned as he followed Peter in from the barn, but he was smiling. "It's good news, Mum," he told her as he gave her cheek a smacking kiss. "Be happy."

Amidst the continuing exclamations of surprise and delight, no one heard the sound of someone coming up the front steps. Ellen turned only when the front door was flung open, hard enough to bang the wall, and Caro stood there, panting, her face flushed and her hair in disarray.

"Ellen," she cried, "you must come quickly. It's Iris Wilson. I think she has the Spanish flu!"

Everyone fell silent as they took in this dreadful news. They'd all read about the deadly disease sweeping through the world, killing millions, more even than the war, but so far tiny Amherst Island had escaped its terrible notice.

"Are you sure, Caro?" Ellen asked. "How would she ever have managed to catch it?"

"She went to Kingston, before she took ill, to sell something, I think. Maybe then?" Caro shrugged helplessly. "I don't rightly know, but she's taken a turn for the worse and she's ever so hot." Caro's face was pale, her golden-brown hair in tangles as she gazed at Ellen anxiously. "I read about the symptoms in the newspaper."

"We all have," Rose interjected, her face drawn into frowning lines of concern. "It's terribly serious. Have you called the doctor?"

"Iris can't afford a doctor's fees," Caro said grimly. "And neither can we, for that matter. And you know Dr. Stephens won't be called out anymore if you haven't got the money."

"He can't afford it, poor man," Rose said quietly. Gone were the days when services could be paid for with a sack of potatoes or a chicken.

"Doctors can't seem to do much anyway," Sarah remarked quietly. "There have been some cases of influenza in Gananoque—it really can be terrible."

"Will you have a look at her, Ellen?" Caro implored, wringing her hands in a most un-Caro-like way. "You're a nurse. You're the most experienced one among us. Surely you would know."

"It's never been up to me to diagnose anyone," Ellen warned her shakily. "I just gave medicine and changed bandages. But I'll have a look at her. Of course I will."

Andrew hitched the wagon and drove them across the island, up to Emerald, where the Wilsons had a small, shabby farmhouse of weathered clapboard, half-hidden beneath some overgrown ash trees. The fields that rolled down to the sparkling blue-green waters of Lake Ontario had once been neatly tilled and sown, but now all but two were fallow, choked with goldenrod and wild sumac.

"Iris hasn't had any help," Caro explained quietly as she and Ellen alit from the wagon, and Andrew tethered the horses. "She's not able to make ends meet on her own, with no one to farm the land. She had a vegetable garden, and she sold some eggs, but that's all. And now this…" She shook her head. "It's bad."

It *was* bad, Ellen realized with a rush of pity, as she stepped across the threshold of the Wilsons' small farmhouse, so different from the busy, happy bustle of Jasper Lane, and saw what greeted her. Three woebegone figures sat at the kitchen table, all tangled hair and runny noses, with nothing but a few slices of stale bread between them smeared with a bit of lard. The jam Caro had bought that morning had already been eaten, with their fingers in the jar, judging from their sticky hands and faces.

They gazed at Ellen with wide eyes, too hungry and frightened to say anything or perhaps even feel curious about this new stranger entering their lives.

"Hello, little ones," Ellen said with a kindly smile. "I'm here to help your mother. You know Caro already. She'll see to you." She turned to Caro and whispered, "Tell Andrew to ride back to Jasper Lane and bring a basket of food. Rose will make one up. They look half-starved, poor things."

"I fed them beef stew last night," Caro said with some affront, "and bread and jam this morning."

"They still look as good as hollow," Ellen replied, and reluctantly Caro nodded.

"There's nothing in the larder as far as I can see. I'll tell Andrew to bring more."

She hurried out and Ellen waited until she'd come back to see to the children before she headed upstairs. Iris was in the front bedroom, the windows overlooking the sea, although they were now closed, the curtains drawn shut so the room was stifling, the air stale, smelling of sweat and sickness and damp.

"Hello, Mrs. Wilson," Ellen said as she took in the wasted figure lying on the bed, her nightgown soaked with sweat and her eyes glazed and dilated from fever. "My name is Ellen Copley. I trained as a nurse and served on the Front, in France. I'm going to look you over now, and see how you are."

Ellen didn't need to do much of a checkup to see that Iris Wilson was dangerously ill. Besides the bright spots of color on her gaunt cheekbones, her face was pale and waxy and her breath rattled through her lungs, each one drawn with terrible effort. Her skin was hot to the touch, and she barely seemed to notice Ellen as she checked her reflexes, her pupils, and listened to her lungs and heart.

Caro appeared at the doorway, her hands knotted together. "She wasn't like this yesterday," she said unhappily. "I wouldn't have left her like this."

"I know, Caro," Ellen replied gently. She could see well enough that Caro felt guilty for the state of Iris Wilson and her children, even though she'd been by every day with food and medicine. "From the cases I saw during the war, I know it can come on quickly."

"So you do think this is influenza?" Caro dropped her voice, even though Iris had fallen into a restless slumber, her eyelids fluttering, her hand twitching against the sheet.

"It might be," Ellen agreed heavily, "but I can't be sure. Whatever it is, it looks bad. Let's do our best to make her comfortable, at least. We can sponge her off, and change her nightclothes and sheets."

Half an hour later, Iris seemed a bit more comfortable, dressed in a fresh, albeit patched and faded, nightgown, with the only other set of sheets on the bed and the dirty ones bundled downstairs, which Caro promised to put through the mangle later in the day.

"Are you going to stay here?" Ellen asked as the three children, revived by a meal of thick slices of ham, fresh bread and butter, and an apple crumble from Rose's own larder, tumbled outside to play. Caro had washed their faces and plaited the girls' hair, warming to her role as substitute mother.

"What else can I do?" she asked as she began to wash the dishes. Ellen found a broom and started to sweep. "Someone has to look after these children, and I don't see anyone else offering."

"There's no kin, I suppose?"

"I asked Iris that before she took so poorly. Her husband's brother is in Oshawa. He's injured, though, and can't do any farming work, as far as she knows." She sighed. "This place belonged to Iris's family. They bought it in '05, having come from Hamilton. Her parents are dead now and she has no brothers or sisters anymore. They've all died—one in the war, one from a fever before, and one as a baby." She shook her head as she listed the litany of grief. "So, no, there isn't anyone."

"Perhaps you should let the brother know?" Ellen suggested. "Just in case?"

Caro nodded soberly. "I could try, although I don't even know his name, and Iris isn't sensible enough now to tell me. Do you think she might..." She swallowed. "Do you think she might die, Ellen?"

"It's in God's hands." Ellen sighed as she swiped at the loose strands of hair that had come out of her bun. "I know that sounds trite, but it's the truth. There's only so much a person can do, even the most skilled doctor, and I am far from that. If she does have influenza, and in truth I think she does, then I honestly couldn't tell you her chances, but I'll warrant they're not good."

Caro's face took on a pinched look. "Poor woman."

"Yes. All we can do is pray."

"It feels like precious little now," Caro returned bitterly. "After everything that's happened... I sometimes wonder what God is doing about all this." She swept one arm out towards the dirty kitchen, yet encompassing so much more.

"Don't lose your faith, Caro," Ellen said softly. "Heaven knows, I've struggled too. But it's at times like this when it can be the only thing keeping you upright."

"I suppose so."

For a second, Ellen thought about asking Caro if she was angry with her, and seeking to mend whatever had been broken between them, but with Iris so ill upstairs, and the children just outside, it hardly seemed the right moment. She kept sweeping the floor instead, her heart heavy with the weight of others' sorrows.

"And if she does die?" Caro asked eventually. "What will happen to these poor children?"

Ellen shook her head helplessly. She had no idea what would become of the Wilson children, but she could guess. They'd be shipped off to St Mary's in Kingston, an orphanage for the destitute, or perhaps Toronto's House of Industry, where the poor were given food and shelter in exchange for work. Neither option was at all desirable, and yet Ellen doubted there was anyone on the island who could take in three more mouths to feed, no matter how many good intentions they might have.

"I'll do my best to take care of Mrs. Wilson," she promised Caro. "But in the meantime, you should find out her husband's brother's name and address, if you can. He's the most likely person to help, even if he is injured."

CHAPTER ELEVEN

When Ellen returned to Jasper Lane, having left Caro in charge of the Wilsons, she was hit by a wave of nostalgia and thankfulness that, in her tired and grimy state, nearly felled her. She swayed against the kitchen door, taking in the sunlight slanting through the windows, a bowl of shelled peas on the table, the cat curled up in front of the old blackened range. Everything about the scene was so homely, and threadbare though it all was, Ellen felt it was rather wonderful, and she was so grateful that she'd been given the chance to live here and be part of this family. Would the Wilsons be given such a chance?

"Ellen, you look done in," Rose exclaimed as she came into the kitchen. She took Ellen by the shoulders and gave her a quick, tight hug. "I've just heated some water for a wash. Go upstairs and have a few moments to yourself. There's so much to do."

"Is there?" Ellen felt too weary to think about what those tasks were. Briefly, she recalled the bookings they'd been so excited about, before Caro had rushed in with her awful news. "When are the first guests coming?"

"They want to come in just three days, would you believe," Rose said as she bustled around the kitchen, pulling out pots and pans. "But don't worry. We'll be ready this time. Now that I know what to expect, I feel much more confident. And the Gardener sisters must have had a nice time, to recommend us? A woman is coming all the way from New York, with her daughter! Apparently she's school chums with Viola from long ago, and Viola sent her a telegram telling her she had to come and stay."

"Imagine," Ellen murmured.

"Who would have thought it could all happen so quickly! But you look as if you could fall asleep right there against the door," Rose half-scolded. "Go upstairs, Ellen, for pity's sake, and have a wash and a sleep. The world will wait."

"Thank you, Aunt Rose." Ellen smiled, feeling quite suddenly near tears.

"My goodness," Rose exclaimed as she took her by the shoulders once more. "Is it poor Iris, Ellen, that's affecting you?" Her expression grew somber. "Will she pull through, do you think? I've never seen a case of the 'flu, just read the stories in the paper like everyone else."

"It's the children, actually," Ellen confessed shakily. "They're so little—the oldest one can't be more than eight. What will happen to them, Aunt Rose, if Iris dies? There's no family, not to speak of…" She shook her head as a shudder went through her. "I can't help but think that it could have been me, facing an orphanage or worse after my father left. If Ruth and Hamish hadn't taken me in… if you hadn't sent for me… I'd have been shipped off to an orphanage or workhouse. They're terrible places, especially for children—"

"But we did send for you," Rose said firmly. "You were a far cry from an orphan, Ellen Copley, even though I know you often felt like one."

"I know." Ellen smiled through the mist of tears she hadn't expected to shed. "I'm so blessed, and yet when I was younger, I resented Aunt Ruth and Uncle Hamish so much! Aunt Ruth was so stern and severe, but she could be kind, too, and I never really got a chance to tell her how grateful I was. I've never thanked them, not properly…"

"They knew," Rose said quietly. "And they loved you, in their own way. Some things don't need to be said." She pursed her lips as her eyes took on a similar sheen to Ellen's. "Dyle didn't tell me he loved me all that often. He wasn't that kind of man. He whistled as he worked and he loved a joke, but when it came to finer feelings… But I knew, Ellen. I always knew. I never doubted for a minute that the man adored the very air I walked on, and glad I was of it, too. And your Aunt Ruth knew you loved her, too. She had a funny way of showing her own feelings, I'll grant you, but she loved you like a daughter. It was hard enough trying to keep you here when she wanted you, and not just to tidy after her! I know you thought that, but it wasn't true. She loved you." Rose gave her another hug. "Now, upstairs with you, before we're both bawling like a couple of babies."

Upstairs, Ellen washed off the worst of the dirt and grime, stripped down to her petticoat and lay on the bed, the sunlight streaming through the windows, and was asleep within minutes.

When she awoke, it was to sounds of excitement and laughter downstairs, making her feel for a second as if she'd tumbled back in time. She was a child again, listening to the loving sounds of a big, busy family, longing to be a part—and she could be.

Smiling in expectation, Ellen dressed hurriedly, tucking her hair up as she came down the stairs to a kitchen crowded with McCaffertys.

"What's going on?" she asked, looking at Gracie's bright, snapping eyes and Sarah's shy smile. Andrew was loitering by the door, along with Peter. "Has something happened?"

"Tom Howard has firecrackers," Gracie told her. "For Dominion Day. He's going to set them off down by the beach across from Nut Island tonight." She tossed her dark ringlets. "And we're all going to go. We'll take lemonade and cookies, and the boys will build a bonfire. It will be such fun, Ellen."

"I'm too old for such nonsense," Rose said with a smile. "And in truth I can't abide such a racket. But the rest of you ought to go along. It's a treat, to be sure."

"You will come, Ellen, won't you?" Sarah implored. "It wouldn't be the same without you."

Ellen could think of better things to do than stand in the dark listening to loud things go off, but she could see how excited Sarah and Gracie were, and they had few enough treats as it was. A bonfire would be nice. "Of course I'll go. What about Caro?"

"Andrew rode over to the Wilsons and asked her if she wanted to come, but she won't leave Iris. I said I'd come and stay, but she's adamant." Rose smiled faintly. "The truth is, I think she's taken a liking to those three tykes. God bless their mother."

"And Andrew? Peter?" Ellen asked. "You're both going?"

"We'll all go," Peter said as he came into the kitchen, with a smile that did not quite reach his eyes. "Why not?"

Ellen glanced at him uncertainly; there was a strange, almost wild glitter in his eyes that she didn't understand. She certainly hadn't seen it in her months at Jasper Lane, yet she could hardly remark on it, or ask Peter if he really wanted to attend the outing. Why would he go if he didn't want to?

It was already dark by the time they set off down Jasper Lane for the beachfront across from Nut Island, where Tom Howard had proposed for everyone to meet.

Even though it was the first of July, there was a coolness to the night air, and clouds covered the stars, the moon sliding between them like a stately ghost. Despite the cheerful and excited chatter of all those around her, Ellen felt a touch of foreboding, although she couldn't have said why. Perhaps it was from seeing Iris so ill that morning, or worrying about what would happen to the

Wilson children, or simply that she was still so tired. Or maybe just old, Ellen acknowledged with an inward, rueful grimace. She was twenty-eight years old, and Tom Howard, if she remembered correctly, was barely twenty.

As they walked down the dirt road towards the beach, the wind whispered in the maples and birches and the moon, when it emerged from behind the clouds, cast a pearly sheen to the placid surface of the lake in the distance.

"All right, Ellen?"

Ellen turned in surprise to see Jed coming alongside her.

"Jed! I didn't realize you were coming to see the fireworks as well."

"Tom Howard was in my regiment," Jed answered. "A young lad—he joined up in '16, as soon as he turned eighteen. His brother Neal died at the third battle of Ypres."

"I'm sorry," Ellen said quietly. She remembered Neal, a quiet, bookish boy compared to his younger brother's more boisterous personality. It was hard to imagine him in the trenches with a rifle in his hands, clambering over the top...

"We all lost someone," Jed answered with a shrug. "More than one, in many cases."

"Yes," Ellen agreed.

They walked in silence for a few moments, and a surprisingly companionable one at that, considering how Ellen never knew what to expect from Jed.

"I spoke to Peter," Jed said after a moment. They'd dropped a bit behind the others, who had moved ahead, eager to get to the beach and see the firecrackers. "Like you asked me to."

"You did?" Ellen was surprised; somehow she hadn't expected Jed to follow through, and Peter certainly hadn't mentioned it. "Thank you, Jed, for doing that. Did it... did it help?" The worry in the pit of her stomach felt like the slow seep of acid. "Do you think he does have shell shock?"

"He didn't seem like it, when I saw him," Jed answered frankly. "No thousand-yard stare, no sudden shakes or upsets, but it was a sunny day in the middle of a farmer's field." He shrugged. "Like I told you before, I'm no doctor, Ellen."

"I know."

"No one fights in a war and comes home without scars," Jed continued quietly. "Peter's are just a different kind to mine." He gestured to his empty sleeve and Ellen's heart twisted at the grim, resigned look on his face.

"Does it… does it pain you very much?" she dared to ask, hoping he wouldn't get angry the way he once might have.

Jed was silent for a moment. "Sometimes," he said at last. "Ghost pain, like I can feel my fingers. Odd, really, like a mockery."

"I remember men experiencing that back at Royaumont," Ellen told him. "Phantom pain, they called it. It was so disconcerting for them—it gave them a sort of terrible hope, for a few moments anyway, when they forgot…" She trailed off, realizing she might have said too much, for Jed's face had closed right up.

"Well, you get used to it," he said in a final-sounding tone.

"Yes," Ellen pressed, "although getting used to something doesn't make bearing it any easier."

Jed did not reply and they lapsed into a silence that was not entirely comfortable, but not as fraught as others had been, and they walked the whole way to the beach together.

Moonlight spilled over the sand and the gentle shush of the waves lapping the shore were a comforting backdrop to the excitement buzzing among the young people gathered there, eager for some entertainment after so much hardship and suffering.

Tom was brandishing the promised firecrackers as everyone chatted and laughed, waiting for the show to begin.

Ellen and Jed hung back, content to be on the fringes of the group. Ellen was conscious that she was older than most of the people there by nearly ten years, and Jed by even more. And she *felt* older, wearier and more careworn than those whose faces were alight with excitement at the prospect of seeing the precious firecrackers shooting off. Yet Ellen knew she couldn't begrudge them their fun. Life had been hard, and promised to continue to be so. Everyone needed to get their pleasure where and when they could, however small it was.

She looked around for Peter and Andrew, but she couldn't see either of them in the darkened crowd.

"Here it goes!" Tom called out in excitement, and there was a collective intake of breath as the firecracker lit up and then went fizzing upwards with a loud bang, lighting up the night sky with a shower of brilliant sparks. Ellen glanced at Jed, who was watching the show with his usual impassive expression. Everyone else was laughing and pointing, enjoying the bright display.

Tom let off another firecracker and another, with accompanying bangs and sparks, to many cheers and lots of laughter, and Ellen began to relax, enjoying the unexpected show, when Jed suddenly grabbed her arm.

"*Ellen.*"

"What is it?" She turned to him in alarmed surprise, and Jed nodded at a familiar figure at the edge of the beach, stumbling away from the firecrackers. "It's Peter," he said in a low voice. "The noise and light must have reminded him of the war. Those firecrackers sound a lot like shells going off."

Ellen's stomach clenched with worry. "Oh, no—"

"I'll go after him," Jed said, and Ellen watched in misery and fear as he hurried after Peter, and then was swallowed up in the darkness.

CHAPTER TWELVE

The next morning, Jed appeared at the back door of Jasper Lane, looking even more grim-faced than usual, and Ellen's heart started to thud. She hadn't seen him since he'd taken off from the beach after Peter; by the time Ellen had arrived home with the others, a pale-faced Rose had told Ellen that Jed had brought Peter home and tucked him up in bed.

"He talked to him as if it was still the war," Rose had whispered, wringing her hands. "As if he was his officer, and he was taking him back to his bunk. It was... it was so odd, Ellen, because Peter believed it. He was talking about the trenches, as if they were right *there.*" She gestured to the front yard, looking as if she could cry.

Ellen had pressed Rose's hand in sympathy and comfort. "It was the firecrackers, Aunt Rose. The noise and sound. It brought it all back."

"But he didn't seem to realize the war is over..." Rose had pressed her lips together and turned away. There could be no denying that something was really wrong, no matter how much Caro or anyone else wished it otherwise. The thought did not bring any relief, just more sorrow.

Now Jed stood in the doorway, his hat in his hands, his expression serious. "May I talk to you, Ellen? Rose? Where's Caro? She ought to be present, I think."

"She's stayed at the Wilsons, to take care of those poor children as well as Iris," Ellen said. Caro had been spending more and more time at the Wilson farmhouse, and Ellen wondered if she preferred it—being the only one in charge, the one to swoop in and save everyone. It wasn't a particularly generous thought, and yet she couldn't help but feeling a twinge of resentment that Caro seemed set on reminding her of her place outside the family, and yet then disappeared to take care of someone else's.

It was barely eight o'clock in the morning and Ellen already felt exhausted. She needed to return to check on Iris, and help Rose get ready for the guests arriving tomorrow, and now Peter. There was so much to do, so much to worry about, and she felt as if she could collapse from it all. "What is it, Jed?" she asked. "Are you here to talk about Peter?" Of course he was, and yet she felt the need to ask.

"Come in, come in," Rose urged before he could reply. "I'll make us coffee."

Jed came inside, the screen door banging behind him. "Where is everyone else?"

"Peter's still asleep, and Andrew is out in the fields. Sarah and Gracie have gone into Stella for some shopping. We have guests coming tomorrow."

"Then I'll make this short." Jed stood in the kitchen, not even taking a seat, although Rose had already started to fill the kettle. "Peter's not well, Rose." He gave his neighbor a direct look. "I think he needs specialized treatment."

Ellen felt a wave of relief at this admission, even though the uncertainty filled her with fear. She glanced at her aunt and saw that Rose's face was pale, her lips set, as she put water on to boil on top of the range. "What kind of specialized treatment?"

"There are hospitals for men like Peter," Jed said quietly. "Men who have trouble recovering from everything they saw and heard and did."

"You're talking about shell shock." Her voice trembled, but she gave Jed as direct a look as he'd given her.

"Yes," he answered steadily. "I am." Rose didn't say anything and he added quietly, "There's no shame in it. Plenty of brave men experience the same. It's no reflection on them or their courage or fortitude."

"I know there's no shame," Rose answered sharply, drawing a ragged breath. "I'm not like that, Jed Lyman. It's just... *Peter.*" Her voice broke. "How can he... and yet I should have realized sooner. I knew something was wrong, but I just kept hoping it would get better on its own." She shook her head, looking near tears. "How long has he been suffering like this, and I haven't done anything?"

"The important thing, Aunt Rose," Ellen said gently, "is that he gets help now. I'm glad Jed has told us."

"But what kind of help? Will he have to go away?" She looked between them, her eyes wide with apprehension.

"There's a military hospital in Toronto," Jed said after a moment. "I could write to Lucas about it." He glanced at Ellen, his expression inscrutable. "Or you could, Ellen, seeing as you're such friends." It almost felt like a rebuke.

Ellen shook her head. "I don't mind who does it, Jed. I just want to help Peter."

"We all do," Rose said. "Whatever needs to be done." She looked troubled, and Ellen knew she was thinking about the money such a hospital would cost. She wanted to tell her aunt that she would pay for it out of the money Henry McAvoy had left her, but she knew Rose would resist and, in any case, she wouldn't say anything in front of Jed. He was so spiky about certain things, money being one of them.

"I'll look into it, then," Jed decided with a nod.

The water had boiled for the coffee, but Rose seemed too shocked and upset to do anything about it, and Jed didn't look as if he wanted any, anyway.

Ellen looked around the sun-dappled kitchen, everything so familiar and dear, and felt a wave of sadness that they'd got to this point. That Peter might need to be hospitalized, that everyone had changed and suffered. She allowed herself a moment of nostalgia and regret and then she drew herself up, determined to get on with the day.

"I should go to the Wilsons." Ellen glanced at the clock above the range. "Caro will be waiting for me. I do hope Iris has taken a turn for the better in the night. Thank you, Jed, for coming here."

"I'll drive you in the wagon if you like," Jed offered, surprising her. "It will take at least half an hour to walk that far."

"Only if you've time…"

"I've time."

Ellen pressed her cheek to Rose's in farewell before gathering her shawl and a basket of food for the Wilsons. She and Jed started back to the Lyman farm, across the field towards the copse of birches slender and white against the sunlight.

"How is your father?" she asked as they walked the old path, the pond shimmering under the July sunshine. "Is he coping all right? I haven't seen him much of late."

"He's fine," Jed answered. "Struggling on as everyone seems to be these days."

"It's hard, isn't it?" They walked for a few moments in silence before Ellen continued stiltedly, "Thank you, Jed, for coming to see us this morning, and also for going after Peter last night. I'm ashamed that I didn't even think about how the noise of the firecrackers would upset him."

"Why would you?"

"I heard the shells too," Ellen reminded him. "I know I didn't fight like you or Peter or any of the island boys did, but I remember the Front, evacuating from Villiers-Cotterets with the bombs going overhead…" She gave an involuntary shiver as the memory assailed her—the orange sky, the earth-shaking thuds, the fear so overwhelming it had felt as if she were frozen.

"Of course you remember." Jed sighed and shook his head. "I'm sorry, I didn't mean to sound as if you hadn't been there."

"I wasn't fighting the way you were," Ellen said. "I don't mean to compare my experience to yours."

Jed gave her an unexpected quirk of a smile. "It's not a competition."

Ellen smiled back, managing a little laugh. "No, I suppose not." She let out a gusty sigh. "Some days I wish we could all go back to before the war, when we were children. Do you remember how we all played around the pond? It seems like such a simple time now, and I know we're far from children, but I miss those days."

"So do I." Jed's voice was so low Ellen almost didn't hear the three simple, heartfelt words. She glanced at him, startled by how sincere he'd sounded, but he was staring straight ahead as they walked past the pond, and on to the Lyman pasture.

As they approached the farmhouse, Jed went for the wagon while Ellen waited by the front steps, enjoying the sunshine on her face and trying not to give in to the worry that was cramping her stomach—the Wilsons, Peter, the guests coming tomorrow… For a few minutes, she wanted to close her eyes and not to have to think about any of it. She'd enjoyed the walk with Jed, companionable as it had been, a small oasis of comfort in the midst of a busy, care-filled day.

"Ellen." Jed's voice sounded surprisingly light as she opened her eyes. He stood in front of her, the horses hitched to the wagon. "I thought you'd fallen asleep there for a minute."

"For a minute I almost did."

Jed stretched out his hand and Ellen took it, trying to suppress the flurry of feeling his dry palm sliding across hers created in her. The last thing she needed was for her old feelings for Jed to be reignited. He was married, after all, and therefore completely off limits, even if Louisa intended to stay in Vermont. And besides that, her own heart was too battered and bruised to take another round with anyone, much less Jed Lyman. Much better to be an old maid. Much safer.

Jed helped her up in the wagon before hauling himself in next to her, holding the reins loosely with his good arm.

"How are the Wilsons?" he asked, and Ellen shook her head.

"Not good. Mrs. Wilson has the 'flu."

"Is it bad?"

"I can't really say, but it doesn't look good. Fever, delirium, nausea, aches and pains..." Ellen shook her head. "There's not much I can do, but Caro feels better if I have a look, and they can't afford the doctor."

Jed called to the horses and they started down the road from the Lymans' to where the Wilsons lived on the north side of the island. It was a beautiful summer's day, the sky hazy and blue, the sun lemon yellow, the lake shimmering beyond the rolling fields. The air smelled sweet, of hay and daisies.

"It's so peaceful," Ellen said as she looked around. "Never going back to those golden days, I wish I could stay like this forever, just enjoying the moment."

Jed glanced at her. "You sound as if you have the world on your shoulders."

"Not the whole world. Just a few people, perhaps. Peter... and Rose and the others. And the Wilson children... what will happen to them, if Iris dies?" The pressure that had been building in her chest broke out in a sudden, unexpected sob, and Ellen pressed her hand to her mouth. "I'm sorry, I don't know what came over me..."

"Don't be sorry." Jed pulled the wagon to the side of the road and then, to Ellen's surprise, he put his good arm around her, drawing her against his shoulder. The feel of his chest against her cheek, the earthy, comforting smell of him, made another sob escape her and she closed her eyes.

"I really wasn't expecting to cry…"

"You can't take care of everyone, Ellen Copley, although heaven knows you try." His voice was both rough and gentle as he kept her against his chest, his good hand stroking her hair. It felt far too nice to be held, to relax for a moment and let someone else carry her burdens. Someone strong, whom she knew and trusted and even loved.

Yet Ellen knew she couldn't indulge herself for more than a minute or two; someone would see them, and the gossip would fly across the island, as well it should. Jed was a married man. This was wrong. There could be no other way of looking at it, no matter how nice it felt.

She pushed herself away from him for a sniff. "Thank you for that. And I am sorry for falling apart. I didn't mean to. We'd better get on to the Wilsons."

Ellen busied herself tidying her hair, which had come undone when she'd had her head pressed against Jed's chest. She didn't look at Jed, but she felt something simmering from him, something that made her heart skip an uneven beat.

It felt like a very long moment before he clucked to the horses and they started down the worn, dirt track again.

Caro looked both worried and worn out as she came out onto the porch to greet Ellen, her eyes narrowing slightly as she caught sight of Jed, who nodded a greeting to her before turning back to Ellen.

"Will you be needing a ride back?" Jed asked.

Ellen's cheeks warmed as she answered, "No thank you, Jed. I don't know how long I'll be and I'm glad for the walk."

He nodded again and then was off, the horses trotting back down the lane, while Caro gave Ellen an assessing look that she did her best to ignore. There was nothing unseemly about Jed giving her a ride across the island, and Caro couldn't possibly know about that moment when he'd held her, although judging from her expression, Ellen thought she could have guessed.

"How is Iris?" she asked as she came into the farmhouse. It looked much cleaner, thanks to Caro's effort, and Ellen put the basket of food on the table as the three children gathered round. They were all washed and well-dressed, with neat hair and faces that looked filled out even since yesterday, thanks to Rose's good food and Caro's care.

"She seems more peaceful this morning," Caro said as they headed upstairs to where Iris was, in the farmhouse's bigger bedroom. "Although she was suffering terribly last night, moaning and groaning and burning right up. The fever broke this morning, when I bathed her and changed her nightdress, but I think it's started to come back up again."

"You're doing all the right things," Ellen assured her as she glanced at Iris lying so still in the bed, the rise and fall of her chest barely visible under the worn quilt. "And there's nothing more we can do, Caro. Either she'll get better or she won't." Ellen bit her lip. "And I pray that she will, because I know her children need her."

She rested her hand on top of Iris's and gazed down at the woman's face. Her eyes had fluttered open a few times while Ellen had checked her over, but she hadn't really regained consciousness, and that worried her. Iris needed the sleep, but what if she was sinking deeper into her illness—and into death? Ellen wasn't sure if this peaceful stillness was a good thing at all; she'd seen it before, in soldiers with life-threatening injuries. When they stopped fighting against the pain, it usually meant their bodies had given up.

She turned away from Iris to wash her hands at the basin on the bureau. "What about the husband's brother? Have you found anything out about him?"

"I found an address in the kitchen drawer," Caro said. "A boarding house in Oshawa. I suppose he must still be there."

"Will you write him?"

"Have we time? Perhaps a telegram would be better."

Ellen nodded slowly, accepting as Caro was that Iris' days could be very well numbered. "Yes, I suppose it would."

"Could you send the telegram, Ellen?" Caro asked. "I can't leave Iris, or the little ones, for that matter."

"Yes, of course, but, Caro, don't you think you need help? You'll wear yourself out here."

"I'm fine." A familiar stubborn note entering Caro's voice. "I want to stay. Please, just send the telegram, Ellen."

Ellen gazed at Caro for a moment longer—her expression was set, her arms folded, a hard look in her eyes. She thought about telling her about Jed's conversation this morning, and the possibility of Peter going to a hospital, but it didn't seem like the right moment. It never did, she acknowledged, but hopefully Iris would recover, and Caro would come back home. Glancing around the shabby little farmhouse, she couldn't deny that Caro was needed here.

"I'll send it," she said quietly, and then she took her leave.

CHAPTER THIRTEEN

By mid-afternoon the next day, the McCafferty farmhouse was as clean as it could be, thanks to all their efforts, and Ellen was standing on the front porch with the others to welcome their new guests from New York City—Elvira Frampton and her daughter Imogen. A cloud of dust kicked up at the end of Jasper Lane and Ellen squinted to see Andrew coming back with the wagon, and two women sitting next to him, looking fine indeed in their traveling suits and matching hats, all in the very latest fashion.

"Do you think they'll be terribly stuck up?" Rose murmured, her confidence seeping away by the second. "These women look even grander than the Gardeners! And we're so homely here…"

"Viola Gardener liked it here well enough to recommend us," Ellen reminded her. "Homely is what they're looking for." At least she hoped it was. "We'll be fine."

Within minutes of Andrew pulling up to the front of the house, Ellen was reassured in her belief. Elvira Frampton was a kind-looking woman with sandy gray hair piled up on top of her head and a frank, no-nonsense manner. Her daughter Imogen, seventeen years old and made in the same mold, was just as friendly, and despite their fashionable ensembles, there was a down-to-earthness about them that filled Ellen with both relief and hope.

"The view here is utterly delightful," Elvira exclaimed as she stepped onto the front porch. "And it's just as delightful to meet you all. Viola said I would love it here, and I already know I do."

Her gaze turned appraisingly to Ellen. "And you must be Ellen Copley."

"Yes…" Ellen was a bit taken aback at the way Elvira spoke, as if she already knew her.

"My dear. *My dear.*" Tears sparkled in Elvira's eyes as she stepped closer and pressed Ellen's hands between her own. "You cannot know what this means to me. To finally meet you…"

"I'm sorry?" Ellen was truly startled now, as well as a little wary. Had Elvira confused her with someone else?

"Your painting, *Starlit Sea.*"

Ellen looked at her uncertainly; she'd painted that canvas, a darkened sea lit by stars, in 1912, after the sinking of the *Titanic.* It had come from a deep, wounded part of her, and she'd been consumed by the effort of creating it for several months. Even though it had been exhibited by the Society of Lady Artists in Glasgow, Ellen had never expected a woman from New York to have heard of it.

"You know it?" she asked, and Elvira gave her hands a little squeeze.

"I saw it in the newspaper, and I wrote to Glasgow, to ask if it could be loaned to the Metropolitan Museum of Art, in New York. They agreed, and it was brought to New York right after the end of the war."

"It was?" Ellen had had no idea. She'd donated the painting to the Glasgow Society of Lady Artists right after its first exhibition; in a strange way, creating the canvas had served as a catharsis, and she'd had no desire to deal with it again. Yet to think her work had been in the Metropolitan Museum of Art…!

"It's there to this day," Elvira exclaimed. "I'm amazed you didn't know." Ellen shook her head, and Elvira pressed trembling lips together. "It meant so much to me, for our firstborn, Charles, died on that terrible ship."

A wave of understanding rushed through her. "Oh, Mrs. Frampton, I'm so sorry."

"Call me Elvira, please, my dear. I'm just so pleased to meet you. That painting offered me such comfort and hope. It reminded me that even in the darkest of days, there can be light. Hope."

"I'm so glad."

"You lost someone too, didn't you?" Elvira said with a knowing nod. "I could sense it, from the painting."

Ellen could only nod back. She hadn't spoken of Henry McAvoy to anyone, beyond the barest of details; his family had only given her the briefest of acknowledgements, as his marriage proposal had been a secret, but at least they had honored his will in bequeathing her a modest yet still substantial amount that had allowed her a certain level of financial freedom.

"I'm so sorry for your loss," Elvira murmured.

"Sarah will show you to your rooms, and after you've refreshed yourselves you can take tea in the parlor," Ellen managed to say before she stepped aside to let the two women into the house.

"It all sounds enchanting," Elvira assured her as the two women came inside.

"Ellen, you really are famous," Gracie exclaimed as she and Ellen began to prepare the tea and cakes. "To think we have a celebrity right here on the island! Fancy that."

"Oh, but I'm not, Gracie," Ellen protested. She felt oddly shaken that Elvira had recognized her painting and had actually arranged it to be brought to New York; it was as if something she'd been keeping secret had been exposed. "It's just an amazing coincidence that Mrs. Frampton knew my painting."

"I don't think it is," Rose returned as she came into the kitchen. "But, Ellen, did she say you'd lost someone on the *Titanic*? I never knew." She looked both surprised and hurt by the omission, but Ellen knew she couldn't tell her about Henry McAvoy right then. She'd hinted at it before, and she suspected Rose knew she'd had her heart if not entirely broken then badly damaged, although Ellen had never gone into the particulars.

"Yes, I did," she said, and began slicing the cake, her gaze lowered.

Rose seemed as if she wanted to ask more questions, but as Ellen kept slicing, she just gave a little shake of her head and got out the cups.

Soon, the two Frampton women were happily having tea; it only took a few moments of conversation for Ellen to realize Elvira and Imogen were much more accomplished than Viola or her sisters, and intended to have a full program of art tuition.

"I hope I am up to the task," Ellen returned with a smile, although in truth she was apprehensive of the extent of the Framptons' ambitions.

"I'm sure you are," Elvira replied. "Were you not a lecturer at the Glasgow School of Art?"

"I never actually took up the position." No doubt Elvira had gleaned all her information from that newspaper article, written so long ago. Ellen felt like an entirely different person from the worldly young woman who had been about to step onto the stage of Glasgow artistic life. Here she was in homespun clothes, worried about what they would serve for lunch tomorrow, and whether Iris Wilson would pull through, never mind what she could paint or draw. "It all seems a very long time ago," she told Elvira frankly, and the woman gave a commiserating smile.

"I'm sure it does. Do you intend to return to Glasgow soon?"

She asked it so expectantly, as if it were a foregone conclusion, that for a second Ellen could only blink. "Oh no... no, I don't think so," she said.

Out of the corner of her eye, she saw Rose give her a thoughtful, troubled look, and she reached for the teapot, intent on refreshing everyone's cups as well as changing the conversation.

*

The next two days passed well enough; the Framptons were easily pleased, and both mother and daughter took to Ellen's gentle instruction with enthusiasm and alacrity. Ellen had even shown Elvira some of her old sketches, along with a few new ones she'd done in recent weeks, the desire to draw reignited in her once more. Elvira had enthused about them all, making Ellen feel both embarrassed and pleased.

Amidst it all, she'd even had time to check on Iris Wilson, who had recovered a little, and Ellen was hopeful she might make a full recovery in time. Iris's husband's brother, Jack Wilson, had not yet responded to the telegram Ellen had sent, which made the Wilsons' situation all the more precarious, and the need for Iris to get well all the greater.

Jed stopped by one evening when Ellen and Rose were sitting out on the porch, watching the stars come out, their guests having already retired after a long day of walking and painting. Caro was still at the Wilsons, and Gracie and Sarah had gone visiting friends, while Andrew was seeing to the animals in the barn.

"Jed," Rose called as he walked across the barnyard with his slow, steady tread. "Come join us. I've just made coffee."

"I won't stay," Jed began, but Rose was having none of it.

"You must," she said firmly and went into the kitchen to get him a cup.

Ellen gave Jed a wry smile as he took a seat on the rocking chair next to Rose's. "She won't take no for an answer."

"So it seems." He managed a small smile back, which heartened her. After that surprising moment on the road to the Wilsons, Ellen was starting to hope she and Jed might be getting their friendship back—friendship, and nothing more. "Do you still have the weight of the world on your shoulders?" he asked quietly as they settled into their chairs.

"Just the weight of one island," Ellen quipped. "Although tonight I feel carefree indeed. Isn't the sky lovely?" She glanced at the palette of blue and violets with a dreamy smile. "It's like a swathe of watered silk."

"I'm afraid I don't know what watered silk looks like," Jed returned, "but I'll take your word for it."

Ellen let out a little laugh. "I love the island skies. I know I wasn't born here and that I moved away, but I'll always feel like an island girl at heart."

"Has someone told you you weren't one?" Jed asked, far too shrewdly, and Ellen thought of Caro's comments that still stung. She still hadn't had a chance to speak to her about Peter, although perhaps that was Rose's responsibility now.

"No," she told Jed. "Not really. I'm just happy to be home."

Rose came out with Jed's coffee cup, handing it to him before sitting down. "So, have you got something to tell us?" she asked, a thread of anxiety running through her friendly tone. "About Peter?"

"Not about Peter directly," Jed replied, "but I have written Lucas, and I received his reply today. He knows the military hospital, and he's acquainted with one of the doctors there. He's coming back to the island next week, and he told me to let you know that he'll talk to you then."

"Lucas is coming back? For a visit?" Ellen felt a little lift of excitement and pleasure at the thought of seeing Lucas again. It had only been a month since the barn dance when he'd first given her the idea of having guests, but it felt like an age.

"Yes, just for the weekend, though." Jed's eyes narrowed slightly as he gazed out at the tranquil, twilit scene. "He can't spare more time than that."

Ellen thought she heard a note of bitterness in his voice, and wondered again at the two brothers, one stuck struggling on the farm, the other living the seeming high life in Toronto. Ellen knew Lucas wasn't suited to farm life, and never had been, but surely he could have helped more than he was? It was a sore point with her, and one she didn't feel she could mention to anyone, although she knew that if she and Lucas were truly friends, she should be able to say something of it to him.

"Thank you, Jed," Rose said. "You've been so kind. Peter's seemed more himself these last few days, don't you think, Ellen?"

Ellen gave her aunt a smile of sympathy. She knew what Rose wanted to believe… and what was true. While Peter did have his good moments, ones where he was alert and even cheerful, the truth was he was often living in his own dazed reality, stuck somewhere in Flanders. Some days it was more apparent than others—when he seemed to retreat into himself entirely, or spent the night in the rocking chair or wandering the fields—but he wasn't well. She hoped Lucas would be able to help Peter get an appointment at the hospital.

"I should get back," Jed said as he drained his coffee cup and rose from his seat. With a sigh, Ellen rose from the rocking chair on the porch. "I'm glad Peter seems a bit better."

"Thank you, Jed," Ellen said, and Rose thanked him again as he gave a single wave and then headed back into the darkness.

"Poor man," Rose said softly as Jed rounded the corner of the barn. "He seems so lonely. It's a tragedy, what happened with him and Louisa."

"What *did* happen, Aunt Rose?" Ellen asked. "Because I don't feel as if I ever heard the whole story."

Rose's mouth tightened as she continued to gaze out into the distance. "I don't want to gossip…"

"Nor do I," Ellen said quickly. "I just want to understand."

Rose sighed. "Of course you do. I haven't forgotten that you two were such close friends." She paused meaningfully and Ellen blushed. Rose had comforted her after Jed and Louisa had announced their engagement, but Ellen hardly wanted to remember, much less talk about that now.

"I only want to help," she murmured as she looked away.

Rose was silent for a moment as the night drew in and the stars came out in the velvety sky. "The truth is, and I'm sure you know it as well as I do, Ellen, that Jed and Louisa weren't really suited to each other. It was a case of opposites attract, perhaps, although I can't blame Jed for letting his head be turned. Louisa's pretty and sociable, after all."

"Yes…" Ellen had always been surprised by the unlikely romance, but she'd made her peace with it years ago, or thought she had.

"Of course we all knew Louisa wasn't suited to farm life. I don't think there's a person on the island who thought otherwise. But we all hoped she'd take to it eventually, and I think Jed tried to be as accommodating as a man in his position could, although I know he can be a bit sullen when it suits him." Rose let out a sigh. "In any case, there was only so much he could do… and only so far a person could expect Louisa to bend. I don't blame her for wanting to move back to Seaton, and to have Jed work in a bank. But he put his foot down on that one quite quickly. He knew he wouldn't manage it, and he'd see it as charity, which he never could stand."

Ellen had been told the vague outline of it all, but she'd never heard Rose speak so plainly or so dispiritedly before. "It must have been very difficult."

"And then when dear little Thomas came… she'd had a hard pregnancy, and the little lad came early. He was always a bit frail, and Louisa coddled him, which anybody could understand. But she kept him from Jed, if I can put it like that… it was as if she had to have him all to herself. It just made things worse between them, in the end. And then when Jed joined up when the lad wasn't much more than a bairn… well, no one was surprised Louisa went back to Seaton." Rose shook her head sorrowfully. "I'm not surprised the 'flu took him. Poor little man."

They were both silent as they contemplated the tragedy that had befallen Jed and his wife; Ellen had visited the little headstone the Lymans had had placed outside the Presbyterian church when she'd first arrived on the island, and laid a bouquet of daisies by it.

"I think," Rose said at last, "that if it hadn't been for that dear child departing this world too soon, Jed and Louisa might have made a go of it, after the war. I hoped they would, anyway. Hardship can bind people together just as much as it can pull them apart."

"They still could," Ellen protested. "If Louisa comes back...?"

"Yes." Rose was quiet as she gave Ellen a rather knowing look. "Whether she comes back or not, they've said their vows, good and proper. Jed Lyman is a married man, Ellen."

An icy ripple of shock went through Ellen as she took in the implication of her aunt's words. "I—I know that, Aunt Rose," she said after a moment, stammering in her surprise and unease.

"I know you do," Rose answered quietly. "I just thought I should say it, is all."

CHAPTER FOURTEEN

The rest of the Framptons' visit went by uneventfully enough; Andrew drove them out to the south shore, and another day they took a little skiff out to the bare-swept beaches of Nut Island. Ellen was kept busying overseeing their artistic tuition, and it was Rose who went to the Wilsons' homestead with Peter, to deliver more food and check on both Iris and Caro.

"Iris seems a little better," Rose told Ellen the evening before the Framptons were due to return to New York. "She's sitting up in bed and taking some broth."

"Oh, that is good news," Ellen exclaimed.

"Although I don't know how she will manage the farm, even if she does recover completely," Rose continued frankly. "The place is falling down about their ears, and Iris hasn't planted so much as a potato this spring. She was always such a slight thing, and not up to much, even before she took ill." She sighed. "But there's been no word from her brother-in-law, I suppose?"

Ellen shook her head. "Not that I know of. Did you ever meet him?"

"No, I don't think he's ever come to the island. Iris's folks were island-born, but the Wilsons came from Oshawa way. It would be best if he took on the farm for Iris, but heaven knows if he'd even want to, or if he's ever turned his hand to the plow. As far as I recall, the Wilsons were factory people."

"I suppose we shall just have to wait and see," Ellen said pragmatically.

"And no more bookings till the weekend," Rose said as she glanced at the Farmer's Almanac calendar hanging above the stove. One of the bookings Lucas had arranged had canceled, and the other was only for a few days. "It's just as well," Rose sighed pragmatically. "I think we're all worn out. But the money won't go amiss."

"Mrs. Frampton has promised to recommend us to all her friends," Ellen reminded her. "We might be awash in bookings come August!"

Rose smiled wearily. "I hope so."

Just then, Elvira herself came into the kitchen from the parlor, startling both Ellen and Rose.

"Mrs. Frampton," Rose said hurriedly. "Do you need anything? Another cup of tea or—"

"No, no." Elvira waved her away. "I am perfectly content, I assure you. I merely wished to speak with Ellen before I retired upstairs."

Ellen shot Rose an uncertain look before replying, "Of course. Shall we go into the parlor?"

Rose looked as confused as Ellen felt as Mrs. Frampton led the way into the front parlor, which was empty; Imogen had already gone upstairs and the McCaffertys did their best to make themselves scarce and give their guests an evening of privacy.

"Is everything all right, Mrs. Frampton?" Ellen asked uncertainly.

Elvira was standing by the fireplace, empty now for the night was warm, her hands laced across her middle as she gave Ellen a rather appraising look.

"Elvira, my dear, please do call me Elvira! And yes, everything is well, indeed. Imogen and I have so enjoyed our time here."

"I'm very glad to hear it."

"And we will recommend Jasper Lane to all our artistic-minded acquaintances, I assure you." She paused, and Ellen had the sense there was more—much more—that she wanted to say.

"But...?" she asked after a moment, managing a little laugh, and Elvira inclined her head in acknowledgment.

"But I do wonder, my dear, as does Imogen, what you are doing in such a place as this."

Ellen stared at her in blank incomprehension. "Such a place as this?"

"Miss Copley, you could be one of the most celebrated women artists of your time, if you so chose it! I am sure of it. I have not seen the like of *Starlit Sea* in all my years, and even the simple sketches you have done here have captured my eye. They could easily be exhibited in New York, along with your wonderful painting. I have already thought of the title—'Island Sketches.' A collection of charcoal sketches of everyday scenes, vignettes if you like, telling a story of life here. I assure you, people would be enchanted."

Ellen let out a huff of incredulous laughter. "I don't think—"

"But I am getting ahead of myself," Elvira continued smoothly. "Speaking of exhibits! The truth is, I wanted to invite you to come and stay with us in the city, perhaps for the month of September? You would be so very welcome, my dear, and I know my husband would dearly like to meet you. You would be our guest—we'd arrange all the details. There are so many people we'd like you to meet, both friends and people we know in the art world. And perhaps then we could discuss a possible exhibition of your sketches. I'm sure you'd like to see *Starlit Sea* for yourself again. Think of all you could do." Elvira smiled at her, clearly expecting an enthusiastic answer, but Ellen could only stare at her dumbly, too shocked to reply.

Go to New York? Be wined and dined by the sounds of it, and meet prestigious people within the art world? It was like something out of a storybook, or a moving picture. A fairy tale, not real life. Not her life.

"I've surprised you, I see," Elvira said with a laugh. "I suppose it is a great deal to take in. But do think on it, Ellen. I shudder to think of you wasting all your days away here! There are so many people you could meet, so many people who would be delighted to meet you, and encourage you in your ambitions."

"That's very kind of you to offer," Ellen began, her mind still whirling. "But I have obligations here, important ones, and I could not possibly leave the McCaffertys for an entire month." She was thinking of Rose as well as Peter, and, she realized, she was also thinking of Jed. Did he need her? No, of course he didn't. And yet she knew she would miss his friendship, if she were to leave the island.

"I understand, but please don't refuse just yet," Elvira entreated. "Not until you've thought about it properly. I know you have duties here, Ellen, and it is quite plain to see how everyone relies on you. But you are a talented young woman and I think you would enjoy seeing more of the world. I know you nursed in the war," she clarified with a quick, conciliatory smile. "And you've had your years in Glasgow, as well. But New York hasn't had the pleasure of your presence, and I think the city would offer you so much. Come to New York, Ellen," Elvira urged, clasping her hands in hers. "Come to New York, and have an adventure."

Ellen barely had time to think of Elvira's surprising and beguiling invitation; the next morning, the Framptons left in a flurry of grateful goodbyes, with Elvira pressing her hand and urging her to send a telegram as soon as she'd made up her mind about visiting her in the city.

"It would be such fun," she insisted. "And such an honor, truly."

An *honor?* Ellen almost wanted to laugh. Elvira Frampton acted as if she were someone special, a famous artist, when she knew she was nothing of the kind. And yet it felt so very nice to be so flattered, to imagine a life apart, meeting important people and doing exciting things. As much as she loved island life, the daily round of chores, the pressing cares, had wearied her, and the thought of going somewhere else—being wined and dined and the rest of it—held a shameful appeal.

She couldn't go, of course. Ellen had known that as soon as Elvira had made the invitation. She couldn't possibly leave Rose and the others, not with Caro still nursing Iris Wilson and her poor children, and the holiday business barely up and running, and Peter's situation so uncertain.

It was impossible. And yet it didn't stop her from daydreaming, just a little, about what a trip to New York would be like. She hadn't spent any time there, not properly. She'd sailed in to the city's harbor as a wide-eyed twelve-year-old, but that felt like a lifetime ago. *Two* lifetimes, when she thought of her time at the Glasgow School of Art, and then nursing in France during the war.

Of course, she'd also done a bit of shopping there before sailing for Scotland eight years ago now, but it had been a fleeting trip, nothing more, two nights in a hotel and a trip to the Ladies' Mile. She still recalled the bustling energy of the enormous city, and how it had invigorated her. To stay in someone's home, tour all the wonderful sights, meet interesting and influential people, for an entire *month*…

"No, Ellen," she muttered as she swiped a strand of hair from her eyes and scrubbed a scorched pan in the sink with even more vigor. "Don't even think of it."

"Think of what?" Rose asked cheerfully as she came into the kitchen with a basket of washing to hang on the line.

"Nothing," Ellen said quickly. "Let me hang that for you, Aunt Rose."

"I can do it, Ellen—"

"But I want to." Ellen left the pan to soak and then took the basket from her aunt. "It's a beautiful day and I'd like to get some air. You sit down and rest for a minute. Have a cup of tea." She put the basket of washing down to fill the kettle and hauled it onto the stove.

"Well, I suppose a cup of tea would be nice."

"Good." Ellen couldn't keep from noticing how tired and careworn her aunt looked. She was only a little over fifty, but the lines on her face and gray in her hair made her look older and frailer. War, loss, worry… it had all aged her, along with everyone else. The thought of losing her aunt, after having lost so many people already, made fear clutch at her heart in a way that Rose must have seen for she smiled at her.

"Why are you looking so worried, dear Ellen? Things are going well, aren't they?" A letter had come that morning from Toronto with a request for another booking in August.

"Yes." Ellen gave her aunt a watery smile in return. She was being rather ridiculously emotional for some reason. Elvira's invitation had stirred up all sorts of feelings inside her, along with talking to Jed the other day. And she was so very tired. But Lucas was due to arrive tomorrow. Ellen looked forward to seeing him with both enthusiasm and some dread, for what he might say about Peter's condition and the likelihood of him going into hospital. "Yes, things are going well."

Outside, the day was fresh, the sun warm, light glinting off Lake Ontario, making the ruffled waves sparkle as if strewn with diamonds. Ellen started to peg the laundry on the line, willing her heart to lift at this simple pleasure. Caro was still with the Wilsons, and Jed was to ask Lucas about a hospital for Peter, and the farm's future still felt precarious, but… the sun was shining, the day was warm, and she wanted to be happy.

"Ellen."

Ellen looked up in surprise to see Lucas striding across the front yard, dressed in his business clothes, his hat in his hand, a smile on his handsome face.

"Lucas…" She shook her head dumbly. "What are you doing here? You weren't meant to come until tomorrow evening."

"I decided to come today. I thought the matter was pressing, and should be dealt with directly. And I was able to get the time off work."

"You didn't…"

"Ellen, this is about Peter." Lucas stood in front of her, his expression both serious and smiling, blue eyes crinkled at the corners, everything about him so wonderfully familiar and dear. "Of course I came. I've known Peter since he was born. He's like a brother to me, and…" He paused, and cleared his throat.

Ellen stared at him in confusion. "And?"

"And I'd do anything to help him," Lucas said simply, although Ellen had a feeling he'd been about to say something else, although she had no idea what. "I've already spoken to the hospital in Toronto, and they're willing to see him as soon as Monday, if need be. We can all go together, if you like, on the train."

"Monday!" That was only in four days. Ellen had never expected things to happen so quickly, and with a holiday booking next week…

"Why not? The sooner he gets the treatment, the better, surely?"

"Yes, I suppose." She struggled to articulate her hesitation, even to herself. "Perhaps he's not as bad as all that…"

"Ellen." Lucas put his hand on her shoulder, warm and comforting, as he looked somberly into his face. "I know we both want that to be the case, and heaven knows everyone else does as well. But what we want and what is true are two separate things, aren't they?"

"You haven't even seen Peter yet," Ellen pointed out, the words squeezed out through her suddenly too-tight throat.

"No, but then I'm not a doctor. This is just for an initial assessment, you know. No decisions would have to be made. Nothing would be final."

"That's good." Ellen managed to nod, although in truth the reality of a hospital appointment in just a few days was completely overwhelming. Just like Caro, she realized, she'd been trying to convince herself that Peter might be all right. He'd had his good days, after all, and there had not been, as far as she knew, another episode of confusion since that dreadful evening with the fireworks.

Lucas put both hands on her shoulders and bent down to peer into her face. "Are you coping?" he asked quietly, his compassionate gaze sweeping over her. "You look done in, Ellen."

"I'm fine..." Ellen knew she sounded feeble. When had she become so weak? Coming over all emotional with Jed a few days ago, and now with Lucas. She wasn't working any harder than Caro or Rose, or even Gracie or Sarah, who had taken over all the garden and kitchen work while their guests were in residence. She really needed to regain her composure, her resilience. "Just a bit tired, that's all, but no more than anyone else."

"Come walk with me," Lucas suggested. "You can spare half an hour, can't you?"

"I shouldn't..."

"Twenty minutes, then."

Ellen glanced back at the house, looking peaceful enough in the sunlight, and then nodded. "All right. We don't have anyone coming until next week. But let me finish pegging this washing out first."

"I'll help you."

She couldn't help but laugh at the incongruity of that. "You, in your fancy suit, hanging out the washing?"

"Why not?" Lucas returned with a smile that held a touch of both whimsy and sorrow. "I've certainly done it before." Mrs. Lyman had died when Jed and Lucas were little more than children; they'd taken over much of the housework after that.

"I know you have," Ellen answered softly. Although they had fathers living, she suspected that, in some ways, Lucas, like her, felt like an orphan. She had lost touch with her father long ago, and hadn't had a letter from him in over a year, a realization that still brought her, after all this time, a pang of grief.

It felt both strange and companionable to finish the simple chore with Lucas, shirts and sheets waving in the warm breeze. After they'd finished, Ellen hurried inside to tell Rose where she was going, and then fell into step with Lucas as they started down Jasper Lane, the oak and maple trees overhead shading them from the bright summer sun.

They'd walked together so many times before, Ellen clutching her sketchbook, and Lucas with his notebook full of scribblings on all the animals and plants he saw and observed.

"Where should we go?" Lucas asked with a mischievous smile as they walked along the ground dappled with sunlight, the air full of birdsong. "Down to the south shore, or out to Emerald? Or into Stella?"

At one time or another, they'd walked all the roads and lanes of the island, exploring its meadowlands and forests, its sandy beaches nestled against the aquamarine waters.

"I don't mind," Ellen said. "I'll go anywhere."

Lucas's gaze rested on hers for a lingering moment that made Ellen's heart flip in her chest in a surprising, disconcerting way, and then he nodded towards the road that led to the brow of a hill.

"How about to Kerr Bay?" he suggested. "I haven't been out there in a long while."

CHAPTER FIFTEEN

Kerr Bay was one of the smaller inlets of the island off the north shore; Ellen hadn't been there in a long while, either. They walked in silence for a few moments, arms swinging at their sides, enjoying the sunshine.

"How long are you here for?" Ellen asked eventually. "Will you return to Toronto for good when we take Peter?"

"Yes, I can only manage the weekend," Lucas replied. "I offered to help Jed with the farm's accounting. He does an admirable job, but he asked me to look it over. If it's amenable to you, I thought we'd take the ferry over on Monday morning. I'll accompany you to the hospital to introduce you to Dr. Stanton, and then I'll return to work."

"I didn't know you helped with the farm's accounts," Ellen said, and Lucas gave her a surprisingly sharp look.

"Why do you sound so surprised by the notion?"

"I just mean…" Ellen began, trying to frame her thoughts into words, and Lucas interjected shrewdly,

"That Jed stayed to help and I didn't?"

She couldn't quite gauge his tone, seemingly matter-of-fact but with an undercurrent of… bitterness? Sorrow? "It's true, isn't it?" she answered after a moment. "I don't mean that unkindly, Lucas, but you aren't here and Jed is, working the farm even though…"

"He only has one arm." Lucas sighed heavily. "No, I'm not here," he agreed after a moment. "That is true."

"I feel I've offended you somehow."

"Not you." Lucas sighed again and then sat down on a stretch of tufty grass, under the spreading branches of a maple tree. "I suppose it's all a bit of a sore point with me."

"How so?" Ellen asked as she joined him under the tree.

"The work I did in the war… well, it was important, but I stayed away from the Front, didn't I?"

Ellen gazed at him uncertainly. She'd sensed this kernel of bitterness in him before, but she'd never truly understood its source. "I'm not even sure what you did in the war, to tell you the truth."

"It's still classified, so I'm afraid I can't talk about it." Lucas sighed and ran a hand through his rumpled hair. "But I know some people felt I was taking the easy way out, not fighting on the Front the way so many island boys did, just as I know there are plenty of people here who think I'm doing the same thing again, leaving Jed and my father to manage the farm as best as they can while I lark about in the city, having a grand old time." Ellen stayed silent, not quite able to disagree, and Lucas turned to look at her searchingly. "Do you think that, Ellen?"

Ellen's heart turned over at the intent look in his eyes. "Lucas…"

"Because it's you that I care about most. As a friend," he clarified with a wry smile, although Ellen hadn't even been thinking about *that*. At least, not precisely. "You'll always be one of my dearest friends."

"As you will be mine," Ellen assured him, her voice slightly choked with emotion that always felt close to the surface these days. "I'll always admire and be grateful to you, Lucas, truly. You're the one who has saved the McCafferty farm—"

"Now that is not true," Lucas answered with a smile, clearly trying to lighten the moment. "I won't take credit for something I most certainly did not do. You've saved it, along with the rest of the McCaffertys."

"I'm not actually a McCafferty, you know—"

"Yes, you are, Ellen. You assuredly are."

She smiled at that, still far too near tears. Impatiently, she dabbed at her eyes. "That's a very nice thing to say, Lucas."

"It's true." He was still looking at her intently and for some reason Ellen's breath caught. A few days ago, Jed had touched her hand and made her heart turn over, and now here she was, feeling things she most certainly shouldn't for his brother. Perhaps it was simply all the excess emotion she felt, the worry for the Wilsons and Peter and the McCafferty farm, everything in life both precious and precarious.

"Let's keep walking, or we'll never get to Kerr Bay," Lucas said after a moment, and he rose from his place on the grass.

They walked in silence that was not quite as companionable as before, although neither was it unpleasant. Ellen was still wondering at her reaction to Lucas—Lucas!—when he nodded to the sandy path ahead of them that led down towards the bay.

"Look, we're almost here."

"So we are."

If there had been a moment between them, it had clearly passed on, and Ellen didn't know whether she was glad or sorry. She picked her way among the rocks to stand with Lucas by the shore, staring out at the placid surface of the lake.

Only that morning Elvira and Imogen had taken the ferry back to the mainland, and then the train from Ogdensburg all the way to New York. In the midst of all this tranquility, Ellen could barely imagine the tall buildings known as skyscrapers, the bustling city, and yet she was. She was picturing herself there, walking on its streets, visiting her own painting in the Metropolitan…

"What is it?" Lucas asked quietly, his perceptive gaze resting on her. "You're thinking of something."

Ellen gave a little laugh as she shook her head. "How do you know?"

"I know you," Lucas replied, and for some reason that simple statement had the power to render Ellen speechless.

Lucas did know her... in a way that no one else ever had, not Jed, not Henry, not Rose or Caro or Amy or Ruby, her friends from Glasgow. He'd always seemed to guess her thoughts before she'd realized them herself, and he'd encouraged and even pushed her when, out of fear, she would have stayed still.

"I've had an invitation," she admitted quietly. "And I don't know what to do with it."

"An invitation?"

"To stay in New York City for a few weeks. Elvira Frampton, who holidayed here, has invited me to stay for the month of September. She believes she can arrange an exhibit of some of my sketches—just little ones I've done, to give an example of perspective, or something like that. Nothing will come of it, I'm sure." She wanted to tell Lucas about *Starlit Sea* being exhibited at the Metropolitan Museum of Art, but it sounded boastful and so she kept silent. In any case, Lucas was staring at her incredulously, and Ellen gave a small, self-conscious laugh. "What is it?"

"Ellen, that's marvelous, truly marvelous!" He reached for both her hands, taking them in his own. "I'm so pleased for you. Of course I'm not surprised. Not surprised one bit."

"I wasn't planning on going," Ellen told him, and he frowned. "Not go? But why?"

"Because of everything. Peter and the art holidays, the farm and the garden, not to mention poor Iris Wilson... I'm needed here, Lucas. I can't just hare off to New York."

"Surely they can all manage without you for a month."

"Perhaps, but it would be difficult, and I don't want to seem as if I'm abandoning them to go gadding about."

Lucas gazed at her, frowning, her hand still clasped in his. "But it's such a wonderful opportunity, Ellen. Surely you can't turn it down."

"Can't I?" Ellen returned a bit sharply, tugging her hands out of his. She felt prickly all of a sudden, and she wasn't even sure why. She knew Lucas was speaking sense.

He shoved his hands in the pockets of his trousers as Ellen reached for a smooth, flat stone and skipped it across the water, taking an almost savage sort of pleasure in seeing how far it flew across the placid surface of the bay. "Why did you tell me, if you weren't going to go?" Lucas asked after a long moment, when she'd skipped another stone, and Ellen let out a weary laugh.

"I don't know."

"You want to go."

She didn't answer, and he took a step towards her.

"There's nothing wrong with that, Ellen. Why won't you admit it?"

"I don't know," she said again as she flung another stone.

"Ellen—"

"All right, I can admit it." She wheeled around to face him, agitated now. "Of course I can. Who wouldn't? Mrs. Frampton was talking about all sorts of things—art exhibitions and the opera, meeting important people, *feeling* important—" She broke off with a despairing laugh. "Why wouldn't I want all that?"

"So why are you fighting against it?" Lucas asked urgently. "Why do you seem as if you feel guilty, for wanting such things?"

Ellen didn't answer; she didn't think she could. Her chest hurt and her eyes stung and everything felt far too close, far too fragile. She tried to shake her head, but then she somehow ended up gasping instead, and suddenly she was enfolded in Lucas's arms, her cheek against his chest, her eyes closed… just as she'd once been with Jed.

"Why can't you go?" he asked quietly, his arms still around her.

"Because…"

"Because why?"

"Because Rose needs me. Caro… Peter…" She spoke falter-ingly, and she knew Lucas heard her hesitation.

"And I said they could do without you for a month. They did without you for seven years, after all, Ellen." He spoke gently, not to hurt her, but to remind her that she wasn't as indispensable as she seemed to believe.

"I know. I don't actually think I'm invaluable."

"Then…"

Ellen didn't know if she had an answer, at least not one she could articulate. Why was she so reluctant to leave the island for a month? What was she afraid of?

"It's just," she said after a moment, stepping out of Lucas's embrace, "that there's much to do, and I'm so grateful to Aunt Rose for letting me call this wonderful island home—"

Lucas raised his eyebrows as if she'd said something revealing, and Ellen gave him a challenging look.

"What is it?"

"Ever the orphan," he remarked quietly, and Ellen stilled, annoyed and even hurt by his comment.

"What is that supposed to mean?" Not that she actually wanted to know.

"Isn't that how you feel?" he challenged. "Like you have to keep proving yourself, so they'll keep you?"

Quite suddenly, the emotion she'd been trying desperately to push back spilled over and two tears slipped silently down her cheeks. She'd never quite thought of herself that way, not know-ingly at least, and yet in that moment she knew it was true. She was trying to be indispensable, so she'd belong. Even now, on her beloved island, in the bosom of the McCafferty family, part of her still felt like an outsider.

"Maybe," she whispered, and Lucas offered her a smile, full of compassion.

"You know you don't need to feel that way, Ellen. You belong here as much as any of us do, if not more."

"Do I, though?"

He frowned. "What do you mean?"

"A little while ago," she explained, sniffing, "when Peter had his first funny turn, Caro as good as told me I wasn't family. She's still been cool with me, making the point that I'm not quite a McCafferty. I know I'm probably being too sensitive, but it hurt more than I dreamed possible."

Lucas's frown deepened. "She didn't mean it, Ellen. She couldn't have. She's most likely just afraid, because of Peter, and it's making her act out in ways she doesn't even realize."

"Perhaps, but it was more than once. She made a point of it, at least it felt that way, and I can't help but feel there's some truth to it." She sniffed back the last of her tears and raised her chin to give Lucas a direct look. "After all, it's true, isn't it?"

"No, it isn't, and any of the McCaffertys would tell you so. It's you who keeps feeling like the outsider. You're the one who's afraid."

Ellen managed a shaky laugh. "Are you trying to make me feel better?"

"I'm trying to tell you the truth. You're welcome here, Ellen. You're loved." He paused, and again, just as before, she felt as if their friendship, so very precious, might slip into something else, something that made her heart lurch in a way that was not unpleasant. She thought Lucas might say something, something of *them,* and yet he hadn't spoken of romance or love in years. "By all the McCaffertys," he finished with a smile as he stepped back, and that strange, edgy feeling of tottering on the precipice of something vague yet immense vanished. "Trust me," Lucas said, taking another step back, as if he needed to distance himself. "Caro spoke in a moment of fear, that's all."

Ellen drew a deep breath as she let the moment pass, like a wave receding. "That's what Jed said," she told him, and it felt as if the words dropped into the stillness, like the stones she'd just skipped into the water, sinking beneath the surface without a trace.

Lucas's gaze swept slowly over her. "Did he," he remarked after a moment, and it was not exactly a question.

"I spoke to him about Peter, as you must know, since he spoke to you. We talked of it then." She waited, sensing something from Lucas she didn't entirely understand. "What has happened between the two of you?" she asked eventually. "Because sometimes you seem… hostile towards one another. Resentful."

"I don't resent Jed." Lucas's voice was toneless; Ellen could not tell anything from it.

"Does he resent you?" she asked.

Lucas reached down for a smooth stone and skipped it across the water in one forceful movement. It went twice as far as Ellen's had. "I don't know. I don't think so."

"Have you talked about it with him?"

He gave her a humorous look, although his eyes were still hard. "Why would I? You know Jed, Ellen. He's not one for cozy chats."

"But you're brothers."

"We'll always be brothers."

She paused, feeling frustrated, finding her way. "Do you think he resents you being in Toronto? Not working the farm?"

Lucas was silent for a moment as he skipped another stone, the wind off the lake ruffling his hair. "I spent four years at Queen's training as a lawyer. It would be a poor job if after that I came back to the island to plant corn."

"But the farm needs your help."

He gave her a searching look, something dark in his expression. "You think I don't know that?"

"Sometimes I don't know if you do," Ellen replied honestly. "You hardly ever come back… Jed and your father had to do the whole planting by themselves."

"They hired a man to help."

"It's not the same."

Lucas blew out a breath as he shook his head. "You don't understand, Ellen."

"Then tell me—"

"No." He sounded surprisingly like Jed then, his voice flat and firm as he skipped a final stone; it fell into the water with a plop. Lucas turned away from the lake. "We should head back."

Ellen gazed at him unhappily. "I didn't mean to quarrel with you."

"You didn't." He gave her a quick smile that didn't reach his eyes. "Come on, I'll help you across." He reached out one hand and after a second's pause Ellen took it as they scrambled across the stony beach that led to the path. "In any case, I still think you should go to New York," Lucas said briskly once they'd reached the lane. He dropped her hand, and oddly Ellen found she missed it. "Who knows what might happen? And I think it would be good for you to have a rest. The McCaffertys can manage by themselves for a bit."

"I thought I was a McCafferty," Ellen reminded him. She felt unsettled by Lucas's vague coolness; barely perceptible as it was, she knew him well and she felt it.

"And so you are. Besides, you know Rose would want you to go. She'd be cross with you if she knew you had the offer and refused it."

"You won't tell her—" Ellen began anxiously, and Lucas shook his head.

"No, that's not my place. But stop being so afraid of life, of grabbing for it with both hands. You've spent enough time in the shadow as it is. Step out into the light."

"I haven't been in the shadows—"

"Metaphorical shadows, and you have." He gave her a faint smile as Jasper Lane came into view.

Ellen paused at the turning, but Lucas had taken a few steps on, down the road.

"Aren't you coming up—" Ellen began, and he shook his head.

"I should get back. Jed and Dad are expecting me."

"All right." Ellen gazed at him uncertainly for a moment, wanting to say something more although she knew not what.

Lucas lifted his hand in farewell. "I'll see you tomorrow. I'll talk to you and Rose, and Caro too, about Peter and the hospital."

As she watched him head down the road towards the Lyman farm, she couldn't keep from feeling a faint, lingering disappointment, but she could not identify its source.

CHAPTER SIXTEEN

There was no time for Ellen to dwell on such vague, restless feelings, for the next morning a telegram arrived from the guests due tomorrow, containing a list of fussy requirements for meals, furnishings, and entertainments, leaving Gracie practically spitting in fury, and Rose at a loss.

"They must have oolong tea, Ellen, but I don't even know what that is, or where to get it."

"And they would like to attend a concert?" Gracie added, her eyes sparkling with defiance. "Shall I play them something on the piano?"

"Oh Gracie, you know you can barely bang out a tune," Sarah protested with a smile. "Besides, half the keys on that old piano don't even make a sound."

"I feel they're going to be terribly disappointed," Rose said worriedly. "They have quite an elevated view of island life! I fear they won't recommend us to anyone."

"Then let them be disappointed," Gracie flashed back. "We haven't pretended to be something we're not, and we shouldn't start now. If they want fancy teas and all the rest of it, they can go to New York or Paris!"

New York. Ellen had barely been able to give Elvira's invitation a thought since she'd spoken to Lucas; he was coming that afternoon to talk about Peter, and on Monday, all things well, she, Rose, Peter and Lucas would all go to Toronto. By the time their next lot of guests left, it would be halfway to August. It was just as well, Ellen thought, that she'd already decided she couldn't go.

That afternoon, Lucas walked over to Jasper Lane while Peter and Andrew were out in the fields; Gracie had gone visiting and Caro was still at the Wilsons, but Sarah sat in on the conversation around the scrubbed pine kitchen table, the day as dark and cloudy as everyone's somber mood.

"Dr. Stanton is a good man," Lucas said as Rose stared at him unhappily and Sarah remained silent, looking troubled. "I knew him in the war. He is very sympathetic to men suffering from shell shock."

"But do you really feel Peter has that?" Rose asked. "He's seemed so well lately…"

"I couldn't say, of course," Lucas answered. "I've barely seen him. But based on what Jed and Ellen have said, I do think it's a distinct possibility. Dr. Stanton will be able to assess him properly, and offer him the treatment he needs, if he needs it. Surely there's no harm in going to see?"

"But all the way to Toronto? The train fare is dear and we'd have to spend the night…"

"I'll take care of all that," Ellen said firmly, "and I won't have you arguing with me, Aunt Rose. I would despise myself if I didn't offer help when I could! You must let me. I really do insist."

"Very well," Rose answered after a moment, with a shaky smile. "I can hardly say no, considering the circumstances. If it can help Peter…" She turned to Lucas. "You say you have the appointment already? For Monday?"

"Yes."

"And it can't be changed? With guests coming tomorrow, we couldn't possibly—"

"I can manage the guests while you're gone," Sarah interjected. "You'll be back Tuesday afternoon at the latest, or even Monday evening if you can make the train, so it wouldn't be for long. They can scribble on their own for a day."

"I'll leave them lessons," Ellen promised. "They'll be so busy they won't have a moment's rest."

"And Gracie and Andrew will be here to help," Sarah added. "There's plenty of us to manage. This is more important, Mum."

"I know it is." Rose dabbed her eyes. "It's just… I'm so afraid." She gave them all a shamefaced smile. "At my age, after everything I've seen and been through, I'm still afraid. For Peter's sake."

"I know," Ellen said softly, and reached for her aunt's hand. Rose clasped it with a grateful smile.

"Then it's all settled," Lucas stated, and Ellen hesitated, her hand still in Rose's.

"What about Caro? Everything has happened so quickly, and with her being at the Wilsons all this time, we haven't had a chance to speak with her. She doesn't even know…"

"Caro will want what is best for Peter," Rose declared. "I know she resisted the notion of treatment before, but surely she can see there's no harm in at least having the one appointment."

"Perhaps not," Ellen murmured, although personally she had her doubts. "But I think she still needs to know what's going on."

"As does Peter," Lucas reminded them quietly. "You can hardly spring this on him with no warning."

"I know." Rose slipped her hand from Ellen's to clasp her own together tightly. "Who should tell him?"

"I can, if you'd rather. Man to man, from someone who understands what the war was like." He paused, his inscrutable gaze moving briefly to Ellen. "Or Jed can do it, if you prefer."

"I don't know what I prefer," Rose replied, agitation creasing her forehead. "It's not something I've ever had to think of before. What do you think, Ellen?"

Ellen shook her head slowly. "It's not my decision to make."

"But you know I value your advice—"

Ellen glanced at Lucas, who gazed back levelly, giving away nothing. How could she say which of the brothers should talk to Peter? It felt like a loaded choice, one that would mean so much more than it was meant to, something far too personal, even intimate. Or was she imagining the undercurrents she felt from Lucas?

"I really don't know," she stated. Lucas looked away, and something in her compelled her to say, "I suppose you, Lucas… since you know the hospital and the doctor. And you're closer in age to Peter, if by only a little…" She shrugged, spreading her hands helplessly.

"Very well," Lucas replied. "I'll speak to him today."

As soon as they'd finished their discussion, Ellen hitched up the wagon herself to go to the Wilsons. She hadn't gone there for several days, and Caro hadn't returned, so she had no idea how Iris was doing, although she hoped she was continuing to improve, as Caro had said she was the last time Ellen had gone.

Now she packed a meat pie and an apple crumble, fresh bread and milk, and a jar of Rose's lemonade into a wicker basket to take with her.

Although she didn't know what awaited her at the Wilsons, it felt like a relief to leave Jasper Lane, and all the cares there, for a little while—Peter, and Lucas's conversation with him, and the guests who would surely prove to be a trial with their needless demands.

As Ellen drove up the rutted track to the Wilsons' house, Caro flew out of the house, her face pale with alarm.

"Oh Ellen, I'm so glad you're here! Yesterday, Iris took a turn for the worse. She was doing so well—even talking to the little ones, and saying how she might try to get out of bed on the morrow, and then…" Caro shook her head and Ellen clambered out of the wagon.

"And then what?"

"The fever returned, and she went back into that awful sort of doze. I wanted to fetch you, but I daren't leave her for a moment, and Lizzie doesn't know the way."

"How is she now?" Ellen asked as she came into the house. The three Wilson children were sitting around the table, looking dazed and glassy-eyed. Ellen put the basket on the table with a sorrowful smile for each of them and was heartened to see them brighten a little at the sight of the food.

"The same, just more still. Last night, she was tossing and turning, but now she's gone into a deeper sleep. Do you think that's a good thing?" Caro asked anxiously. "Or bad?"

"I couldn't say, not without looking at her. What about the doctor?"

"They can't afford—"

"I'll pay," Ellen said. What was left of her meager savings would not go very far at this rate, but she didn't care. She was all too aware of her own limitations—a single year of nurse's training, and then the years in the war. She wasn't qualified in the way Caro and so many others seemed to think she was.

"I'll send Lizzie," Caro said, hope flaring briefly in her eyes. "She knows the way into Emerald, at least."

Upstairs, Iris lay in bed, her body as still as a waxwork, her face pale and lifeless, the rise and fall of her chest barely visible.

"What do you think?" Caro demanded as Ellen took the poor woman's pulse.

"I couldn't say," she said again, although she feared she could. She'd seen soldiers in Iris' condition back at Royaumont—men who had been conscious and even cheerful one day, and then slipped into rest that seemed peaceful, yet with the slow breaths and clammy pallor that so often preceded death.

"It doesn't look good, though, does it?" Caro said quietly. "She's barely stirred all day, not even to open her eyes."

"It's usually not a good sign," Ellen admitted quietly. "But let's leave that to the doctor."

The doctor, when he did come, agreed with Ellen's assessment. A tired, harried man with too many patients and not enough time, he checked Iris over, took her pulse, and then gave them a level, not unkind look. "I'd give her twenty-four hours, not much more."

"*Oh.*" Caro put her hand to her mouth, her eyes wide. Even though she'd been speaking practically, she hadn't expected such a blunt assessment, and neither had Ellen, despite her fears. "What shall we do?"

"There's no kin?"

"A brother-in-law in Oshawa," Ellen said. "I sent him a telegram last week, but there's been no reply."

The doctor shrugged; the children were not his concern. "I don't suppose you'd take them in?"

Ellen gave Caro a quick, questioning look. "We can't," Caro replied regretfully. "We haven't the money or the space."

"Then they'll have to go to an institution. St Mary's in the Lake is well run by the nuns of the House of Providence. I would advise sending them there, if they have the space."

"Thank you, Doctor," Ellen said, and with a brief nod, he took his leave. When Ellen was sure Iris was comfortable, she headed downstairs to see Caro, who was bustling about, making supper for the children, who remained silent, no doubt sensing the somber mood.

The oldest, Lizzie, had a quiet, worldly-wise air at only eight years old that made Ellen's heart ache. The younger two, a tow-headed boy and girl, couldn't be more than five or six. She couldn't imagine them in a place like St Mary's, no matter how efficiently it was run. It was still an institution, not a home.

Ellen glanced at Caro, noticing how worn out and grim-faced she looked. "Caro, why don't you come back to the farm?" she suggested. "I can stay here."

Caro shook her head, the movement almost frantic with determination. "No, I want to be here."

"You look so tired. It doesn't have to be your responsibility, Caro—"

"But it is," Caro said with sudden, surprising fierceness, rounding on Ellen with an aggressiveness that made her take an instinctive step back. "I know I'm unlikely to get married or have children of my own, not with the war having taken so many men. But here are three children who need me, and a woman besides, at least—at least for a little while—and I'm not beholden to anyone otherwise. You can manage the farm without me, can't you? And the guests?"

"Yes, of course—"

Caro lifted her chin, her eyes glittering with both frustration and tears. "Thank you. Then I'll stay."

Ellen hesitated, knowing she needed to tell Caro about Peter, yet unwilling to broach such a thorny subject when the moment was so fraught, and Caro already seemed so fragile.

"I'll be back tomorrow," she promised. "To check on Mrs. Wilson… and on you."

CHAPTER SEVENTEEN

As Ellen drove up the lane, her breath caught as the screen door slammed and Peter strode out of the house towards the fields, his face darkened with fury. A few seconds later Lucas followed, remaining on the porch as Ellen drove the wagon up.

"You spoke to Peter, I see," Ellen said as Lucas came down the steps to her from the wagon.

"I did, and you no doubt also saw that it didn't go very well. I suppose he needs a bit of time to get used to the idea."

"Should I talk to him…?"

"I'd leave him be for now. Let him cool down." He took the reins as Ellen started into the house. "Shall I see to the horses?"

"Thank you, Lucas."

Inside the kitchen, Rose was slumped at the kitchen table, looking despondent. "Oh, Ellen," she said as Ellen came into the room. "Peter was so very angry."

"I don't blame him," Ellen told her aunt with a small, sorrowful smile. "It must have been a surprise to him."

"Yes, I feared it was, but even so. He was angry at our interfering, and at Lucas for talking of hospitals and doctors. He wouldn't hear a word of it. What shall we do?"

"Perhaps he'll come round, once he's had a chance to think about it," Ellen suggested, although she wondered whether it was very likely.

"Perhaps," Rose agreed, "but I fear he won't, and it made me realize how ill he truly is. He needs help, Ellen. We need to give it to him."

"I know," Ellen agreed softly.

"Will you talk to him? Try to make him see sense?"

Briefly, Ellen closed her eyes. "I don't know that I'm the right person…"

"It has to be you. He didn't want it from Lucas, and he won't listen to his brother or sister, not when they're all younger than him, and none of them have been over there the way you have. You're family, Ellen, and Peter looks up to you. Please?"

Ellen opened her eyes and gave her aunt a weary smile. It seemed she was as good as a McCafferty, after all, at least when it mattered. "Of course I will, Aunt Rose."

Outside, Lucas had finished seeing to the horses and he came up to Ellen with a wry look.

"I think I made a hash of it, I'm afraid."

"I'm sure it wasn't your fault, Lucas. Thank you for trying." She glanced towards the ripening fields of barley and wheat; Peter had disappeared among their waving golden stalks. "Rose has asked me to give it a try now."

Lucas nodded his agreement. "Perhaps you'll fare better than I did."

"And perhaps not." She sighed, swiping a strand of hair behind her ear, and Lucas touched her shoulder.

"Have you thought any further about New York?"

"Not a bit," Ellen confessed. "I can't—not with everything that has been going on here—Peter, and these guests coming, and poor Iris Wilson likely to die in the next day or two. There's so much to deal with, Lucas. To bear."

"You don't have to bear it all," he told her gently.

"I'm not. Everyone's helping. Caro's worn to the bone." She glanced again at the fields. "I think I'll go find Peter now." She started down the porch steps.

"I want to help, Ellen," Lucas called after her.

She glanced back uncertainly. "I know—"

"Help *you*," he emphasized, and she faltered in her step. "I care about you," he continued quietly. "I always have."

Again, Ellen felt that unexpected lurch of her heart. Not knowing how to answer, she just nodded and started after Peter.

The fields of barley and wheat were golden-green all around her as Ellen walked slowly through them, looking for Peter. It was still well over a month until harvest, but it had been a good summer so far and the stalks were tall and strong, waving in the slight breeze off the lake.

"Peter?" she called out, but there was no answer.

The farmhouse grew smaller in the distance as Ellen continued to wander through the fields, until she was all alone, surrounded by a sea of wheat under a wide, flat sky of shimmering blue.

She stopped in the middle of a field that, from her vantage point, stretched in every direction, and breathed in the still, sun-warmed air. For a few seconds, she let it all fall away—Iris Wilson lying pale and still in bed; the telegram insisting on feather mattresses and fancy dishes; Caro's ongoing veiled hostility; Rose's troubled frown and Lucas's warm, lingering look as she'd walked away across the fields. She stood there, arms outstretched and face tilted to the sky, and didn't let herself think about anything but this—sun and sky, the stalks brushing against her, the chirrup of the crickets hiding among them. Simplicity. Solitude. She almost wished she could stay there forever, simply breathing the summer in.

"Ellen! What are you doing?"

Ellen lowered her head and blinked the shimmering world back into focus and saw Peter striding through the grain, a scowl on his face.

"I was looking for you."

"And they say I'm the one who's mad."

"You're not mad, Peter." She dropped her arms with a wry smile. "And neither am I, although I might look it, standing in the middle of a field in the noonday sun."

"You looked like a statue... or some sort of sacrifice." Peter shook his head as if to rid himself of the image. "In France, the villagers used to hide in the fields, to get away from the shelling. The targets. But occasionally a bomb would flatten them all huddled together, even there. The women and children, too..."

"Oh Peter." Ellen shook her head. "I'm sorry. I didn't mean to alarm you, or bring back memories..."

"It doesn't matter."

"It does." She regarded him silently for a moment, and he stared back, his mouth and eyes both hard. "Lucas only wants to help you," Ellen said finally. "We all do."

"I'm not mad," he said wearily.

"No one is saying you are. But the war... it changes people, Peter. It changed me."

Curiosity flickered briefly in his eyes. "How?"

Ellen paused, considering. "It made me tired," she said slowly, feeling her way through the words. "So, so tired. And not the kind of tired that a good night's sleep helps."

"No," Peter agreed quietly.

"I came back to the island because it felt like a—a safe harbor. But there is a part of me that feels like I'll always be in France—not with the wounded, but with the sense of—of hopelessness. Sometimes I'm afraid that will never leave me, no matter what happens."

Peter was silent, his narrowed gaze scanning the peaceful fields. "Yet no one is telling you to go see a doctor," he said after a moment.

"No, that's true."

He turned to look at her. "But you think I should?"

"Yes, I do." She paused. "There's a part of you that's still back there, Peter, just like there is for me, but it's a bigger part, because you had a bigger role in the war. You have harder things to forget. I can't even imagine what some of them are—"

"There's no forgetting," Peter cut across her. "Ever."

"No," Ellen agreed, "but there's making your peace with it, perhaps. And that's where a doctor could help. Why not go?" she entreated, her voice rising. "If there is any chance it could help, even a little? Surely you don't want to live like this forever?"

"Do you?" Peter challenged, his chin thrust out, and slowly Ellen shook her head, decisive now.

"No, I don't. I want to hope again. I want to remember how to be happy." If she could. All these concerns that had dogged her, beaten her down—they wouldn't have before the war, Ellen realized. They wouldn't have made her feel so defeated, so desperate, as if there was hardly any point in trying. Just like Peter, she was suffering from the years of heartache and hardship that had been France. "You could at least try," she said, "and if not for your own sake, then for your mother's. She loves you, Peter, so much, and she only wants to help. She'd do whatever she could to make you healthy and happy and whole—sell Jasper Lane, sell her own soul. Can't you do this one thing, for her as well as for you?"

Peter stared at her for a long moment. Then slowly he nodded. "I suppose," he said, his voice as flat as ever, "I could try. But the thing about it, Ellen..." He paused, scanning the fields as if looking for snipers, and she tensed, waiting. "What if it doesn't help? You know what the one thing is that is worse than hopelessness?"

Wordlessly, Ellen shook her, although she feared she knew.

"Hoping," Peter answered flatly. "To no avail."

CHAPTER EIGHTEEN

The next morning, Andrew drove Ellen in the buckboard back to the Wilsons', the day overcast and muggy, the lake the color of slate. It had rained in the night and everything was damp and dreary, and Ellen couldn't imagine how the fussy guests arriving that afternoon would take the change in weather. Amherst Island, the jewel of Lake Ontario, looked well and truly tarnished today.

"Captain Jonah says the weather's going to stay damp and gray through August," Andrew remarked. Although hardly an expert on anything, Captain Jonah had, Ellen knew, been predicting the island weather accurately for nigh on fifty years.

"I shudder to think how our guests will find it," she replied, and Andrew grinned as he shrugged.

"Unfortunately for them you can't pay for good weather." He nodded towards the sad little house of weathered clapboard as it appeared around a bend in the lane, half-hidden by a cluster of weedy-looking alders. "What do you think will happen to those little mites in there, if Mrs. Wilson passes?"

"I don't know." Ellen felt a flicker of guilt that she had not considered the Wilson children's predicament more seriously, what with everything else going on. "I just hope her brother-in-law comes, although since he hasn't responded to the telegram, that possibility seems less and less likely. He might not have received it, or…"

"He might not have been able to," Andrew finished grimly. "He did survive the war?"

"I believe so, but no one seems to know anything about him, except he was last in Oshawa." She sighed. "But before we worry about him, there is poor Iris to attend to."

Ellen climbed out of the wagon with trepidation growing inside her as no one came out of the house. There was, she saw, no smoke from the chimney. And where were the children?

"Caro...?" she called softly as she tapped on the door. "Are you..."

"I'm here." Caro opened the door, looking exhausted and grimy, her apron stained with goodness knew what, her hair falling out of its usual neat bun in careless strands. Ellen gave her a quick hug.

"I should have come sooner."

"It wouldn't have done any good."

Ellen stilled, her hands clasped on Caro's shoulders. "What do you mean? Has she..."

"She's gone," Caro said simply. "She passed this morning, without anyone even beside her." Her eyes filled with tears. "I was downstairs with the little ones, and then when I came to check on her, she was already gone."

"Oh, Caro..."

"I knew it was coming, of course, especially after yesterday, but it still feels like a shock. And I didn't even know her very well, poor woman. Poor wretched woman, with so little to hope for, and now these children..." Her voice choked and Ellen pulled her into a tight hug.

"It never gets easier," she whispered, her heart aching with loss. "Never."

"What will they do, Ellen? Where will they go?"

"Let's deal with the present," Ellen said firmly. She felt ready to wilt, but she knew she needed to be strong for Caro, who looked as if she could drop where she stood, as well as the Wilson children, who had gathered in the doorway of the kitchen, staring at them both with silent, apprehensive faces. "We must attend to Mrs. Wilson and the children, and let tomorrow take care of itself, at least for the moment."

Upstairs, Iris lay in bed, her eyes sightless, her face pale, her poor cheeks already sinking inward. Ellen had seen many dead bodies during her time at Royaumont, and she'd never understood how anyone could think bodies looked as if they were sleeping. Iris did not look peaceful or asleep. She looked dead.

Gently, she closed the woman's eyes while Caro hovered in the doorway.

"What should we…"

"We'll need to wash and dress her," Ellen said matter-of-factly, her nursing training thankfully coming to the fore. "Then you can bring the children in to say their goodbyes. I know it might seem ghoulish, but it's important for them to see her. To know."

Caro nodded and Ellen rolled up her sleeves.

It was neither pleasant nor easy to do the tasks required of her, but Ellen knew the importance of dignity and respect for the dead as she washed and dressed Iris Wilson in her Sunday best, a faded dress with a turned-down hem and patches on the elbows. She brushed out her thin, lank hair, the color of ditchwater, and styled it as best as she could, her heart twisting with pity for the poor woman and the short, hard life she'd led.

When she'd finished, Caro brought the children to pay their respects; they came in hesitantly, the youngest one looking confused, the oldest, Lizzie, trying to be brave. All of it made Ellen's heart ache and ache—for the children, and for herself. She remembered all too well what it felt like to lose a mother.

"I suppose we should call for the minister," Caro said.

"And the undertaker as well. Andrew can fetch them." Caro nodded. "Shall I stay?" Ellen asked. "Until…"

"Until what? There's no one to take these children, Ellen, and we can't leave them on their own."

"I know—"

"I'm going to stay here," Caro said firmly, "for as long as I need to."

"Why not bring the children back to the farm, Caro?" Ellen suggested. "Then you won't be so alone. I worry for you, stuck out here…"

"I'm not stuck," Caro returned. "And you know it's not possible for me to bring these three back, with guests coming. Besides, this is familiar to them, the only thing that is. I can't yank them away from the only home they've known, not when their mother has just died. I'll have to wait, at least until Iris's brother comes."

"But what if he doesn't?" Ellen protested. "Caro, he might not have even received that telegram. What if he's—"

"Don't say it," Caro cut her off. "Surely we would have heard if he hadn't received it. They would have said it couldn't be delivered. He's our only hope, Ellen. He's *their* only hope."

"Isn't there anyone else?"

"Isn't that what everyone says?" Caro fired back, and Ellen sighed.

"I'm just worried for you, Caro. You look exhausted, and it's so much for one woman to bear—"

"I'm fine," Caro returned firmly. "Now you go back home, and tell Mum I'll be all right. See to those guests." She called to Andrew, who had been waiting patiently by the horses, ready to fetch the minister and undertaker.

"Get home quick, Andrew, and then go on to town," Caro instructed. "Then, if you can, come this evening with some more food." He nodded, and Caro gave Ellen a quick hug. "Go now, and don't worry about me. Take care of yourself, Ellen. You look ready to drop, never mind me."

Ellen managed a smile, although she was conscious she still hadn't told Caro about Peter. It would have to wait—again—and yet by the time she had a chance to tell her, Peter would have already gone. If she didn't say something now…

"Caro, there's something you should know," Ellen blurted before she could think better of it. "About Peter."

Caro's careworn face hardened into something like suspicion. "What do you mean?"

"He has an appointment at a hospital for veterans in Toronto," Ellen said in a rush. "On Monday."

Caro stared at her for a moment, as if she couldn't take in the words. "You arranged it?" she asked finally.

"No, Lucas did. But I asked him." She felt a compulsion to confess her own part. "I spoke to Jed, and he spoke to Lucas. Lucas recommended the hospital. He knows one of the doctors."

"You arranged all this and never thought to tell me?" Caro demanded. "You had no right, Ellen Copley—"

"I'm sorry." Ellen tried not to be hurt by the use of her last name, as if Caro was emphasizing her otherness. "I wanted to speak to you about it, but there never seemed to be a good moment, with how busy you've been with the Wilsons."

"Don't blame the Wilsons! There were plenty of moments you could have told me." Caro's face was flushed, her eyes bright with anger.

Ellen stared at her miserably. "I didn't want to add to your burdens…"

"You didn't want me to know you were interfering, especially as I told you not to!" Caro looked as if she might fly into a rage, and Ellen steeled herself for it. It was no more than she deserved, she knew. She should have told Caro what she was up to long before this. She'd simply been too cowardly to do so.

"I am sorry, Caro, truly…"

"Oh, never mind." Caro sighed heavily as she looked away, her lips pursed. "I can't think of all that now. I suppose my mother has gone along with it?"

"She agreed, yes."

"You had no right." Caro shook her head. "No right. But, like I said, I can't think of it now."

"Miss Caro?" Lizzie peeked her head out the front door. "Can we have some bread and butter?"

"Yes, of course, Lizzie. I'll be right there." Caro gave Ellen a long, level look. "I won't forget this, Ellen."

"It's for Peter's sake, Caro—"

"It wasn't your place."

"Oh, and what is my place?" Ellen demanded, her voice vibrating with hurt, but Caro just shook her head.

"I'm not going to talk about this now," she said, and went back inside with Lizzie, closing the door firmly behind her.

Ellen let out a sound that was half sigh, half cry, and then went back to the wagon where Andrew had been waiting. He gave her a questioning look as she climbed up, but Ellen just shook her head. She couldn't speak of it now. Not to Andrew, not to anyone.

It wasn't her place, Caro had said. Then where, Ellen wondered as they started back down the lane, *was* her place?

CHAPTER NINETEEN

By the time Ellen arrived back at Jasper Lane, everything was in a flurry and she had no time to dwell on her argument with Caro. The guests were due to arrive in Stella in a matter of minutes, so Andrew set off to collect them, while Ellen washed as quickly as she could and Sarah, Gracie, and Rose all hurried around doing their best to keep everything spotless.

"Are you sure you're all right, love?" Rose asked just as the old buckboard turned up Jasper Lane. The woman sitting in the front wore a hat so bedecked with feathers, fruit, and even a stuffed bird that it added another two feet to her height. Inwardly, Ellen quailed at the sight. A woman wearing such a hat could not bode well for the week ahead.

"I'm fine, Aunt Rose," she said with a reassuring smile, determined not to mention anything of the argument with Caro. "Just a little tired."

Soon enough, the guests were disembarking, and it was every bit as bad as they'd all feared, with Isadora Welton of Hamilton, Ontario turning her nose up at just about everything, her carrying voice with its affected accent remarking on all she found lacking.

"If the Framptons of New York enjoyed their stay, I don't know why a Welton of Hamilton can't," Gracie hissed viciously as she came downstairs, Mrs. Welton having returned the pitcher of washing water because it wasn't warm enough.

Ellen plonked the kettle on the stove, her arms aching with the effort. "They'll be gone in a week, Gracie. Let's just do the best we can."

"At least you'll have some respite, going to Toronto," Gracie said, rolling her eyes, and Ellen managed a smile, although she did not know how much respite that particular journey would offer, especially with Caro's harsh words echoing in her ears.

The next twenty-four hours passed interminably. Isadora Welton seemed determined to find fault with everything, and her daughter Elspeth, although apologetic about her mother's airs, was cowed by the woman to the point of meek and subservient silence, and did not make any objection when Mrs. Welton sent back the chicken pie Rose had made, claiming it to be too plain, and then the dessert, saying the cream had gone off.

"Milked this morning," Rose had whispered in despair. "I'm sure it's fresh…"

"Of course it is," Gracie had flashed. "Irritating Isadora simply wants to find fault with everything."

"Gracie, hush—"

"It's true—"

"This is part of having guests," Rose had insisted staunchly. "They won't all be to your liking. We must manage as best as we can. Sarah, give her another bowl of pudding without the cream."

Thankfully, Isadora Welton ate that without too much complaint.

Still, she seemed to take pleasure in elucidating her many complaints at every opportunity—the bedclothes, including Rose's beautiful handstitched quilt, were scratchy, the food was overcooked, the bath water was either too hot or too cold, and Ellen's art lessons were clearly not up to scratch.

"I was expecting someone with a bit more… gravitas?" Mrs. Welton suggested with an acid smile on Sunday afternoon. "A bit more experience and standing. You said you've been to art school somewhere, did you, dear?"

"Glasgow Art School," Ellen clarified as politely as she could. It didn't help that Isadora Welton was a rather uninspired artist herself. "As it happens, Mrs. Welton, I will not be available to instruct you now until Tuesday morning. A pressing matter has called me away tomorrow." Although Ellen had considered staying for the guests' sake, family was more important.

"What!" Isadora looked thunderous. "But I have paid—"

"I have left detailed instructions, of course," Ellen continued, "and the two Miss McCaffertys will be here to see to all your needs. You are in good hands, I assure you."

Isadora continued to complain, much to Rose's alarm and aggravation, but Ellen begged her not to think of it.

"We need to think about Peter now," she told her on Sunday night, after the Weltons had gone up to bed. "He's more important than a few fussy guests." She knew she needed the lecture as much as Rose, especially as she'd been accosted by doubts ever since Caro had stormed at her. "Besides, Isadora and her complaints will still be here upon our return."

"Unfortunately," Rose agreed with a sigh.

Ellen wished there was time to call in at the Wilsons before they left for Toronto; she longed to speak with Caro as much as to hear any news of Jack Wilson. There wasn't any time, however, for they had to wake up just after dawn to make the first train from Kingston to Toronto the next morning. Caro was still with the Wilsons, having sent a message to Rose that Iris' funeral would be a quiet affair as there was no money for a proper service or burial, and Caro would stay at the farm until Jack Wilson arrived—*if* he arrived. Perhaps he already had. Gracie, Sarah, and Andrew would stay at Jasper Lane to manage the demanding Weltons.

"If things get too much, I'll hit Mrs. Welton over the head with a frying pan," Gracie informed them cheerfully as they took their leave the next morning. "That will sort her out."

"*Gracie.*" Rose shook her head, smiling worriedly as Lucas helped them into the wagon. "The trouble is, I think you actually *might.*"

Peter, Ellen saw, was quieter even than usual as they boarded the train in Kingston; he spent the entire journey watching the world slide by as Rose chattered nervously away and Ellen tried to keep up her end of the conversation, although she found it difficult; she felt unaccountably tired and her head ached, no doubt from all the pressing needs and events of the last few days.

"Do you know, I've never been to Toronto," Rose told Lucas. "Have you got used to such a big city, after all this time?"

"I suppose I have," Lucas answered. "The population topped half a million this year. It's the biggest city in all of Canada."

"My goodness." Rose shook her head in wonder. "Half a million. I can't even imagine. Do you suppose you'll stay there?"

Lucas's gaze moved fleetingly to Ellen for a moment before he turned back to Rose. "It's difficult to say."

Several hours later, after alighting at Toronto's Union Station, only just built and taking up an entire city block, they took a taxi—Rose marveling at being in a motorcar—to the Toronto Military Orthopedic Hospital on Christie Street.

It had been converted from an old factory only recently, and looked big and square and gloomy, a severe sort of brick-fronted building that made Rose glance worriedly at Peter, who stared impassively back.

"I know it doesn't look much," Lucas said cheerfully, "but the medical staff is top class. Peter will be in good hands."

"What a relief," Peter said flatly, and Rose bit her lip.

Ellen hoped her cousin would be amenable to being examined by a doctor; although he'd come this far, she sensed his reluctance as if it were as solid and immutable as the brick walls of the hospital.

Inside, the hospital was not much better than its exterior. A smiling young orderly gave them a tour of the wards, with the narrow, military-style beds with scratchy gray blankets drawn up tightly, the walls painted a depressing dark green. But worse than the beds or the walls were the men themselves—some slack-jawed and indifferent, staring sightlessly into space, others seeming tense and tightly wound, their eyes wild, their fists clenched, as if they were ready to spring.

"And this is the day room…" the orderly said as he led them into a large, open room scattered with sofas, chairs, and about a dozen men staring blankly in front of them. Two men sat at a table with a checkerboard in front of them; neither man so much as picked up a piece.

"What a lovely, bright room," Ellen said, although her heart felt as if it were faltering within her. As cheerful as they'd tried to make the room, it felt stifling and almost unbearable in the grim sorrow that permeated the place like an invisible fog. How could they possibly want Peter in a place like this?

After the tour, Lucas's acquaintance from the war, Dr. Stanton, greeted Peter, shaking his hand and welcoming him, although Peter did not reply.

Rose, Lucas, and Ellen all waited anxiously while Dr. Stanton took Peter to his office for a private interview.

"Will he… examine him?" Rose asked in a whisper.

"I believe they'll just talk," Lucas said. "As you know, neurasthenia cannot be diagnosed through a physical examination."

"No, I suppose not." Rose sighed and shifted on the hard bench where they'd been asked to wait. "It would be easier, in a way, if it could be. Or if he'd been damaged physically. Lost an arm or—*oh*." She glanced apologetically at Lucas. "I'm sorry. I wasn't even thinking of Jed just then."

"I understand your thoughts completely," Lucas assured her. "The invisible wounds can be the most difficult to treat."

Ellen thought of what Jed had said, about how every soldier had scars, some more obvious than others. What, she wondered, were Lucas's?

After nearly an hour, Dr. Stanton opened the door and welcomed them into his office, a small, friendly room that was cluttered with books and papers and seemed quite homely after the grim sterility of the wards.

"It's a pleasure to meet you all." He sat behind his desk, lacing his hands together in front of him. "And I very much enjoyed meeting and talking to Peter." He gave a smiling nod towards Peter, who was sitting silently, his hands resting on his thighs, his expression unreadable. "After our discussion, I think it would be of benefit for Peter to stay with us for some time."

"How much time?" Rose asked anxiously, and the doctor spread his hands helplessly.

"I could not say, Mrs. McCafferty. As long as needed, one hopes. My initial estimation would be three months, but of course, that can change."

"Three months…"

"I am sure you have questions about a residential stay," he said kindly, his eyebrows raised.

Rose, clutching her handbag tightly, threw Peter an anxious glance before admitting hesitantly, "The hospital… it's not quite what I expected."

"No," the doctor agreed, "I'm afraid it never is."

"I thought… I thought…" Rose shook her head. "I thought the patients—the men—they'd all be a bit happier, if I'm to tell the truth."

"They can be, sometimes, Mrs. McCafferty," Dr. Stanton said, his tone gentle. "We've had some quite jolly times here. But it's also difficult, and sometimes it feels endless." He glanced at Peter, his expression softening into a deep compassion that made Ellen's anxiety ease a little bit. Dr. Stanton looked like a man who understood. "Doesn't it, Peter?" he asked quietly, and Peter's glance flicked to him, his expression inscrutable, before he gave the tiniest of nods.

"What types of treatment do you use here, Dr. Stanton?" Lucas asked, his tone friendly and reasonable, as if they were talking about any particular matter of interest. Ellen was glad he'd come. He was a steadying presence when she so desperately needed one, as did Rose, and of course, Peter.

"We try to use psychotherapy as much as possible," Dr. Stanton answered, and Rose blinked.

"I don't think I've…"

"The talking cure, it's sometimes called," he explained with a smile. "Some of my colleagues have reported success with electric shock treatment, but I am not yet convinced that such measures are either helpful or necessary."

"So Peter would just… talk?" Rose looked doubtful; she glanced again at Peter, whose face remained impassive.

"Yes, in a contained, unpressured environment, with the opportunity to remember and discuss elements of his war years that would, in time, I hope, help him to make sense of all he has experienced. In the meantime, he has full medical support, as well as the companionship of men who understand what he is experiencing, which, I must say, can go a long way towards helping men to recovery." Dr. Stanton gave Peter another warm look.

"I don't know." Rose bit her lip. "I feel like he might be better at home with us, just getting on with things." She glanced again at Peter, who had remained silent all the way through this unsettling interview. "What do you think, Peter?"

Peter looked at his mother for the first time. "I want to stay," he said quietly.

Rose's mouth opened silently, her eyes filling with tears. "Peter…"

"I know I'm not right," he said quietly. "Even if I pretend that I am. Even if I wish—and I do, so much—that I was. I can't hide it all the time, and to tell you the truth, I'm sick to death of trying. Of feeling different, of feeling like an outsider… here they understand me. They're *like* me. I want to stay."

Rose's lips trembled before she pressed them together and she nodded. "If you're sure, Peter…" Her expression clouded as she glanced nervously at Dr. Stanton. "Except… I'm afraid I don't know how much it costs. Three months…"

"Aunt Rose," Ellen interjected, "Remember, I said I could—"

"The costs have already been covered," Dr. Stanton informed them easily. "For the foreseeable future."

Ellen's jaw dropped along with Rose's.

"*Covered?*" Rose repeated in disbelief. "But how…"

Dr. Stanton smiled. "An anonymous donor. We have them sometimes, by God's grace. So I am not at liberty to tell you who it was."

"But… but…"

"Let's accept it in the spirit it was given," Ellen said. She'd been ready to offer to pay, but she didn't know whether the rest of her savings would cover three months in hospital. She was glad for this solution, although she wondered who on earth had paid, even before they'd arrived. It felt too wonderful to believe, but she was too tired to do anything but trust it. "This is for the best, Aunt Rose."

"Yes, of course." Rose still looked shaken, both to realize Peter would be staying, and that it was already paid for. "When shall Peter come back to begin his… his stay?"

"He can stay now, if he likes," Dr. Stanton said. "Everything is ready. You can send his things on. It's often the best way."

"Oh, but—"

"This is what I want, Mum," Peter said, sounding almost gentle. "I'll stay from today. Don't worry about me. I'm going to get better and come home to you, I promise."

Rose did her best to hold back her tears. "If you're sure…"

"I am."

It felt surreal to be saying their goodbyes only moments later. Dr. Stanton showed Peter to his room, which he would share with another patient. Rose looked around the sterile surroundings, clearly trying to come to grips with it all and failing.

Peter, however, seemed content enough, and more than ready for them to leave, and soon enough they were out on the street, a depressing drizzle blanketing the cityscape in yet more gray.

"It's happened so fast," Rose said, pressing one hand to her cheek. "So much faster than I ever expected. I thought today would be just to look, to see…"

"But like Dr. Stanton said, it's better this way," Lucas said kindly. "And it's good news for Peter. We know that, even if it is so very hard to say goodbye."

"Yes." Rose smiled at him gratefully. "Thank you so much, Lucas. You and Jed both have been such a support to us."

"As you have, through the years, Rose. Now, let me take both of you ladies to tea before you make the train." Lucas had suggested they stay the night, but in the end neither Ellen nor Rose had wanted to stay away from the farm for that long, and they would be leaving on the evening train in just a few hours.

The hotel Lucas took them to was fancy indeed, all velvet chairs and damask tablecloths, with crystal and silver as well. Lucas ordered tea and scones, sandwiches and cakes, yet Ellen found she could barely eat a bite.

Her head continued to ache, and her whole body as well. Perhaps she was coming down with a cold, or maybe she was just exhausted. Either way, she looked forward to collapsing into bed that evening, even though that seemed like a long time away, with the train to Kingston to catch, and then the ferry.

"Ellen, you really do look worn out," Rose said when Ellen had refused a delicious-looking éclair. "Perhaps I shouldn't have had you come with me today. Sarah could have come—"

"She's looking after things at home," Ellen reminded her. "And our guests, which is a far more demanding occupation, I fear." Besides, they both knew Sarah possessed too gentle and sensitive a nature for such a visit as this.

"Still." Rose frowned. "You need some rest."

"We've the Weltons to deal with when we return." Ellen shook her head, trying to be cheerful, even though she felt like wilting. "I'm fine, Aunt Rose, honestly."

But she had to admit she didn't *feel* fine, and when she stood up from the table, to leave for their train, her head swam and for a brief moment she staggered. Lucas reached out to steady her with one strong arm, and Ellen tried to smile at him.

"Thank you, I don't know what came over me…" she began, only to have her head swim again, and the world begin to blur at the edges in a way that felt most alarming, as if everything were slowing down, losing focus.

"Ellen!" Rose said, her voice rising in a cry of frightened distress, and then Lucas's arms were around her as the world blurred completely and Ellen crumpled to the floor.

CHAPTER TWENTY

The world was fading in and out. Every time Ellen blinked, she felt as if something had shifted or tilted, colors, lights, and sounds all blurring together into an indistinguishable mass. She heard voices, sometimes close, sometimes distant, and on occasion the sound of sobs suppressed, choked tears.

Periodically, she felt a cool hand on her forehead or cheek, fingers laced with her own, and a feeling of comfort, of safety, would suffuse her, although she couldn't speak of it or even open her eyes. Any impressions were fleeting, however, and she always sank back into oblivion after only a few moments, craving the enveloping darkness like a warm tide washing over her, drawing her under.

For the few moments she was awake, she felt as if she were swimming through treacle, each breath labored and difficult, before she gave up and returned to the comforting depths of darkness—and sleep.

And then slowly, so slowly, the world around her began to sharpen into focus; she felt as if she were swimming up towards a light or a sound, searching, searching, trying to remember what had happened…

"Ellen… Ellen?" Rose's tearful, incredulous voice hit all her senses and she felt Rose's hand press her own.

Ellen blinked slowly and saw she was in a large, bare room; tall, sashed windows let in bright sunlight. Her whole body ached, and her mouth was desperately dry. The sunlight was so bright she had to turn her head away, the pillowcase scratchy under her cheek. In the distance, she heard the low murmur of voices, the squeak of a wheel.

"Where…" It was all she could manage, her voice no more than a thread of sound.

"You're in the hospital, in Toronto," Rose said, hurrying to explain, her voice still full of unshed tears. "Ellen, you've been in and out of a fever for nearly a week! Oh my darling, we've been so worried. So very worried. We thought we might lose you…"

Ellen's eyes fluttered closed as her aunt's words sank in. A week… she'd been ill for a whole *week*. She tried to sift through the blur of memories and finally latched upon the last clear thing she could recall… standing up in the restaurant where she, Aunt Rose and Lucas had had tea after they'd admitted Peter to the military hospital for soldiers suffering from shell shock. She and Rose had been meant to catch the train, but all Ellen could remember was looking at Lucas as the world went woozy.

She opened her eyes again and licked her dry lips. Rose peered at her in eager concern, new lines of worry furrowing her dear forehead.

"What… what happened?" Ellen managed in a rusty croak.

"Let me get you some water first." Rose poured a glass of water from the pitcher by Ellen's bed, one of six in the ward. The others, she saw blearily, were occupied by patients like herself—most of them asleep, looking wan and pale, barely moving or even visible under their sheets.

"Thank you, Aunt Rose," Ellen said after she'd taken several life-sustaining sips while her aunt held the glass to her lips. "I feel… much better."

"I think it will be a while before you feel that," Rose answered with a shaky smile. She sat back down on the chair she'd pulled up to the side of the bed. "But thank goodness the fever has broken and you're going to be all right. We feared the worst, you know."

Rose's lips trembled and she pressed them together. "I hate to confess it, but we did, Ellen. We really did. For a while, when the fever just wouldn't break…"

"We…?" Ellen repeated, frowning. Surely the others hadn't come all the way from the island to sit by her bedside, even if she had been as ill as Rose said?

"Lucas and I. He's been here every day, Ellen, coming after work to sit with you, and sometimes staying through the night, even though one of these starchy nurses didn't think it proper. But he was that worried, and it was that close, I'm afraid to say. I don't know what I would have done without him here. He's been a rock, truly."

"Oh…" Ellen flushed and squirmed inwardly to think of Lucas being so devoted, and while she had been so ill, so helpless, tossing and turning, feverish and moaning…! She must have looked a complete fright the whole while. She felt like one now, as weak as a kitten, and as wrung out as a wet dishrag. When she glanced down at her hand resting on the bedsheet, she saw how it looked like a claw, skin stretched tautly over bone.

"And of course everyone back at home has been worried, as well," Rose continued. "I sent a telegram when you first took ill, and the whole island's been praying for you. I'll send another today, to let them know you're out of the worst." Rose let out a shuddery sigh. "Thank the good Lord."

"How is Peter…" Ellen asked. She hated to think of everyone concerned for her when it was Peter who needed attention.

"He's doing well, I think. I visited the hospital after your fever had broken. Dr. Stanton said Peter was settling in well, but it was best if we didn't see him for a little while." Rose's voice hitched, but she continued determinedly, "We can write letters, of course…"

Ellen nodded slowly, doing her best to absorb all the news. Her brain felt as if it were working so slowly, like the laborious turning of gears. "And what of the Weltons…"

"Oh, don't you worry about them. They're long gone, thank goodness. In the end, Mrs. Welton said she quite liked her stay, or so Caro said in her letter. She wrote yesterday."

Caro… was she still angry at her, Ellen wondered, for interfering with Peter? She couldn't ask Rose.

"Who knows," Rose said, smiling, "perhaps Mrs. Welton will book again?"

Ellen tried to laugh, but only managed a throaty rasp. "Have I had the influenza?" she asked, and Rose nodded.

"That's what the doctors said. You must have caught it from poor Mrs. Wilson, when you were nursing her, God rest her soul."

"Yes…" Ellen remembered Iris Wilson's poor, desiccated frame with a tremble. Had she been as ill as *that*? "I only hope no one else catches it," she managed in a whisper. "Those poor, frail children… they wouldn't last a minute…"

"Caro said everyone was as right as rain so far. She's decided to take the children back to Jasper Lane until Iris's brother turns up, since our last booking cancelled, and she wrote that there has been no end to the bread and butter and gingerbread they're all putting away." Rose smiled at this, and Ellen smiled back—or tried to.

"I'm glad to hear it, although I'm sorry about the booking."

"It doesn't matter, Ellen. We've enough put by for now."

She drew a ragged breath, words becoming an effort, her vision darkening at the edges. "Will Iris' brother ever turn up? Caro wasn't even sure she knew where he was…"

Rose nodded soberly. "Yes, who knows if he even received that telegram. The last address Mrs. Wilson had for him was from before the war. But, still," she reached for Ellen's hand and gave it a gentle squeeze, "all that matters is that you're on the mend, Ellen. I'm so, so glad." A tear fell from Rose's eye and she dashed it away with a little laugh. "Look at me, falling to pieces, and when you're getting better. What a daft woman I am sometimes."

"I'm sorry to have given you such a scare, Aunt Rose."

"Oh love, what could you have done about it? We've worked you too hard, I fear. You'll be needing a good, long rest once we get you back."

Ellen smiled faintly, unable to respond for she felt herself falling back into sleep, as if being tugged by some invisible yet determined hand. It felt good to sink back into those welcoming depths of oblivion.

"Sleep now," Rose said softly, patting her on the shoulder as Ellen felt herself slip away. "Sleep, my dear Ellen."

Four days later, Ellen sat in a chair in the ward's day room, a rug over her knees as the summer sunshine poured through the window and bathed her in its needed warmth. She'd been in the hospital in Toronto for ten days, spending most of them asleep or in a doze, and now still feeling as weak and helpless as some poor, newborn creature.

When the nurse had brought a washbasin and a mirror to her in bed, Ellen had stared at her reflection in ill-concealed horror.

"I'm nothing but skin and bone!" she'd exclaimed. She'd touched her once glossy chestnut waves, now straggly and limp-looking, hanging down in dirty ropes. "And I'm going gray…" she exclaimed as her fingers found a few unwelcome, glinting strands.

"You'll get your looks back," the nurse had said robustly, and dipped a flannel into the warm water in the basin before handing it to Ellen. "Or most of them, at any rate."

It was hard to feel so tired and worn out, Ellen reflected as she gazed out at the buildings of Toronto, now gleaming under the sunlight. She'd been ill before, seriously so, back when she'd been a nursing student in Kingston. It felt like a long time ago, ten whole years, and all she wanted now was to be back on the island, being of use to those she loved, instead of sitting here like a lump, utterly useless, and so far from Jasper Lane.

"Hello there, lazybones." Ellen turned at the sound of Lucas's laughing voice, a smile lighting her face as he came towards her, taking off his hat as he did so. He'd visited her every day she'd been in the hospital.

"I do feel lazy," she admitted. "I've done nothing but lie about for well over a week, and yet I don't feel strong enough to do anything else."

"The doctors don't want you doing anything else, and neither do I," Lucas answered firmly. "You've been very ill, Ellen. You need to rest."

"Yes, but I want to get back to the island. To home." She spoke the word with feeling, realizing afresh how much she meant it. "Aunt Rose told me that the last booking was cancelled, and she's been stuck in Toronto for so long, having to look after me—"

"You speak as if you're a burden," Lucas said gently as he drew up a chair next to her. "And you're not."

Ellen bit her lip, not wanting to revisit their old conversation about her place in the McCafferty family, or how insecure she sometimes felt about it, especially in light of the argument she'd had with Caro before she'd left for Toronto. "I just want to get back," she insisted. "There's so much to do."

"And if Aunt Rose or any of the McCaffertys have anything to do with the matter, you won't be doing any of it." Lucas studied her, a serious look in his light blue eyes. "Do you know how close we came to losing you, Ellen?" The throb of feeling in his voice had Ellen biting her lip and looking away.

"I suppose I'm stronger than I look," she said a bit unevenly.

"And I thank God for that. It was the hardest thing I've ever done, to have to watch you toss and turn in the height of a terrible fever, and know there was nothing I could do but watch and wait and pray. I felt completely powerless, and I hated it."

"Sometimes that's all anyone can do," Ellen said. "Watch and wait and pray." She turned to look back at him, willing the slight flush to fade from her cheeks, and the intensity of the moment to ease. "Thank you, Lucas, for being with me when I was ill."

"There wasn't any other place I'd rather be." The intent look in his eyes had the flush returning to her face.

Surely Lucas didn't feel that way about her anymore? No matter how he'd told her he cared about her, she couldn't believe he still had the youthful romantic notions from their days at Queen's. They'd both lived what felt like several lifetimes in the years since then, and Ellen had always assumed Lucas had moved on from his romantic affections for her. She'd *hoped* he had. But now…

"You'll always be one of my dearest friends, Ellen," Lucas added, and Ellen smiled, doing her best to ignore the slight flicker of disappointment his words caused her. She was being silly, thinking there was more going on than Lucas's kind and sincere friendship, for which she was so very grateful. She depended on him. She didn't want or need anything more from him than that.

"And you mine, Lucas, truly."

He nodded, smiling, and Ellen smiled back, doing her best to banish the strange, stubborn feeling of something close to disappointment she felt. Of course she was glad he was her friend. What more could she possibly want from him?

"I spoke to the doctor before I came in here," Lucas resumed after a moment, "and he said he thought you could be discharged in another few days. Convalesce at home instead of here."

"Oh, really?" Everything in Ellen brightened at that welcome news. "That's wonderful, Lucas! I would so much rather be at Jasper Lane. I can't wait."

"Yes." Lucas's smile was whimsical and just the tiniest bit sad, making Ellen wonder what he was really thinking. "Yes, it really is the most welcome news, I know."

*

Three days later, a weak and wobbly Ellen boarded the train to Kingston with Aunt Rose. Lucas had accompanied them to the station in a taxicab, ever solicitous and concerned for Ellen's still flagging health, and promising to return to the island to check on her as soon as he could free himself from work.

"You will take care of yourself," he admonished sternly. "And not run about, trying to do everything. The world does *not* rest on your shoulders, you know."

"I'll make sure she doesn't," Rose promised, holding onto Ellen's arm. "She's to stay at bed for at least another week."

"A whole week—" Ellen protested, albeit feebly. The journey from the hospital to the station had tired her out considerably, and she already longed for bed.

"Yes, a whole week, and two or three if necessary," Rose said rather fiercely. "Everyone insists, Ellen. We won't lose you."

"And I shall be visiting as soon as I can, to make sure you're doing as you're told," Lucas informed her.

"You don't have to—"

"I want to," he interjected, his voice both gentle and firm as his gaze rested on her for another moment. "And I will."

As Ellen settled into the second-class carriage and watched Lucas wave goodbye from the platform, a lump came to her throat. She was so very fortunate, so very blessed, to have friends and family who cared for her so deeply. No matter what Caro had said in a moment of anger, she knew she belonged on Amherst.

Impulsively she turned to Aunt Rose and clutched her hand. "Thank you, Aunt Rose, for staying with me all the while I was ill. It was so very kind of you."

Rose smiled, looking both surprised and a bit misty-eyed. "Why, child," she said. "Where else would I be?"

"You could have gone back to the island. There are so many demands on you—the guests as well your own children—"

"My own children?" Rose repeated, her voice sharpening with incredulity. "Ellen, my dear, surely you know you're as good as my own child by now? I've raised you, Ellen Copley, and I've loved you just as my own, right from the first moment you arrived at Jasper Lane, all those years ago." Rose's voice was fierce. "I hope you know that, and know it well."

Tears crowded Ellen's eyes and when she blinked, a few trickled down her cheeks. "I do," she whispered in a choked voice.

"But somehow I think you'd doubted it," Rose answered shrewdly, even as she gave a tear-filled laugh. "Oh Ellen, how could you doubt even for a moment? I feel I've aged a decade in the last week, worrying over you. I'm so very glad you're well, my darling. So very glad."

By the time they arrived at Ogdensburg to catch the ferry to Amherst Island, Ellen was feeling completely wrung out, limp and exhausted. Simply sitting on a train, having it jostle and jolt beneath her, had exhausted her, and she leaned heavily on her aunt's arm as they boarded the little tugboat to the island and took their seats.

It was late afternoon, with golden sunlight coating the lake like syrup, the sky a soft, hazy blue above them, the air fresh and clean, especially after the smog and choking traffic of Toronto's city streets. Captain Jonah's dire prediction that all of August would be wet and gray had, for once, not come true, although he refused to admit as much, predicting with relish that it would rain that day, just wait and see.

"Oh, I've missed being here," Ellen exclaimed as she leaned against Rose's shoulder and the little boat started across the lake. "I feel as if I've been away an age."

A few other passengers had boarded the ferry, including several familiar faces who inquired after Ellen's health and wished her well, pressing her hand and giving her glad smiles.

"Andrew will be waiting with the wagon," Rose told her as the boat approached the landing at Stella. "And then as soon as we get back to Jasper Lane, it's right into bed for you. You must be exhausted."

"I won't protest," Ellen admitted with a wry smile. "I am well and truly worn out."

They were just leaving the ferry when one of the passengers approached them, his hat crumpled in his hands, his head slightly bowed so they couldn't see his face. He wore a well-worn suit whose fashion was from before the war, and although he looked tired and scarecrow-thin, when he spoke, Ellen felt there was something kind about him, in the timbre of his voice.

"Pardon me, ladies," he said, "but do you know where the Wilson farm is?"

"Wilson…?" Ellen spoke so sharply that the man looked up, and she did her best not to recoil at the sight of his face; half of it was normal, with a straight nose and a kind eye of faded blue. The other half looked as if it had melted like wax, the flesh lumpen and reddened, his eyes swollen shut and his mouth pulled into an unpleasant rictus by scarring. He must have been burned by poison gas in the war, and while she'd seen the like before, both in Toronto and during her time at Royaumont, it still came as a shock. "Are you Iris Wilson's brother-in-law?" she asked gently. "Jack Wilson?"

"Yes, that's me." He looked up, a light entering his good eye, brightening the blue. "I only received the telegram a few days ago. They had to track me down. I'd been out west looking for work. Is Iris…?"

"My dear boy," Rose said quietly, laying one hand on his arm. "I'm so sorry, but your sister-in-law passed away a few weeks ago. My daughter Caroline sent the telegram before she'd passed, bidding you to come…"

John Wilson's face contorted, the muscles drawn sharply across his good cheek, and pulling the other painfully before he gave one terse nod. "And the little ones?"

"They're all well, and staying with us, at our farm on Jasper Lane," Rose said. "If you want to accompany us in our wagon, you are more than welcome to do so, Mr. Wilson."

"I thank you for that," he said with another quick nod. "I will accept your offer."

CHAPTER TWENTY-ONE

The trip back to Jasper Lane through a gathering dusk was silent; Andrew had taken one surprised look at John Wilson's face before shaking his hand and asking no questions. Rose had explained matters and Ellen had collapsed into the wagon seat with an audible sigh of relief. She felt as if she could fall asleep right then and there.

As Andrew drove up Jasper Lane, Caro came out onto the porch, followed by Gracie and Sarah, all of them looking anxious.

"Is Ellen all right?" Sarah called.

Rose called back gaily, "She's as right as rain, or soon she will be! And, Caro, look who we found on the ferry."

As Andrew pulled the wagon up to the front of the farmhouse, they all clambered out; when Ellen faltered, John Wilson took her arm with a small, sympathetic smile.

"It's Iris Wilson's brother-in-law," Rose exclaimed. "He received the telegram and he came right away. Isn't that good news?"

"Oh, yes—" Caro began, and then fell suddenly silent as John Wilson turned and she caught sight of his face.

For a few awful seconds, everyone was speechless and staring; with an attempt at a wry smile, John touched the misshapen side of his face with his fingers in acknowledgment.

Then, thankfully, Caro gathered her wits once more and came down the steps to greet him. "You're very welcome here, Mr. Wilson, I'm sure."

Ellen was too tired to stand around listening to their pleasantries, and with Rose's help, she made it up to her bedroom, half-collapsing on her bed.

"Oh Ellen, I fear the journey has set you back terribly!" Rose exclaimed as she bustled about, helping Ellen to remove her shoes and then turning back the covers. "You must rest. If you get out of that bed even once before Sunday, I shall be having cross words with you!"

"I shall be having cross words with myself," Ellen returned sleepily as her head hit the pillow. Her eyes fluttered close and she was asleep before Rose had even closed the door.

Several days later, Ellen was feeling stronger—she'd taken Rose at her word and had stayed in bed the whole time—when a soft knock sounded at her bedroom door.

"Come in," she called, and then tried not to show her surprise when Caro peeked her head around the door. "Caro… is everything all right?"

"Yes and no," Caro answered frankly as she perched on the end of the bed. She looked unhappy, and Ellen tensed, unsure if she had the strength to have another complicated conversation with her cousin.

"What is it?"

"I need to apologize, Ellen," Caro said in her frank way. "I have a terrible feeling I've treated you horribly. In fact, I know I have."

"You haven't…" Ellen began, so unconvincingly that Caro laughed.

"I have and you know it! I shouldn't have railed you about Peter, and I never should have acted as if you of all people were interfering." Caro shook her head, her face full of regret. "I don't know why I did. I suppose because I was scared."

"That's understandable…"

"And more than that," Caro admitted in a rush. "I was… jealous of you."

Ellen stared at her, shocked. "Jealous?"

"Mum looked to you to save Jasper Lane, and you did. You came back into our lives after seven years and it was wonderful—truly it was—and I was as grateful as Mum for all you did." Caro sighed heavily. "But at some point I started to feel resentful, I suppose. Frustrated that I didn't have all the answers, or even any of them. And whenever there was a problem Mum looked to you, not me. She valued your advice far more than mine."

"Oh Caro, I don't think that's true—"

"That was in part why I spent so much time at the Wilsons'. The family needed my care, but I needed *them*. I needed to be needed."

"Caro, you are needed," Ellen said quietly. "I know you are. If you didn't feel so, it's because Aunt Rose simply depended on you without ever saying so. Took you for granted, perhaps. You've done so much for the family, the farm."

"Perhaps," Caro allowed, "but I know my mother has always valued your experience, especially as you've had so much more than I have, what with moving to Glasgow, and serving in the war. But the Wilsons need *my* experience," Caro continued, her voice hardening with conviction. "My experience of the island, and of farming, and even of raising little ones. I may not have had any of my own, but I helped with Sarah and Gracie and Andrew. I can help them."

Ellen searched her face, noting the resolve she saw there. "You've been very good to them, Caro," she said. "But what can you do now that Mr. Wilson has returned? He will take them on, won't he?" Ellen hadn't seen much of Jack Wilson since he'd come to the island with them. He was staying at the Wilson homestead, and trying to get the farm going, as well as visiting the children at Jasper Lane at least once a day.

"I hope he will," Caro said slowly. "But there might be some trouble."

"Trouble—"

"The Presbyterian Ladies' Benevolent Society is taking an interest in the children," Caro explained, an edge of anger to her voice. "They didn't seem much interested when Iris was struggling and they were near to starving, but now that a good man has come to take care of them, they've decided to show some neighborly concern."

"Concern? Why?" Ellen asked, even as she silently registered Caro's opinion of Jack Wilson. Did she really know the man that well? He'd seemed nice enough, but Ellen had no idea whether he was suitably placed to take care of three motherless children.

"Because he's a stranger, and because of—because his face." Caro shook her head. "It's cruel of them."

"That does seem rather narrow-minded," Ellen answered after a moment. "There are many men who have scars like Mr. Wilson's from the war."

"It's just because they don't know him," Caro exclaimed in frustration. "And because he's not from the island. Sometimes this place feels so ridiculously *small.*"

"I'm sorry, Caro," Ellen said quietly. "I can see you've come to care for the Wilson children. But surely the Ladies' Society is concerned for their wellbeing, too? You don't actually know Mr. Wilson, do you, or whether he'd be a suitable father for those children?"

"He'd be better than an asylum, surely," Carol fired back.

Ellen stayed silent. It was a conundrum, to be sure, but not one she thought either she or Caro would be able to solve.

"In any case, you should rest," Caro said as she rose from the bed. "I'm sure something will sort itself out." She did not sound convinced. "You do look worn out, Ellen." She patted her shoulder before leaving the room, and Ellen leaned back against the pillows as her eyes fluttered closed and she abandoned herself to the comforts of sleep once more.

A week passed in a similar fashion before Ellen felt strong enough to venture out of bed. Rose insisted she not lift a finger in the house, which Ellen both appreciated and resented. She felt useless, and yet exerting herself more than a little still exhausted her.

There had been no more holiday bookings made for the rest of August, and Rose had already cancelled several due to Ellen's illness. Although Ellen had insisted she would be well enough when they came, Rose refused.

"We've made enough money off the bookings we had to see us through the winter," she declared. "And that's enough for now."

Still Ellen worried. Unless they had a full summer of bookings every year, the McCaffertys would be as good as living hand to mouth.

"Hey, Ellen, are you feeling well enough to join us?" Caro called as she came onto the front porch, where Ellen was sitting in a rocking chair, enjoying the afternoon sunshine.

"Join you…?"

"Mr. Wilson and I are taking the children for a walk." A familiar, steely note of determination had entered Caro's voice even though she was still smiling. "I thought it would be nice for us all to spend time together, get the little ones to know their uncle better. He's been visiting them nearly every day, you know."

"Yes, I remember." Ellen smiled as Jack Wilson appeared at the porch steps, his hat in his hands, his face slightly averted so she couldn't see the worst of his injury. "How nice to see you, Mr. Wilson. I don't know how far I'll get on a walk, but it would be lovely to have a bit of a stroll."

"I'll get you a hat," Caro said, and went inside with a flounce of her skirts.

A few minutes later, the six of them were walking down Jasper Lane, the sunlight dappled by the oak and maple trees that lined either side of the familiar dirt road. Ellen walked slowly, taking care with her steps; it was the most exercise she'd had in weeks, and it was tiring her out more than she wished or expected, weeks after her illness.

The children scampered ahead, grateful for an afternoon's adventure, and Caro had dropped behind with Mr. Wilson. She appeared to be talking to him quite insistently, making Ellen wonder what her intentions were. Did Caro want Mr. Wilson to fight the Ladies' Society and their belief that the children should go to an asylum? How could he? A bachelor with no fixed income or abode who was a stranger to three young children was hardly the likeliest candidate for their guardianship, and yet Ellen could not wish them into the asylum.

She found out a short while later, while Mr. Wilson went ahead to walk with the children, stooping slightly so he could hear them better.

"Nothing is as easy as it should be," Caro said with a frown as she folded her arms, her stroll practically turning into a march. Ellen struggled to keep up with her.

"Does this have to do with what you told me about the Ladies' Benevolent Society? Was that what you were talking to Mr. Wilson about?"

Caro threw her a fulminating look. "You can call him Jack, you know."

"I don't know, actually. He hasn't invited me to do so." Ellen was a bit surprised by Caro's familiarity. It had been a little over a week since Jack Wilson had arrived on the island, and he'd spent most of the time at the Wilson homestead.

"He's very kind," Caro said in a low voice. "He's just quiet because of his face."

"That's understandable. I saw many men like him during the war. It's a terrible burden for them to bear."

"Yes, and it's so unfair," Caro burst out. "Everyone judges him for something on the outside that wasn't his fault. It doesn't change who he is."

"No, of course it doesn't." Ellen eyed her cousin uncertainly. Caro spoke with so much passion, but what was its source? "What's really going on, Caro?"

Caro let out a frustrated sigh, pursing her mouth tight. "The Presbyterian Ladies' Benevolent Society have decided the children should go to the asylum in Kingston, and they won't be moved on the point. They made their decision yesterday." She'd lowered her voice so the children scampering ahead couldn't hear. "They don't think it's appropriate for them to be placed with their uncle as long as he's a bachelor. They say it's not because of his face," she continued in an angry rush, "but I know that's part of it. One of them—Mrs. Lewis—said he'd scare the children." She nodded towards the happy group ahead of them; the littlest girl had slipped her hand in her uncle's. "Do they look scared now?"

"That's unkind of the Ladies' Society," Ellen said quietly, and Caro glared at her, clearly needing to take her anger out on someone.

"It's more than unkind, it's positively cruel. Condemning those children to the orphan asylum instead of a loving home? Jack could take care of them, I know he could, with a little help."

"I didn't think you knew him that well," Ellen pointed out as gently as she could. "You only met him last week, Caro, and he's only been to Jasper Lane a few times since he arrived. A bachelor taking care of three young children as well as a farm—it's a big responsibility."

"Still, I know," Caro insisted stubbornly. "And, more importantly, he wants them with him. He and his brother grew up as orphans themselves. They spent their childhood in an asylum and then, as soon as he was old enough, Jack took a job and did his best to make his own way. His brother married Iris and came here, and then they lost touch during the war. It wasn't his fault."

"You seem to know a great deal," Ellen remarked, slightly stunned by the depth of Caro's knowledge—and her feeling. She hadn't realized Caro had spent so much time with Mr. Wilson over the last week, but it was clear that she had.

"Jack told me the whole story a few days ago. If only there was something I could do…"

"Could you speak to the Benevolent Society?"

Caro shook her head. "They won't listen."

"Do they have that much control?" Ellen asked hesitantly. She didn't know about such matters, despite being as good as an orphan herself, growing up. At least she'd had the McCaffertys to take her in, along with her Uncle Hamish and Aunt Rose.

"Yes, the children are still in the society's care even though they're staying with us." Caro sighed and shook her head. "It's just so unfair. I really wish there was something I could do."

Ellen laid a hand on her arm. "It sounds as if there isn't, Caro, and you've done so much already. Sometimes you simply have to let Providence have its way."

"Sometimes Providence needs a little help," Caro answered, and shaking off Ellen's arm, she hurried ahead to join the Wilson children—and Jack.

By the time Ellen returned to the farmhouse, Caro and the others having gone ahead, she was feeling entirely worn out. The walk had done her good, but it had also exhausted her. Her legs trembled and her breathing came in labored gasps.

"You shouldn't have gone so far," Rose scolded as she helped Ellen up the steps. "It's straight to bed with you, but first I have some news."

"News?" Ellen eased herself into the rocking chair with a sigh of relief. Her whole body ached. "What news?"

"I've just heard from Elvira Frampton, and she is ready to receive you in New York next week!" Rose's hands were clasped together as she beamed at Ellen in excited delight.

"What on earth..." Ellen stared at her aunt blankly. "Visit? But..." She'd never told Rose about the visit, and she'd assumed, with her illness and everything else, that it would never happen.

"Lucas told me about her invitation to you, when we were back in Toronto," Rose explained. "How you wanted to go but didn't feel you could."

Ellen flushed with anger. "He shouldn't have told you that, Aunt Rose. He said he wouldn't."

"I'm glad he did." Rose laid a hand on her arm. "You've worked so hard for so long, Ellen, and carried the weight of the world on your shoulders. And the truth is, we couldn't have managed without you. I've come to depend on you, more than perhaps you'll ever know." Rose's lips trembled as she smiled. "But you've worked yourself down to the bone and you need a proper rest. New York is the perfect answer. I insist that you go."

Ellen blinked back sudden tears, feeling like a child. "Why do I feel like you're sending me away?" she whispered.

"Oh Ellen, dear Ellen, no!" Rose gathered her into her arms. "Never that. I'm doing this for your sake, because I love you so very much." She leaned back to gaze intently into Ellen's tear-filled eyes. "I told you before that I love you like one of my own. My very own daughter. Never doubt that, Ellen. Never." Rose pulled Ellen back into her arms and hugged her fiercely.

Ellen closed her eyes as she pressed her cheek against Rose's shoulder, savoring her aunt's loving comfort, her arms around her. "Thank you," she whispered. "I love you too, Aunt Rose. So much."

"Then it's settled. You'll go next week, when you've gained back a little bit more of your strength."

"But the farm—and the holidays—what if more guests book?"

"We'll manage, Ellen. Guests can still sketch if they need to, or take country walks. Andrew has often given a tour of the island, and in any case, we've made enough this summer already to tide us over."

"I could help more—" Ellen protested.

"I don't want your money," Rose said firmly. "Save it for a shopping trip in the city! You must have some new dresses, of course. Mrs. Frampton mentioned the theater as well as the opera."

Rose's eyes sparkled as Ellen sat back in the rocking chair, dazed by this sudden turn of events. Before she'd fallen ill, she'd daydreamed about traveling to New York at Elvira Frampton's invitation, but she'd never thought it would become a reality. She felt a mixture of growing excitement and trepidation at the prospect. Despite the fact that she'd lived in Glasgow, France, Vermont, and on her beloved island, she still felt like an inexperienced homebody. How would she manage in the big city? She'd never even heard opera before.

"You'll be fine, Ellen," Rose assured. "And you'll have a wonderful time. I can't wait to hear about all your adventures when you return."

CHAPTER TWENTY-TWO

Four days later, Andrew drove Ellen to the ferry landing at Stella, her trunk in the back of the wagon. She was wearing one of her best dresses and a wide-brimmed picture hat that Rose had adorned with some lavender ribbon and a few silk flowers. Ellen felt both elegant and ridiculous, especially sitting next to Andrew on the old buckboard, the horses trotting down a dusty road. Although she still felt somewhat fatigued, a new excitement was firing through her veins at the prospect of the adventure ahead.

She'd said goodbye to all the McCaffertys, as well as the Wilson children, who were still at Jasper Lane while the Ladies' Society debated where to send them, and last night Jed had walked over from the Lyman farm to say his own farewell.

"Jed!" Ellen hadn't been able to stop smiling as she saw his familiar figure on the front porch as dusk dropped over the fields. "I wasn't expecting you." As it was the busiest time of a farmer's year, Jed hadn't stopped by Jasper Lane since Ellen had returned… not that she'd been expecting him to call.

"I thought I should say goodbye." A small smile tugged at his mouth. "Who knows how long you might be gone?"

"I've only been invited for a month," Ellen answered as she stepped aside to let him into the kitchen. "Would you like some coffee?"

"Yes, please."

Jed had leaned against the kitchen table, one booted foot crossed over the other, while Ellen made the coffee. The McCaffertys were all in the front parlor, but Ellen didn't call to them to let them know Jed had arrived. He'd come to say goodbye to her, after all, and she was grateful for the quiet moment.

"So, are you going to get notions into your head, now that you'll be staying in such a big city?" Jed had asked her, that old teasing lilt in his voice that Ellen remembered so well.

"I promise I won't." She'd handed him a cup of coffee and then cradled her own between her hands. "The truth is I'm practically petrified about going. I feel like country mouse."

"You've been a city girl before."

"Yes, and I was just as frightened then. But I came back to the island, didn't I?" She'd cocked her head as she'd looked at him. "I'll come back again."

"I hope so."

Jed had held her gaze for a moment until Ellen had looked away and they'd both sipped their coffee. She'd felt a prickle of something—pleasure and trepidation mixed together. There was nothing untoward about their conversation, nothing at all, and yet…

"Jed!" Rose's voice had rung out sharply as she came into the kitchen, her narrowed gaze moving between Jed and Ellen. "I thought I heard voices. You should have come in and said hello."

"I was just saying my goodbye to Ellen," Jed had replied. Ellen saw that there was a faint flush of color to his cheeks. He'd drained his coffee and put the cup in the sink. "But I'd best be off now. I've still got the animals to see to. Good evening, Rose." His gaze had skated towards Ellen and then away again. "Ellen."

"Goodbye, Jed," she'd murmured.

The only sound was the squeak and slap of the screen door, followed by the heavy tread of Jed's boots on the porch steps before a rather chilly silence had descended on the kitchen. Ellen went to the sink and began to wash the cups. She could feel Rose standing behind her, staying silent, and she'd felt compelled to say something.

"It was nice of Jed to come by."

"Yes." Rose had paused. "Very nice."

Ellen had half-turned and saw how disapproving her aunt looked. "Aunt Rose…"

"Jed is a married man, Ellen, even if Louisa never steps foot on this island again."

"I know that!" Ellen had flushed with humiliation as well as some anger. "Of course I know that. I have never done anything untoward in that regard, and neither has Jed."

Rose had nodded slowly. "I know," she'd said, and then her voice had gentled. "Of course I know. But our hearts are wayward things, Ellen. They can lead us astray without us even realizing where they're going."

"I know that," Ellen had said stiffly, and with another nod, Rose had left the kitchen.

Ellen had finished the washing up, seething with resentment that Rose had felt compelled to give her such a warning, as well as a guilty shame. *Did* she have feelings for Jed? She didn't think she did anymore, but she'd enjoyed even just those few moments together. It had felt, with such bittersweet poignancy, like old days, when Jed had teased her, when they had smiled and laughed together, when they'd been such good friends. She hated that Rose's words had tainted it, turned it into something almost sordid.

Now as they approached Captain Jonah's little tugboat, Ellen tried to push the whole episode out of her mind. Rose had been her usual, loving self this morning, and Jed she had not seen at all. She had a month ahead of her to explore and experience, and she didn't want to waste time thinking about the what-ifs of the past.

"Take care of yourself, Ellen," Andrew said as he loaded her trunk onto the ferry. "Don't forget us in New York."

"As if I would!" Ellen exclaimed. "I'm not going for as long as that, Andrew." Although she hadn't yet booked her return ticket, and Elvira Frampton had assured her she could stay for as long as she wanted, Ellen had already resolved not to stay for more than the month originally planned.

"Even so," Andrew said, and gave her a quick hug, before touching his hat in farewell.

It felt strange to be leaving the island again so soon. The lake whipped up into lacy white froth as the boat churned through the waters. Ellen held onto her hat as the sprightly breeze threatened to blow it right off her head, and her feelings veered between hope and sorrow, fear and joy.

The train journey to New York felt like traveling through time, all the way back to where she began, when she'd landed on Ellis Island with her father and her heart full of dreams. Dreams that had been broken and then remade; would the same happen again? What dreams did she even have anymore?

She'd told Peter she was tired from the war, tired in a way that made it hard to hope or to dream. Yet as the train pulled into a busy Grand Central Station, Ellen felt her spirits lift in a way they hadn't in a very long time. Here was a new chapter, another chance. Who knew what kind of dreams she could have here?

Certainly her experience of New York was far grander than before. Thomas, Elvira Frampton's manservant, met her at the platform, took her valise and led her to a gleaming Pierce-Arrow coupe parked right outside the station.

It was a short drive to the Framptons' opulent townhouse on Fifth Avenue, overlooking the park, now a lush, verdant green in the last halcyon days of summer. Elvira was waiting in the front hall as Ellen mounted the steps.

"Ellen, dear Ellen!" She hurried forward to embrace her, kissing her on both cheeks. "I'm so very glad to see you. And so very sorry to hear of your dreadful illness. Thank heavens you are well again!"

"Yes, thank you," Ellen murmured, trying not to gape at the entry hall's luxurious decorations, everything gilt and marble, a sweeping staircase leading to the upstairs. She hadn't been in a house as nice as this since she'd gone to a ball in Glasgow with Henry McAvoy, back in 1911, and she'd felt entirely out of her element then.

"There's tea and cake in the parlor," Elvira continued as Thomas took Ellen's things upstairs. "But first you'll want to refresh yourself. Let me show you to your room."

Elvira led her up the stairs, while Ellen marveled at all the paintings and antiques, the plush carpets, the burnished wood. The anxiety she'd been feeling about this trip eased, replaced by a burgeoning excitement.

"You must be exhausted," Elvira said as she guided Ellen along the upstairs corridor. "Train journeys are always so fatiguing, and when you've been ill... Here we are." She threw open a door and led Ellen into an enormous bedroom with a canopied bed with jacquard bed coverings and a matching wardrobe and bureau set in gleaming mahogany. It was the largest and most elegant bedroom Ellen had ever seen. "There's an adjoining bathroom," Elvira said, opening a door to a room with a deep bathtub and a sink with gold taps. "Feel free to wash the worst of your journey away."

Then, with a flurry of silk and a whiff of perfume she was gone, and Ellen sank onto the canopied bed in the center of the room, feeling overwhelmed by it all. She'd known the Framptons were wealthy, of course, but she'd had no idea of the depth of luxury she'd been catapulted into. What must they have thought of shabby Jasper Lane!

She let out a little laugh at the thought, shaking her head, and then she rose from the bed and went to the window, pushing aside the drapes to take in the view of a bustling Fifth Avenue, the wide street teeming with cars, the cobblestone sidewalk along the park with people. Everyone, Ellen thought, was going somewhere.

A spark of excitement kindled in her soul and she unpinned her hat and took off her suit jacket, rolling up her sleeves so she could wash her face. Perhaps later she would try the bath—she'd never had one with running water. At Jasper Lane, they still had to heat water over the stove and haul it upstairs for a bath.

Once she'd dried her face and fixed her hair, she decided to find Elvira. She looked forward to becoming reacquainted with her hostess, and discovering what plans she had for her in this great and gracious city.

"You look much refreshed," Elvira exclaimed as Ellen came into the drawing room, an elegant space of generous proportions, with silk drapes at every window, and a grand piano tucked in one corner.

Ellen paused to examine several objects displayed in a Chinese curio cabinet. "You have so many lovely things," she remarked as she admired a small, perfectly carved jade elephant. "I could spend every day simply taking in all the beautiful things in your home."

"Well, I would be very disappointed if you did that," Elvira replied with a laugh. "I have such plans for you, my dear. Of course, the city completely empties in August—everyone removes to the Hamptons, and there's very little society to be had, thanks to this wretched heat. Are you wilting?"

"I'm fine," Ellen assured her as she took a seat on an armchair with a pattern of striped silk.

"Still, there are some amusements to be had," Elvira promised her. "The Van Alens are having a ball at the end of the month, and afterwards we are going to Sands Point. We have an invitation from the Guggenheims to stay at Hempstead House."

Ellen smiled faintly as she took a sip of the iced tea Elvira had poured for her. It was surprisingly sweet. "That all sounds amazing, Mrs. Frampton—"

"Elvira, of course!"

"I fear I am not used to such high society," Ellen felt compelled to confess.

"Oh, you shall fit right in, Ellen, I assure you," Elvira replied. "And I have already spoken to the curator of a small gallery on Madison Avenue to exhibit your sketches. You did bring them?"

"Yes," Ellen admitted, although she'd felt a bit arrogant for doing so. "But I don't think—"

"Nonsense! I insist. You are going to be the belle of the ball, my dear. The belle of the ball." Elvira glanced at the door as it opened and her daughter Imogen came into the room. "And here is the other belle of the ball! Imogen, come and say hello to Ellen."

Ellen rose from her chair as Imogen clasped her in a light hug and kissed her cheek. She was far quieter and less vibrant than her mother, but there was a frankness about her face and a sincerity in her eyes that Ellen liked.

"How lovely to see you, Ellen. My mother has been so excited."

"I just hope I don't disappoint," Ellen said. Already she was feeling overwhelmed by all of Elvira's plans.

"You could never do that," Imogen assured her, and Elvira rang the bell for the maid to bring more cake.

The next week passed in a flurry of excitement and outings. Elvira took Ellen everywhere—parading through Central Park, shopping on Fifth Avenue at the grand block-long department stores of Bergdorf Goodman and Arnold Constable and Company.

"When I was last in New York, in 1911," Ellen told her, "all these stores were downtown, in the Ladies' Mile. How it has all changed!"

"The city is constantly changing," Elvira agreed. "I remember the Ladies' Mile, back when I went shopping in a horse and carriage!" She let out a little laugh of incredulity, and Ellen hid her smile. Back on the island, she still traveled around by horse and wagon. "It's all warehouses there now," Elvira continued.

"Completely unfashionable. Everyone has moved uptown, to be closer to the park."

Despite Elvira's lamenting of the lack of society during the hot summer months, there were parties to attend, and trips to the opera and theater; twice they dined out at elegant restaurants, being served by white-jacketed waiters. And as she'd promised, Elvira had shown her sketches to a gallery owner, who had thought they held much promise, and was considering having them be part of an exhibit in the autumn, although Ellen wasn't entirely sure he hadn't simply been trying to placate a wealthy and well-connected customer.

At first, as she'd navigated this glamorous and glossy new world, Ellen had felt clumsy and gauche, and was sure everyone else could notice. How could she, a railwayman's daughter from the sooty yards of Springburn, have ended up here?

But as the days passed and Elvira's easy affections smoothed every interaction, Ellen felt herself relax, and the luxury that had overwhelmed and shocked her at first began to simply be enjoyable. Three weeks slid by with her barely even realizing they'd gone.

Since she'd arrived, she'd received several letters from Amherst Island—Rose had written twice, filling her in on all the island news—the Wilson children were still at Jasper Lane and Jack Wilson was fighting for them, Sarah had gone back to Gananoque and Peter had written a cheering note and thought he might return by Christmas.

Lucas had written her from Toronto, describing his regular visits to Peter and amusing her with his little asides and anecdotes, so she could almost imagine he was sitting right next to her, chatting in his easy way. He'd commanded her to "suck the marrow out of the city," whatever that was supposed to mean, although whatever it was Ellen thought she was surely doing it. She was glad he'd told Aunt Rose, in the end; she realized she'd needed this adventure.

Even so, while she knew Lucas thought she was wasting her talent on Amherst Island, she still couldn't imagine living anywhere else. Although, she admitted ruefully, after several weeks immersed in this luxury, she certainly was starting to.

One humid, hazy afternoon, while they were taking tea in the elegant Palm Court, Elvira reminded her of the trip to Sands Point in a fortnight.

"It will be so lovely to get out of the city, after all this heat."

Ellen paused, conscious that she could not continue imposing on the Framptons forever, pleasant as that sometimes seemed. "I don't know if I shall be here then, Elvira," she felt obligated to say. "I've already been here for nearly a month. I wouldn't want to overstay my welcome."

"Nonsense, my dear girl, you know you could never do that. In any case, I've barely started on all the things I want to show you."

"Barely started?" Ellen repeated with a laugh. "I've never been as busy as I have these last few weeks!" She'd been to the opera, amazed at the sheer scale of the production as well as the beauty of the voices, and attended several tea parties; to the Bronx Zoological Gardens and the huge department store, Macy's, on Herald Square. She'd strolled through Central Park and wandered through the galleries of the Metropolitan Museum of Art, stopping in front of her own painting, hung, admittedly, in a distant, dusty gallery, but amazed nonetheless to see it there. Really, there had barely been a dull moment.

"There's still so much to do," Elvira pressed. "You can't possibly leave yet, Ellen."

Ellen smiled and murmured her thanks. It was hard to resist Elvira Frampton's energized determination; she was like an ocean liner in full sail, bearing down on everyone with steely enthusiasm. You either had to get out of the way or get on board.

"Shall we walk back?" Ellen suggested once they'd left The Plaza Hotel. Outside, it was a hazy day, a gentle breeze blowing down Fifth Avenue. The stifling heat had lessened a little with the onset of late afternoon, but her hostess still looked horrified.

"Walk… but it's nearly ten blocks!"

"I haven't done much walking since I've been here," Ellen said with a smile. "And I want to get my strength back." Although she'd toured much of the city, it had always been from the back of the Framptons' gleaming Pierce-Arrow. She longed to stride down the city's wide streets, taking in all the incredible sights, drinking in the city. She'd been an invalid for too long.

"Oh, very well," Elvira said, still looking slightly scandalized. "I suppose it is always beneficial to one's health to take some exercise."

They set off down Fifth Avenue, passing the steel towers on every block that were to be the city's first traffic lights, a development of which Elvira did not approve.

"They look ghastly, don't they?" she said as she and Ellen maneuvered past one. "And I shall miss the friendly police officers on every corner. But something simply *must* be done about the traffic. I read in the paper that it can take forty minutes to drive from Fifty-Seventh Street to Thirty-Fourth."

"Shocking," Ellen murmured. There was only a handful of cars on Amherst Island, and traffic of any sort was never a concern. A pang of homesickness assailed her suddenly, and she wondered yet again when she would go home. If Elvira had anything to do with it, it wouldn't be anytime soon. And as much as she missed the island, it was so pleasant to be in such congenial surroundings, with little to do besides amuse oneself, and nothing to worry about except what to wear.

Back in the cool, dim foyer of the Framptons' townhouse, their butler handed a letter to Ellen. "This arrived while you were out, madam."

"Thank you, Thomas." Ellen smiled self-consciously, still unused to having servants wait on her. Her smile widened as she saw the Ontario postmark and Rose's familiar handwriting. "Do you mind if I read this upstairs?" she asked Elvira.

"Of course not, my dear. Dinner's at seven. We're dining in tonight."

"Thank you, Elvira."

Upstairs in her room, Ellen unlaced her walking boots and unpinned her hat. A glance in the mirror showed her flushed cheeks and wisps of hair framing her face; it had been hot outside, but her bedroom was deliciously cool, thanks to the electric ceiling fan that Ellen considered a marvel. Elvira's husband had had the whole house wired for electricity twenty-five years ago, but it was still somewhat of a novelty to Ellen. Electricity had yet to come to the island, although there was talk of it happening soon.

Ellen curled up in an armchair by the window overlooking Central Park and slit open the envelope, taking a moment to savor Rose's beloved, loopy handwriting before she began to read.

Dear Ellen,

So much has happened and I've only written a few days ago! How funny it seems, to have so much news on our sleepy little island. I can only imagine how exciting your life in New York is, parties and balls and afternoon teas… I am so very happy for you, Ellen, for goodness knows how much you need and deserve a rest as well as a treat.

But onto my news! You remember Jack Wilson, of course, the brother-in-law of poor Iris, and how he wanted to keep her children with him. He'd been going back and forth with the Ladies' Benevolent Society for all these weeks, but they'd finally insisted the children were to go to the asylum in Kingston. They'd even booked the train tickets, and Mrs. Lewis was to take them, although I don't think she even knows their names!

Ellen paused in her reading, a frown puckering her brow as she imagined such a sad fate for the poor children. Caro would be furious as well as heartbroken, as would Mr. Wilson. It did seem so dreadfully unfair.

Caro felt it was not to be borne, Ellen continued reading, *as you can imagine, and she has suggested quite the surprising solution! Ellen, you will hardly believe it, but she and Mr. Wilson are to marry!*

The letter nearly slipped from Ellen's fingers at this bit of news. Caro was to marry Jack Wilson, with his ruined face and taciturn manner, a man she barely knew? Ellen was too shocked for words, and yet at the same time she was hardly surprised at all. Caro had always been determined, to the point of orneriness, and she'd already shared with Ellen how unlikely it was for her to find a husband in these bleak times. Besides, she'd treated the Wilson children as her own. But… Jack Wilson! And yet of course Jack Wilson. Smiling, Ellen decided it made perfect sense.

Of course it caused a bit of a scandal, mainly among the aforementioned ladies, whose noses were put out of joint at having their plans put awry. You'd think they almost wanted those poor children to be shipped off to an orphanage, but I can hardly think something so uncharitable about Christian women. In any case, the marriage is to take place at the end of the month, and they shall live, all five of them, at the Wilson farm. I asked Caro if she was certain, and she said she'd never been so certain of anything in her life! I do fear, Ellen, that she is marrying Mr. Wilson simply for the children's sake, and not her own, but I pray in time the two of them will develop an affection for each other,

and even a deep and abiding love, such as I knew with
your Uncle Dyle.

A pang of grief assailed Ellen at the memory of her beloved
uncle, almost always with a mischievous glint in his eye and a ready
smile on his face. Like her aunt, she hoped Caro and Jack could
learn to love each other in time, with a deep, abiding love. Caro
deserved happiness; she'd worked so hard, and the best years of her
life had been given to the war, yet she'd never complained. Perhaps
this sudden family—a husband and three children—would be
her chance to find a new and lasting happiness.

Ellen read on.

In other news, Peter seems to be doing well at the military
hospital. He has written several times and is learning new
skills, even typewriting! I miss him every day, but I am so
thankful he is getting the help he needs.

We have not had any more bookings for the autumn,
which is just as well since I'm not sure we could manage
any, with you, Caro, and Peter all gone and the har-
vesting to be done! But don't worry, Andrew, Gracie,
Sarah, and I are coping quite well. In any case, we
earned enough already to tide us over till winter, if
we're careful. Please don't worry, Ellen, and don't come
rushing back! I am so happy that you are able to have
this well-deserved rest.

All my love, Aunt Rose.

Ellen laid the letter in her lap, her unfocused gaze resting on the
blur of green that comprised Central Park, now touched with reds,
yellows, and golds. Gauze curtains ruffled in the breeze from the
open windows, and the sounds of the city—both horses and cars,

pedestrians and workmen, a policeman's whistle or the blare of a car horn—were settling down as evening stole over Manhattan.

Dinner was still not for several hours, and Ellen had time to read the novel Elvira had lent her—*My Antonia* by Willa Cather—and have a bath before getting dressed. All of it sounded wonderfully lazy and pleasant, and yet in that moment with Aunt Rose's letter in her lap, all Ellen longed for was to be back in Jasper Lane, listening to the cluck of chickens and the slap of the screen door as the breeze came off the lake and twilight settled over the fields of golden green.

With a sigh, she rose from her seat, tucking Rose's letter away.

CHAPTER TWENTY-THREE

A week later, Ellen found herself standing on the edge of the Van Alens' magnificent ballroom in a mansion even grander than the Framptons' on Fifth Avenue. All around her, men and women laughed and danced; Ellen marveled at the women's sleek hairstyles and new fashions—baggy dresses with hems that barely skimmed their ankles, and long ropes of pearls or beads that swung nearly to their waist. Ellen had never seen the like, and she felt more than a bit fusty in her dated gown from before the war, with its nipped-in waist and puffed sleeves.

Elvira had practically insisted she buy something new, but Ellen had been adamant that this gown, from her time in Glasgow, would suffice. It wasn't as if she needed a ball gown in her everyday life, and she could not justify the expense, even for Elvira, who could well afford it.

This was her first ball since coming to New York, and just as she had at the beginning of her stay, she felt as gauche and out of place as she knew she looked. While she'd attended plenty of outings in the last few weeks, a proper grand ball was, Ellen realized, another prospect entirely.

The Van Alens' ballroom had a twelve-piece orchestra playing at one end, and a champagne fountain in the shape of a swan, the likes of which Ellen had never seen before, at the other. The floor-to-ceiling windows overlooking the park were bedecked with heavy satin drapes, and candles glimmered from every available surface, making the room stuffier than it already was, pressed close with bodies on a hot summer's evening.

With Elvira firmly ensconced in a group of matrons, Ellen had taken the opportunity to retreat to stand by the wall, where she could hopefully be ignored. It seemed easy enough; a few people had taken in her old-fashioned gown with a wry twist of their lips, but said nothing, and Ellen knew she was as good as dismissed. She didn't actually mind and chose to slip out of the ballroom onto a terrace overlooking the mansion's private garden, a small, verdant oasis in the middle of the city.

It was cooler outside, the still night air like soft velvet against her heated skin, the evening wonderfully peaceful. Ellen waved a hand in front of her flushed face and let out a deeply held sigh of relief. She had enjoyed so many of the outings Elvira had arranged for her, but not, she decided, this one.

"Now that," a voice from behind her said in a tone of dry amusement, "was a sound I like to hear."

Ellen whirled around, her hand now pressed to her chest, her widened gaze taking in the sight of a dapper young man lounging in the open French windows.

"I beg your pardon?"

"No need to sound so frosty." He smiled easily, his eyes glinting with ready good humor. "I only meant it is refreshing to think that a young lady feels as I do about these wretched balls, with everyone parading about as if they own the world, or at least the bit of it that matters."

Ellen eyed him uncertainly, loitering there as if *he* owned the world. He wore a white tie and tails, and his blond hair was brushed back from a pleasant, handsome face—blue eyes, straight nose, wide smile. He looked like one of the city's privileged few, the highest echelon of society, a touch of arrogance to his slightly louche manner.

"You don't seem as if you are having difficulty enjoying the evening," she ventured, her tone still a bit cool.

"On the contrary, I find it quite excessively dull, which is why, like you, I am out here." He stepped onto the terrace, and Ellen resisted the urge to step back. As charming as this man was, something about him felt a little reckless and far too assured.

"Perhaps you should introduce yourself."

"Indeed I should. William Hancock Turner the Third."

"Goodness." Ellen raised her eyebrows. "And here I am, plain old Ellen Copley."

"There is nothing plain about you, Miss Copley."

A blush warmed her cheeks and she looked away. This William Hancock Turner was far too forward, and yet she knew she was not entirely immune to his charms. After being ignored for most of the evening, it felt nice to be admired.

"What do you do for a profession, Mr. Turner?" she asked.

"A profession?" He looked amused. "How terribly quaint. I'm afraid I don't have one of those, Miss Copley." One blond eyebrow arched. "Are you disappointed?"

"Disappointed?" Ellen considered his question. She knew far too many men who were desperate for gainful employment, men with mended boots and work-roughened hands and despairing eyes. Yet here was a man who clearly had as much money as he could want, and was simply looking for ways to spend it. But was it his fault? William Hancock Turner the Third had been born into wealth, that much was glaringly obvious, and she should not despise him for it. "A bit, I suppose," she said at last. "Although I am not surprised that you don't have any gainful employment."

"Touché!" he exclaimed with a laugh, one hand clutched to his chest as he pretended to stagger. "A double hit. I am mortally wounded."

"I didn't mean—" she began, not wanting to offend him, but he simply smiled.

"You are different than the usual vapid socialites, Miss Copley. Is it because you yourself have a profession?"

Ellen blushed again. He made her sound like a snob in reverse. "No, I'm afraid not."

"You are not from the city, though."

"No, I live in Canada, but I'm from Scotland originally."

"Which explains your charming if not easily distinguishable accent."

She laughed, enjoying his easy manner despite her intention not to. "I'm here visiting the Framptons. Do you know them?"

"Only by acquaintance. How long will you be staying?"

Ellen thought of Rose's letter, and Elvira's insistence that she accompany them to the Hamptons in a few days. "I'm not quite sure."

"Well," William said, his gaze lingering on her for a moment longer than necessary, "I hope it's for a good while yet."

Ellen looked away, unsure how to respond to such bold flirtatiousness. She had not encountered it before, although she'd mingled with the wealthy and privileged when she'd been a student at Glasgow School of Art and engaged, ever so briefly, to Henry McAvoy.

The thought of Henry sent a pang of grief through her. It had been seven years since he had died on the *Titanic,* and their relationship had been short and uncertain, due to the difference in their social stations. But he had loved her, Ellen had never doubted that, and in the long and lonely years since, she had wondered if another man would ever love her in the same way.

A brush of fingers against her cheek had her startling. "I beg your—"

"I'm sorry," William said gently, "but you looked as if you were miles away, and it didn't seem a very nice place."

Her cheek burned where he had touched it. "Where I was or what I was thinking is no business of yours," Ellen said stiffly, "and I resent your forwardness, Mr. Turner. Goodnight."

Bristling with affront, she stalked past him into the ballroom.

*

That weekend, the Framptons took the Pierce-Arrow out to Sands Point, where they were staying at the enormous, opulent Hempstead House, home of the famous Guggenheim family, who had made their fortune in mining and were known for their support of philanthropic causes.

As the car pulled into the estate, Ellen could not keep her jaw from dropping. Hempstead House was more castle than house, with a crenellated roof and imposing tower, and had been built only seven years earlier, by the equally wealthy Gould family. Elvira had told Ellen on the drive out that the Goulds had not liked the house, so upon its completion they'd sold the entire estate to the Guggenheims. Ellen could not imagine such reckless, lavish spending, tossing money about as if it were confetti, when so many struggled and starved.

"Hempstead House is considered to have the best parties on the Gold Coast," Elvira confided as seventeen house servants lined up for their entrance into the magnificent building. "We'll have such fun, Ellen."

Ellen managed a faint smile. She knew she was quite out of her depth here; she had neither the wardrobe nor the confidence, never mind the desire, to take part in such an extravagant exercise. This was a far cry from afternoon tea in the Palm Court, or a tour of the Metropolitan Museum of Art. Perhaps she could plead a headache and miss out on the evening entertainments, which she feared would emphasize the difference between her and her hosts all the more.

The opulence continued inside the house, which was even grander than the castle-like exterior. Ellen paused inside the huge foyer with a Wurlitzer organ on proud display, the pipes stretching towards the vaulted ceiling.

"Isn't it magnificent?" Elvira whispered. "The pipes are only for show. The music is heard through spaces in the floor."

"I've never seen the like," Ellen whispered back, which was certainly an understatement.

Their hostess, Florence Guggenheim, greeted them with a flourish and kissed them on both cheeks in the European style before showing them to their rooms herself; Ellen's room overlooked the Sound and was nearly twice as large as her bedroom back at the Framptons', with an adjoining bathroom, a dressing room and private sitting room. The excess bordered on absurd. The Wilsons' entire farmhouse was not as large as her suite, she realized. It made her homesick for the simplicity of life on the island, and all the people there.

With several hours before afternoon tea was served, Ellen decided to walk down to the beach, visible from her bedroom window. She missed being close to the water, and as she slipped out of the house and wound her way through the gardens, she savored the breeze coming off the sea, possessing a tang of brine.

Leaving the manicured gardens behind, she picked her way across the sinuous sweep of a sand dune to the pale stretch of beach, a few twisted pieces of driftwood cast upon its sands like strange sculptures. Sailboats and pleasure yachts dotted the slate-blue sea, and a woman's laughter from somewhere—either the sea or the house—floated on the breeze.

Ellen took a deep breath of the fresh sea air as the tension banding her shoulders started to ease.

She belonged here even less than she did in New York, and the thought of spending an entire week rubbing elbows with the crème de la crème of New York society made her want to hightail it back to Amherst Island. She wanted to talk to Caro about her upcoming marriage, and sit on the front porch with Rose and Sarah and Gracie, shelling peas. She wanted to walk past the pond with its copse of birches, their leaves no doubt already tinged with yellow, to the Lymans' farmhouse and visit with Jed, sitting at their kitchen table and drinking coffee served from an old tin pot.

Jed. Her heart twisted as she thought of him. He hadn't written, but then Jed Lyman had never been much of a letter writer. She thought of Rose's quiet yet steely concerns when she'd found Ellen and Jed in the kitchen alone. Nothing improper had happened, of course, and yet, alone on the beach, Ellen could acknowledge that she had had such feelings, or at least the faint possibility of them, in her heart.

Now that Jed's marriage to Louisa was as good as over, could she even think of rekindling those feelings for him? Did she want to? As ever when it came to Jed Lyman, she felt confused, caught in a battle between old longings and more grownup sensibility. Sometimes she wondered if she'd made Jed into more than he'd ever been in her head and heart, simply because he'd chosen someone else. Were the feelings she remembered ever as tender as she thought them?

But no matter what she felt for Jed, Ellen knew she wanted to go home. She'd had a lovely adventure and a good rest, but she was done exploring and experiencing. After they returned from Sands Point, she'd tell Elvira she needed to book her ticket for Ogdensburg, and then onto the island. Home.

Ellen was just turning back towards the house when a lone figure coming down the beach called out to her.

"I say, it isn't Miss Copley, is it?"

Ellen froze as the tall, lithe figure came closer, with his familiar wave of blond hair and eyes as brightly blue as the sea. Willian Hancock Turner the Third, wearing a white summer suit and doffing a straw boater with a little ironic smile.

"What are you doing here?" she blurted. She had given William Hancock Turner the Third more thought than she'd liked since she'd last seen him, unable to decide whether she liked his easy charm or not.

"What a welcome!" William laughed lightly. "I'm a guest of the Guggenheims, as it happens. What are you doing here?" He spoke with gentle mockery, making her blush. What was it about this man that unnerved her so?

"I'm a guest of the Guggenheims as well," she admitted reluctantly. "Through the Framptons, that is. We were not personally acquainted before my arrival."

"Well, then! We shall have a splendid time this week, don't you think?"

Ellen could not think how to respond and William laughed again as he started to stroll towards the gardens, leaving Ellen with little choice but to fall in step with him.

"Do you know, Miss Copley, I have an awful feeling that you don't like me very much."

"I don't know you well enough to say one or the other."

"What would you like to know?"

Ellen shrugged. "How do you fill your time, if you don't have a profession?"

"Oh, but there's any manner of ways to fill my time! Horse racing, hunting, card-playing, parties and balls…" He let a shout of laughter as Ellen could not hide her horrified expression. "What a louche and dissolute character I must seem to you."

"You are very different than the men I know in my regular life," Ellen replied as tactfully as she could. She thought of Peter, of Jed, of Lucas. Yes, William was different from all of them.

"And what is your regular life?"

"I live on Amherst Island, in Ontario," Ellen said a touch primly. "Really, I'm a simple farm girl at heart, as incredible as that might seem to someone who is used to all this." She swept one arm out to encompass the Guggenheim estate.

"Now that I don't believe."

"Why not?" she asked, her tone sharpening.

"Because our hostess has been telling tales about you, garnered, I believe, from your own hostess Mrs. Frampton."

Ellen faltered in her step. "Tales?"

"You nursed the wounded during the war in France, and before that you lived in Glasgow and are the artist of a renowned painting, which I've actually seen, you might be surprised to know, in the Metropolitan Museum of Art."

Ellen was dumbstruck, even though her painting had been exhibited in New York for several months. It still seemed impossible to believe people actually viewed it. "You've seen—"

"Why shouldn't I have? Although really it belongs in one of the better galleries. It's truly magnificent. I am most impressed by your accomplishments." His gaze lingered on hers, suddenly seeming serious and making her blush.

"Oh." Ellen felt completely disconcerted. "Thank you. But, in truth, that all seems like a long time ago."

"I'm sure it does."

They'd reached the house, and William bent lower over Ellen's fingertips, not quite kissing them.

"Until dinner, Miss Copley."

Ellen was still thinking about her conversation with Mr. Turner as she came downstairs for dinner, feeling more than a little self-conscious in her plain frock, with its simple pleats and a touch of lace at the collar.

Dinner at Hempstead House was an elegant affair, and although Florence Guggenheim had assured her it was informal that evening, since they were not entertaining anyone but houseguests, Ellen soon realized that informal at Hempstead House meant her finest gown. She started to apologize as her hostess came up to her dripping in pearls, but Florence would have none of it.

"But, my dear, you're so charming! And I can't tell you how absolutely thrilled I am to have a proper artist in residence! Do you know, Picasso visited here last year and I can't make head or tail of his scribbles. I find him quite an enigma."

"Picasso," Ellen repeated faintly. "I hardly think—"

"Mr. Turner was asking all sorts of questions about you! Isn't he devilishly handsome? It's a shame, really, what happened to him."

"What happened to him?" Ellen repeated, knowing she shouldn't gossip but unable to hide her curiosity.

"In the war. He was a pilot, didn't you know? He was shot down over enemy lines and kept as a prisoner-of-war for over a year. Ghastly. He refuses to talk about it. He only returned a few months ago."

"Goodness," Ellen said faintly. "I had no idea." She'd judged him on appearance and attitude, and he'd certainly given her cause, but perhaps she should have looked more deeply.

"No, you wouldn't, would you? He likes to act like the careless playboy, but he really isn't. Before the war, he was studying physics at Columbia, much to his father's chagrin. He wanted him to follow the family footsteps in banking, of course."

"Of course," Ellen agreed, her mind whirling. Why had William Hancock Turner presented himself to her in a way that was sure not to appeal? If he'd spoken of his learning, or his war years, she would have had a much more favorable impression of him, something he must have surely known.

The question kept her occupied throughout all six courses of the lavish meal; Mr. Turner was on the opposite end of the table that seated twenty and so Ellen did not have the opportunity to discuss it, much as she wanted to.

In fact, it wasn't until the next day, when she took her sketch-book out to the beach and saw him sitting alone on the sand, that she decided to broach the topic.

"Someone's been telling tales about you," she remarked as she stood by him.

William glanced up at her with a wry smile. "Ah, have I been sussed out, then?"

"Why didn't you tell me yourself that you fought in the war?" Ellen asked gently.

"Why didn't you tell me you'd been a nurse?"

Ellen considered the question. "Because people who haven't been there don't understand it, and it's not really a time of life I want to dwell on."

"You have your answer, then." He stared out at the sea, the wind ruffling his hair.

"Why not tell me about studying physics at Columbia?"

William shrugged. "I'm not anymore. I didn't even get my degree."

"Why not?"

"I didn't see the point, I suppose. I don't see the point of much, if I'm honest." He gave her the glimmer of a smile, but Ellen saw a bleakness in his eyes that she found all too familiar.

"Then you're like just about every other veteran I've encountered," she said. "Everything seems frivolous after you've seen warfare."

"Especially my life."

"Is that why you spend your time in such pursuits? Because at least then it's *supposed* to feel frivolous?"

William's smile deepened. "You're far too clever, Miss Copley."

"Not really." Ellen gazed down at him, feeling a mixture of sorrow and sympathy. Despite all his wealth and privilege, Willian Hancock Turner the Third was just as lost and grief-stricken as any other soldier she'd met. Some things money couldn't buy—or take away.

"Don't feel too sorry for me," William said lightly. "All in all, I'm quite a lucky guy."

"Yes," Ellen said slowly, thinking of Jack Wilson, with his ruined face, Jed having lost his arm, and Peter in the military hospital in Toronto, recovering from shell shock. "Yes," she agreed sadly, "I suppose you are."

CHAPTER TWENTY-FOUR

The rest of the week in the Hamptons passed surprisingly quickly, in a blur of golden, sun-soaked days. Although there were plenty of entertainments for those so inclined—croquet on the lawn or sailing on the Sound—Ellen eschewed them for quiet days spent sketching on the beach, enjoying the simple pleasure for what it was and no more, or walks to the nearby village of Sands Point. On many of these lazy sojourns, William Hancock Turner—or Will, as he asked her to call him—accompanied her.

Both Florence Guggenheim and Elvira had looked pleased, shooting each other knowing smiles that Ellen caught, as they observed the friendship that had sprung up unexpectedly between her and Will. Ellen couldn't help but be surprised by it; the last thing she would have expected was to enjoy the company of one of New York City's most eligible bachelors, or find him unpretentious and gently humorous.

But, for her, that was all it was—friendship—and she hoped Will felt the same. After that first bit of flirting, he'd seemed content simply to spend time with her, and although she felt a surprisingly deep affection for him, she did not think she could ever consider him romantically. His life was in the city, and hers was on the island. She knew she could never be the wife of such a prominent man, as down-to-earth as he could seem, and she had no interest in a romance that didn't lead anywhere.

"Shall I see you back in New York?" he asked on the last day, as she stood by the Pierce-Arrow, ready to return to the city.

Already the air felt a touch cooler, and the sky was the color of gun metal. Will's smile was wry, a look of sadness in his usually laughing eyes, as he regarded her.

"Perhaps, but I don't know how long I'll be staying with the Framptons."

"You're thinking of returning to your little island, then?"

"Yes, I am," Ellen answered, but with a touch of hesitation. Even though she felt like a fish out of water amidst all this elegance, there was much she'd miss about her life in New York—Will included. Yet she had to go back. It felt almost like a compulsion, a soul-deep need, to be back on Amherst Island, among her friends and family, the only place where she'd ever felt as if she truly belonged.

"Don't leave without saying goodbye," Will said, and Ellen shook her head.

"Of course I'll say goodbye." Yet the thought made her sad, as much as she longed to return to "her little island".

When she broached the idea of returning to her hosts, however, Elvira would not hear of her leaving before the end of September. "You simply mustn't, Ellen, because I've still so much planned."

"Elvira…" Ellen stared at her hostess, who had become a good friend, in amused exasperation. She felt as if she might never be free to return to the island, and yet she also knew she wasn't protesting all that much. She was looking forward to being able to see Will a little while longer, as well as all the entertainments Elvira would plan. "I really should get back, you know."

"Let's talk about it tomorrow," Elvira said with a touch of coyness. "After our morning visit. Perhaps you'll think differently then."

"Our morning visit?" Elvira had introduced her to a variety of people over the last month, but this sounded like something else entirely.

"You'll see," Elvira said, her eyes dancing, and Ellen gazed at her with both curiosity and a touch of foreboding. What did her hostess have planned?

*

When the Pierce-Arrow stopped in front of an elegant brownstone on West Forty-Eighth Street the next morning, Ellen was nonplussed.

"Where are we?" she asked as Elvira alighted from the car. The tall, stately building didn't look like someone's house, or a museum, or any such building they would enter for whatever entertainment Elvira had planned.

"The Spence School for Girls, one of the best institutions for female education in the entire city, and even the whole country! The headmistress, Miss Clara Spence, is really quite remarkable, and she's keen to meet you."

"Meet *me?*" Ellen repeated in disbelief. "Why?"

"You'll see," Elvira said, leaving Ellen only to wonder. "She has only just returned from The Willows, her summer residence in Maine, but she was insistent I bring you here as soon as she came back to the city."

"She did?" Ellen was completely flummoxed. "But why?"

"You'll see," Elvira said again, and led her into the foyer of the school, where Clara Spence greeted them.

She was a kindly and handsome woman in her late fifties, and she welcomed Ellen with quiet friendliness, talking about the summer she spent at her house in Maine, and the four children she'd adopted with her lifelong friend and companion, Charlotte Baker.

She took Ellen and Elvira through the whole school, showing her the classrooms, the library, and then ending in the art studio, a large, square room on one of the top floors with long, sashed windows letting in the sunlight.

"This is marvelous," Ellen said as she studied some paintings done by current pupils. She'd been impressed by everything about the school, which seemed to have an academic yet friendly air.

Clara Spence had founded the school and lived in an apartment above it with Charlotte Baker and her four children. "Your students clearly have a great deal of talent."

"And, unfortunately, they are without an art teacher at the moment," Miss Spence said. "Which I believe is where you might come in, Miss Copley."

"Me?" Realization was slowly dawning as Ellen turned around to face both Elvira and Clara.

"Can't you guess, Ellen?" Elvira said with a smile, excitement lighting her eyes as she pressed her hands together. "Miss Spence would like to offer you a teaching position here. Isn't it the perfect solution? You can live in New York City permanently!" Elvira smiled as if she'd handed Ellen a treasure, and Ellen stared back, unsure how to respond—whether to take it with both hands or thrust it away. She was honored, of course, and also thrilled... and appalled. Stay in New York?

Stay in New York...

"I don't..." she began, and then trailed off helplessly.

"I can see you are surprised," Clara said with a little laugh. "Why don't we retire to my study for some tea, and I can explain it all a bit more to you?"

Dazed, Ellen managed to murmur her agreement, before following Clara to a comfortable and spacious room at the top of the building, with views over Forty-Eighth Street. A maid brought in a tray, and soon they were all settled in armchairs with cups of tea.

"I founded this school because I believe passionately in girls' education," Clara began without preamble. "And by education, I don't mean finishing school—a bit of sewing, a bit of music, walking with a book atop your head." Clara made a face and Ellen couldn't help but smile. "No, I mean proper learning, book learning as well as discussion of ideas, exploration of every facet of the mind."

"It sounds… daunting," Ellen said. She thought of her years at the one-room schoolhouses in Seaton and on Amherst Island, and then her single year of nurse's training. She didn't think she'd had anything like the kind of education Clara Spence was talking about.

"Daunting? Yes. And so very exciting." Clara's eyes lit up and Ellen found her enthusiasm infectious. She couldn't help but feel a tug of interest at the thought of being part of such an interesting community.

"I have no experience of teaching art," she confessed, and Clara raised her eyebrows.

"You were offered a position at the Glasgow School of Art before the war?"

"Yes, but I never took it up."

"And you have been tutoring students back in Ontario? Elvira mentioned the holiday she went on."

"Yes, but that's hardly…" Ellen let out a little, embarrassed laugh. "I haven't been to university or even high school, Miss Spence. I went to a one-room school until I was sixteen, and I attended nursing school in Kingston when I was eighteen. But I am hardly an academic. Far from it."

"You are an artist," Clara said. "That is what we are looking for."

"Yes, but…" Ellen shook her head.

"What are you afraid of, Ellen?" Elvira interjected. "If Miss Spence is confident in your capabilities, then so should you be."

Was she afraid? Was that what this was about? She thought of Lucas, who would have told her something similar. He'd want her to grab such an opportunity with both hands… wouldn't he? Why did that thought make her feel so unsettled?

"I must think on it," she said, and both Clara and Elvira hastened to reassure her that was indeed a wise course of action.

"You're very quiet, Ellen," Elvira remarked as they headed back across the city to the Frampton mansion.

"I am feeling a bit overwhelmed by this sudden opportunity," Ellen admitted. "I never dreamed such a thing could happen."

"Isn't it thrilling?"

Elvira looked so pleased that Ellen felt a flash of guilt that she was not tripping over herself with gratitude. "Thank you, Elvira," she said, laying her hand on the older woman's arm. "You've been so very kind, in so many ways. I really cannot thank you enough."

"Thank me by taking the position," Elvira said lightly, and Ellen merely smiled. She was not ready to make any commitments just yet.

As they came into the house, Elvira glanced through the post and then slit open an envelope with a silver letter knife.

"Look, Ellen," she exclaimed, waving the single sheet in excitement. "Your sketches are going to be exhibited at the gallery in October."

"Oh my goodness…" Ellen had not really expected the possibility of an exhibition to become reality. "I don't know what to say…"

"It's all happening, isn't it?" Elvira said happily as she showed Ellen the letter. "A position as a teacher… an exhibition at a gallery… isn't it obvious, Ellen? Your life is here now."

CHAPTER TWENTY-FIVE

"A penny for your thoughts."

Ellen turned to smile at Will, although she could tell from the look on his face that he wasn't convinced by her attempt at good humor.

"How about a nickel, then?" he asked lightly as they strolled through Central Park. The heat had broken and the day was bright and clear, with an autumnal crispness to it. "Or, I'll tell you what, I'll give you a whole dollar." He pulled a crisp one-dollar bill from his wallet and Ellen laughed and shook her head.

"I'll give them to you for free, Will. The truth is, I need to make an important decision and I feel very conflicted about it." Just confessing that much had her stomach clenching with anxiety.

It had been three days since Elvira Frampton and Clara Spence had shocked her with the unexpected proposal that she become Mistress of Art at the school, a permanent full-time post, and live in New York City. With the promise of an exhibition as well, it seemed as if her life in New York was lining up perfectly. So why did she feel so torn?

Ellen had thought of little else since the proposal had been put to her, and yet three days on she felt no nearer a decision than she had been in Clara Spence's study.

"I think I can guess what this important decision is," Will said. They were strolling through Central Park, along the terrace by the Fountain of the Angel of Bethesda, one of the first pieces of artwork created by a woman in the park. It was a splendid sight, with a wide terrace in front of the imposing statue with her beatific face and outstretched wings in the middle of the fountain, and a stone staircase leading up to the street above, where motorcars trundled by.

"Can you?" Ellen looked at him in surprise. "Who has been telling tales about me now, then?"

"New York can seem like a very small place sometimes. I heard from a friend of a friend of my mother's that Miss Spence is looking for a new teacher of art. I imagine that might be you?" A teasing smile curved his lips as he eyed her speculatively.

"It really is a small place." Ellen shook her head as she gave a wry laugh. "I can't have any secrets, can I?"

"Do you want to have them from me?" A serious note crept into his voice that had Ellen looking away. She and Will had only been friends for a few weeks, but it had sprung up with surprising intensity, perhaps based on their shared experiences of the war. More recently, she had begun to wonder if his feelings ran deeper—and, in truth, she wasn't sure whether she wanted them to or not. She'd assumed at the beginning that she held no romantic affection for him, but now, as the shimmering possibility of a life in New York stretched before her, she wondered if her feelings for Will could change—and grow.

There was so much she wasn't sure of, so many torturous what-ifs in her mind, about living one sort of life or a very different one. How could she possibly decide?

"Since it seems I don't, I might as well tell you all of it," Ellen said, sidestepping his rather intimate question. "Miss Spence has indeed offered me the position, and my friend Mrs. Frampton has offered me lodgings at her house, or if I prefer, she can help me to find my own apartment." Ellen shook her head, torn between exasperation and a flickering excitement—her own apartment in New York! She pictured herself teaching pupils, going to art exhibitions or the theater, living the life of a young cosmopolitan woman. A flapper, even! It seemed absurd, and yet also exciting. "She's also arranged for an exhibition of my sketches here in the city, in October."

"Ellen, that's wonderful!" Smiling with buoyant, boyish enthusiasm, Will briefly caught her hands in his. "Aren't you thrilled?"

"I should be, shouldn't I?" Ellen stared at him rather despairingly as she slipped her hands from his. On the one hand, it felt as if she were being given everything she'd ever wanted on a shining silver platter… and on the other, she felt like Eve, about to take that first, juicy bite of the destructive apple. How could she turn her back on the McCaffertys, the Lymans, her beloved island, all of it, and pursue her own life here in the city? It felt wrong at the most fundamental level of her being, and yet she knew she was tempted, and Will saw it in her face.

"To be honest, Ellen, I don't really see the conflict." He thrust his hands into his pockets and gave her a smile touched by wry whimsy. "Why would you turn down such a superlative offer? A full-time position, a place to live, and opportunities to showcase your artwork. Not to mention the city's most eligible bachelor to escort you to whatever function you chose." He grinned to show he was joking, although Ellen wasn't entirely sure he was. "What's really holding you back?" he asked more seriously.

"Amherst Island is my *home,*" Ellen answered, a throb of emotion pulsing in her voice. "I moved there when I was thirteen years old, nearly an orphan, and the McCaffertys welcomed me like one of their own. It's the only place I've ever felt completely accepted and safe." And yet she hadn't felt either of those more recently… but that was her own doubt and insecurity, not because she wasn't. Still, it made her wonder.

"Does living in New York change any of that?" Will asked with a shrug.

"No, I suppose it doesn't," Ellen answered slowly, "but I don't want to simply abandon them."

"Fair enough, but what would really keep you on the island?" He cocked his head, his gaze sweeping over her with slow and thorough assessment. "You said yourself there is little work, and the McCaffertys are struggling on their farm as it is. Can you really see yourself there in the long term, Ellen, past the next few months or years, struggling to make ends meet and offering painting holidays to bored housewives?"

Ellen looked away, not wanting to answer his question. She didn't even want to think about the answer, and yet it was already written on her heart. She'd returned to the island, emotionally battered after the war, and the comfort and familiarity, the love and affection of the McCaffertys, had soothed and restored her.

But she'd known all along, if she'd only been willing to face it, that it wasn't a permanent solution, just as the art holidays they'd been offering weren't. The holidays could tide them over for a while, but Ellen had a sure and leaden feeling that they wouldn't be able to make Jasper Lane a going concern in the long run. She sighed heavily.

"Ellen." Gently, Will took her by the shoulders. "What is it you're afraid of, really?"

She resisted the urge to either wrench away from him or melt in his embrace. "I'm not *afraid*."

"Then what is keeping you on that island? If it's not work and it's not a house or home, then it must be a person." A light came into his eyes, followed by a shadow. "Is it a man?"

"There's no one like that, Will." Ellen stepped back from him and he dropped his hands. "There hasn't been for a long time."

"Are you sure about that?"

Was she? In her mind's eye, she first pictured Jed, his face so often cast in sullen lines. He was married to Louisa, even if they were estranged. No matter what feelings still remained on her part, she knew Jed couldn't ever be for her. She kept telling herself that, and yet she remembered the way he'd smiled at her in the kitchen, and every emotion inside her became impossibly tangled.

Did she still love Jed, or did she just yearn for the attention and admiration from him that she hadn't received, all those years ago? She really didn't know.

"Your silence tells me everything I need to know," Will said quietly. "Whether you've admitted it to yourself or not."

"There's nothing to admit, Will—" Yet for some reason then, she found herself thinking not of Jed, but Lucas. Lucas, with his kind eyes and wry smile, his gentleness and his constancy. *Lucas...*

"There is someone," Will stated flatly. "I wonder if even you know who it is."

Will's words reverberated through Ellen for several days as she continued to wrestle with the question of whether to stay or to go. *I wonder if even you know who it is.* Her mind kept skirting around the remark, skating nearer and then darting away. She realized she didn't want to think too closely as to what—or whom—he could have meant, and she didn't even know why. What *was* she afraid of, for surely it was something?

And then it came to her as she stood on the edge of another ballroom, doing her best to be invisible. The city's social season was starting in earnest after an empty August, and Elvira had insisted Ellen attend.

"You know, you really aren't a wallflower, as much as you try to be," Will remarked as he came to stand next to her, by a potted palm.

"I don't want to be a wallflower," Ellen protested. "I just don't belong here."

"You seem to believe you don't belong anywhere," Will replied. "All things considered."

Ever the orphan. It was the remark Lucas had made, and the truth of it shook Ellen to her core. Was *that* what she was afraid of—the thing she most longed for? Belonging. Somewhere. Anywhere.

"Dance with me?" Will asked, and Ellen nodded, grateful for the distraction. As they took to the floor, he gave her a wry yet serious look. "You've decided, haven't you?"

"I... have," Ellen said slowly, because she hadn't until that moment, and yet she realized she'd known all along, and the realization was a relief.

Will gave a small, sorrowful smile. "I'm not surprised, but I am sorry. We could have had such a fabulous time, Ellen."

"You'll always be a good friend, Will—"

"I think you know I was toying with the idea of more than that," he said lightly, and Ellen smiled, even though her heart was aching.

"You need a proper society wife."

"I think that's exactly what I don't need. But don't worry, my heart isn't broken, at least not all the way through. The truth is, if you decided not to stay, and I was pretty sure you would, I told myself I'd move on as well."

"What?" Ellen stared at him in shock. "Where will you go?"

"I've been offered the chance to finish my studies at Stanford University, out in California. I know I'm a bit old now to be an undergraduate, but I've always fancied living in the land of eternal sunshine, and I reckon I ought to turn my hand to something worthwhile."

"Oh, Will," Ellen exclaimed with genuine pleasure, "I'm so glad for you."

He shrugged. "A man has to do something with his time. But enough about me." He gave her a frank, serious look. "When do you leave?"

"As soon as I can book the train fare." As she said the words, she realized how much she meant them. "I need to go home. But how did you know?"

"I think I always knew," Will answered. "I just didn't want to." He spun her around as he added lightly, "I really could have fallen in love with you, you know."

"But you didn't," Ellen returned unsteadily.

"No, but it was a close-run thing." The music ended and Will returned her to the side of the ballroom, a wry smile touching his lips. "A very close-run thing, my little wallflower," he said softly, and kissed her cheek. "Now we'll both be having adventures, and my own is in more than a small part thanks to you. You've helped me, Ellen. You've made me want to live again, or at least to try. I hope you're a good letter writer."

"I am," Ellen assured him, her voice clogged with tears. She would miss Will terribly, she realized.

"Well, I'll be honest with you," Will said. "I'm not. But I'll try, Ellen." He paused, his warm gaze resting on her face. "I'll try," he said again, and she knew he meant more than writing letters, just as she knew this was farewell, and as poignantly bittersweet as that felt, a new determination had taken hold of her. She was going home, where she belonged.

CHAPTER TWENTY-SIX

Three days later, Ellen was packing her bags to return to Amherst Island. Elvira Frampton had begged her to stay on even just a few more weeks, but Ellen was resolute.

"I need to go home, Elvira. As much as I've loved it here, I need to go back to the island. That's where I belong. It always has been."

"But you haven't turned down Miss Spence's offer?" Elvira exclaimed with unaccustomed desperation. "I do think it would be such a perfect fit for you, Ellen."

"I haven't turned it down," Ellen answered with a small smile. Clara Spence hadn't let her. She'd encouraged Ellen to return to the island for a week or two, and then tell her.

"The term doesn't begin for another few weeks, and I have yet to find any suitable candidates for the position." Clara had given her a smile full of understanding when Ellen had stopped by the school to give her decision in person. "Sometimes you need to return home to realize what you really want."

Ellen could only hope that was true. At the moment, with her bags packed and her heart twisting within her, her feelings remained in a positive ferment. She still had no true idea of what she wanted... what—or whom—she *dared* to want. She just hoped she would realize it when she returned to the island.

"You will come back," Elvira said fiercely, sniffing as she pulled Ellen into a tight embrace. "I've so enjoyed having you here, and you must know how much is waiting for you here." She pulled back to give Ellen a look full of meaning. "I am not the only one who will miss you."

Ellen knew Elvira was referring, none too subtly, to Will, and the memory of his farewell brought a lump to her throat. She hoped he found all he was looking for in California, and she rather thought he would.

That lump was still lodged firmly there as she said her goodbyes to the Framptons and climbed into the back seat of the Pierce-Arrow that would take her to Grand Central Station. She'd become so used to the sights and sounds and even the smells of the city, the whole lively, chaotic blur of it, and as much as she ached for the island's peaceful quiet, she knew she'd miss New York's energized, frenetic life. Yet she was ready to return, and see if the island truly was the home she believed it to be.

The hours slipped by on the train, and it was late afternoon when Ellen stepped onto the platform at Ogdensburg, and nearly dusk by the time she reached the ferry landing for the island. The sight of the familiar blue-green waters of Lake Ontario lapping against the rocky shore, the island a green smudge in the distance, nearly brought tears to her eyes. The air smelled fresh and sun-warmed, touched with the sharp tang of cedar, so different from the city's smog-choked fumes. The fading sunlight poured syrup over everything, soaking the world in golden light.

Relief filled her heart, as well as excitement to finally be returning to the place—and maybe even the person—where she belonged.

"Ellen?"

Ellen stiffened at the sound of the strangely familiar voice, and then slowly she turned, her heart turning over in shock. On the dock, waiting for the ferry as she was, stood her friend from former years, decked out in the latest fashionable frippery, a jaunty hat perched on her still burnished, chestnut curls, her dropped-waist ankle-skimming dress the very latest in style.

"Louisa?" Ellen said faintly. She could hardly believe her old friend—Jed's wife—was standing there. "What are you doing here?"

Louisa bristled, her thin shoulders stiffening. "Why shouldn't I be here?"

"I'm sorry, I didn't mean it like that." Ellen's mind was a jumble of mixed emotions; she was afraid to untangle them and realize what they were. "It's only, I didn't expect you. I thought…" But she realized she didn't want to say what she had thought.

"What are *you* doing here?" Louisa challenged. "The last I heard, you were living in Glasgow."

Somehow that stung, even though Ellen knew it shouldn't. Had no one on the island told Louisa of her whereabouts, or had she not been in communication with anyone? Or was it that Louisa was simply being spiteful, pretending not to know where she'd been all these years, that no one had cared enough to tell her? Ellen knew from childhood experience how temperamental Louisa could be… but surely they'd both grown beyond that now. They were nearing thirty, for heaven's sake. It was high time to put such childish notions aside.

"I was in New York City, visiting friends."

"Oh? I was in New York, for a little while." Louisa drew her light summer coat around her, one hand clutching at her throat. Now that Ellen was looking at her properly, she saw how thin her old friend had grown, and she noted the lines that ravaged her face, deepening from nose to mouth. Her eyes looked hard. Louisa was twenty-eight, the same age as she was, but she looked older.

"Louisa, I'm so glad to see you," Ellen said, and impulsively she put her arms around her.

Louisa stiffened, and then hesitantly returned the embrace.

"Are you?" she said with a sniff. "I fear you might be the only one."

"Does—does Jed know you're coming?"

Louisa shook her head, stepping back from Ellen's embrace. "No. I wrote ever so many letters, but I couldn't work up the courage to send even one." Her mouth tightened, her face taking on an unhappy, pinched look, and Ellen squeezed her hand.

"Oh, Louisa."

"I'm afraid everyone must hate me, for running away," Louisa admitted, her voice choking. "But the truth is, Ellen, I didn't know what else to do."

"It must have been so very hard." Looking at her now, seeming so desolate and miserable, Ellen could only feel sympathy for Louisa. "I was so sorry to hear about your little boy, Thomas."

"He was such a good boy…" Louisa averted her head, blinking rapidly. "So full of joy, even though his health was always frail. I know it was a while ago now, but it still feels fresh. I suppose it always will."

"I imagine it is a grief you will bear your whole life."

"Yes." Louisa's shoulders straightened and she nodded towards the ferry. "It's coming now."

Neither of them spoke as the tugboat chugged towards the shore under a darkening sky. Ellen's mind whirled. If Jed didn't know Louisa was coming… was she hoping to reconcile with him? Would Jed welcome his wayward wife? Her mind spun with the possibilities.

The silence stretched between them as they boarded the ferry, the only two passengers in the twilight, the air possessing a decidedly autumnal chill. Jonah eyed Louisa speculatively but said nothing, an unusual silence from a man known for speaking his mind. Although it had been hot in New York, Ellen was glad she'd worn her coat now they were further north and coming ever closer to her heart's home.

The dark green blur of Amherst Island came steadily closer, and with each passing moment, Ellen saw Louisa become more and more tense, her knuckles white as she clutched her handbag, a leather design that looked far fancier than anything seen on the island. Louisa's face was pale, her lips bloodless beneath the bright slick of crimson lipstick she was biting off in her anxiety.

A shaft of sympathy, and even pity, pierced Ellen once more and she reached for Louisa's hand. "Louisa, I'm glad you're back. Truly."

Louisa's eyes narrowed speculatively—she'd long ago guessed how Ellen had once been in love with Jed—and then she gave a regal nod. "Thank you," she said simply.

Neither of them said anything more until the boat reached the shore.

No one was waiting at Stella for either of them, although Ellen had sent a letter several days ago with news of her return. She suspected it had yet to reach the island, and so she suggested they walk, leaving their cases at the little office for Andrew to pick up later.

It wasn't so far, and she had a sudden hankering to walk all the way back to Jasper Lane, just as she'd done when she'd returned here in June, after the war, a true journey down memory's lane. Now autumn was in the offing, a chill in the air; the birches were tinged with yellow, the maples with scarlet. The seasons were turning yet again, on and on, inexorable, towards eternity.

"Walk?" Louisa wrinkled her nose, reminding Ellen of when they'd been children, and Louisa had been accused by more than one islander of putting on airs. "It's a bit far, don't you think?"

"I'm not sure what else we can do. There's no telephone, after all."

"I suppose you're right." Louisa sighed and wedged her case under the old weathered bench of the ferry office. "Jed can come and collect it, if he's of a mind to. Perhaps he won't be. I might be back on that ferry sooner than I can blink."

"Don't you think he'll be glad to see you?" Ellen asked cautiously as they set down the dirt road that led towards Jasper Lane, with the Lymans' farm beyond. Tumbled stone walls lined the road, the trees now just blurred shapes in the oncoming darkness. The sky was violet, the night full of shadows. A whippoorwill called once, mournful and insistent.

"I have no idea." Louisa lifted her chin and quickened her stride. "We haven't exchanged so much as a letter since Thomas died. Not a word since we put him in the ground." Her face crumpled for a second before she smoothed her expression out. "I should have written, I know."

"Oh, Louisa."

"I know it's mostly my fault that we are where we are," Louisa continued flatly. "I know I shouldn't have left all those years ago, but I couldn't stand being on this island without Jed. No one ever took to me, you know, and while it might have been partly my fault, it was theirs, as well. I was never good enough for this island, as much as everyone believed I thought they weren't good enough for me." She paused, her lips trembling before she pressed them together. "I love Jed, Ellen. I always have. But sometimes I wonder if love is enough."

"It can be," Ellen urged her, "if you choose for it to be, especially when life is hard."

"You warned me it would be hard," Louisa reminded her with a bitter little smile. "You were right. I suppose that makes you happy."

"No, of course it doesn't." Ellen shook her head, horrified that Louisa would think such a thing, even for a moment. "My heart has broken for the both of you, Louisa—"

"Has it?" Louisa shot her a darkly suspicious look, even as sorrow swamped her eyes. "I imagine, Ellen, that you might have been tempted to offer Jed some comfort in his loneliness."

Ellen's cheeks burned at such a suggestion, and for a moment she couldn't speak. It was true, she'd felt a shaft of longing for the man she'd once been in love with, but she'd never crossed the threshold of propriety. She'd made sure of that.

"I'm sorry," Louisa said quietly. "That was unkind."

"I've tried to be a good friend to Jed," Ellen said with dignity. "For I know he's needed it."

Louisa nodded slowly. "A good friend, yes. That he's needed. But does he still want a wife? We shall see."

"You and Jed have had your fair share of sorrows, Louisa," Ellen insisted, "but surely things can be different now. If you both want to try?"

"If he does," Louisa answered rather grimly.

By the time they reached Jasper Lane, the lights of the farm-house flickering in the distance, Ellen was aching with exhaustion and also with relief. The tension of walking side by side with Louisa had become nearly unbearable, and she was more glad than she could have ever said to start up the rutted track, the oak and maple trees arching above, towards the welcome glow of the farmhouse.

"Come on, Louisa," she urged as her friend faltered at the gate. "Come and sit down and refresh yourself before you head back to the—back home."

After a tiny pause, Louisa nodded, and they both started up the lane, stumbling a bit in the dark, for the only light besides those from the farmhouse came from a high, thin sliver of moon as it slid out from under a bank of cloud.

"Hello?" Ellen called as she opened the front door. The hallway was empty, and she heard the murmur of voices from the kitchen, suddenly muted, and then the clatter and scrape of chairs being pushed back.

"*Ellen!*" Rose came around the corner, her mouth upturned into a wide, disbelieving smile. "You're back! You didn't even send a telegram or a letter!"

"I did send a letter, but it must not have arrived. I was in such a hurry to get home—"

Rose's eyes widened as she caught sight of Louisa, standing behind Ellen as if she was of half a mind to bolt back out the door. "Louisa. Oh, my child, you've finally come home."

Rose put her arms around the pair of them, and Ellen breathed in the warm, comforting, motherly smell of her with a pang of love and longing. She was so glad to be there that the tears she'd been holding back for so long finally fell, and when she turned to look at Louisa, she saw her friend was weeping as well. They were home, indeed. At last.

The next morning, drinking coffee on the front porch with Rose, Ellen felt almost entirely happy, even though her future remained just as—if not more—uncertain. Somehow she could live with that uncertainty, settled in herself in a way she hadn't been in a long time.

Last night, Andrew had hitched the horses to the wagon and driven Louisa to the Lyman farm; Ellen had no idea what her reception had been, but she hoped Jed had welcomed her.

Now, a cat in her lap and a cup of coffee cradled between her hands, she listened as Rose filled her in on all the island gossip.

"The Hammonds have had another baby—that's seven, would you believe! A lot of mouths to feed in these times, but it's a bonny little boy. And, of course, all the tongues are wagging about Caro and Jack Wilson! But the gossips will shut their mouths soon enough, I warrant. Caro is determined, and you know what she's like when she gets an idea into her head."

"I do," Ellen answered with a smile. Rose had told her last night that Caro was living at the Wilson homestead with the three children, while Jack boarded at a house in Stella until the wedding in just two weeks' time. "Do you think she'll be happy, Aunt Rose?"

"I do," Rose said after a moment. "She's always wanted a family of her own, and Caro needs people to need her. Besides," she added, her voice quiet, "Jack Wilson is a good and decent man. He's had a hard time of it, on account of his injury, but if people can look past it, they'll see a fine man indeed."

"I'm glad to hear it."

"So much is changing," Rose said with a sigh. Her gaze grew distant as she looked down the lane, almost as if waiting for someone to walk down its familiar path. "Gracie is off to Queen's in just a few weeks, and Sarah already back to teaching. And as for Andrew…"

"What about Andrew?" Andrew was just shy of seventeen and had never had much of a hankering for education. He'd always seemed happiest on the farm.

"You'd never believe it, but he's talking about finding work out west, in Alberta. Maybe even settling there on his own homestead, when he's earned enough."

"What!" Ellen stared at her aunt in shock. "He isn't, surely…?"

Rose shrugged her shoulders. "Why shouldn't he? Andrew's waited out the war, too young to do anything but watch, and now he wants to find his own way, his own adventure. Besides, there's more opportunity out west for a young man like him. I can't blame him."

"But you need his help here on the farm."

Rose didn't reply and Ellen felt a tightness start in her chest. "Aunt Rose…"

"I didn't want to tell you like this, Ellen, but I'm planning on selling Jasper Lane. I had an offer from the Glenns on the other side of the island…" Ellen knew of them, one of the island's more prosperous families, with a large holding of their own. "They're expanding and Arthur's son, Alexander, wants his own place. They've always liked the view here at Jasper Lane."

Ellen opened her mouth but found she had no words. Somehow she felt completely shocked and utterly unsurprised at the same time.

Aunt Rose sniffed and sighed. "I wish it could be otherwise, Ellen, but the truth is, I can't manage this place on my own, and I can't tie Andrew or anyone else to it. I thought Caro and Jack might want it, but Jack wants to make a go of his brother's place, and he's too proud to accept what he thinks amounts to charity. As for Peter…" Another shuddery sigh. "He's made so much progress, but in his last letter he's said he hopes to find office work in Toronto, and that will be better for him, I think, to be surrounded by people, with help from the doctors when he needs it. The world is moving on, in so many ways."

"But…" Ellen didn't even know what or how to protest. It was just that she simply couldn't imagine life without Jasper Lane. Even when she'd been far away, whether in Scotland, Vermont, or France, she'd known the farmhouse was here waiting for her, her family with open arms. It was why she'd come back from New York. *Wasn't it?*

Rose touched her arm lightly. "I know you wanted to make a go of the holidaymaking idea, and for a little while I thought we could. But it will never be quite enough, will it, Ellen? And the truth is, I don't want to tie you here, either."

"You wouldn't be—"

"Elvira Frampton wrote me about the offer of a teaching position in New York," Rose said gently and Ellen couldn't keep from letting out a little cry of surprised distress.

"Is that why—"

"No, of course not. But it made me see how selfish I've been, wanting you here. We all need to come home, Ellen, especially when we've been battered by life's stormy seas. But we all need to leave that home at some point too, and stretch our fragile wings again. I think it's time for you to do that."

Ellen blinked rapidly, not wanting to surrender to the threat of tears yet again. "But where will you go, Aunt Rose?"

"I'm going to settle in Hamilton. There will be enough from the sale of the farmhouse to buy a little place, and Dyle has a cousin there. I haven't seen her in decades, it's true, but she's still family. Besides, it's near enough Toronto that I can visit Peter. There should be room for Sarah and Gracie, as well, when they're of a mind to visit. And you too, Ellen, of course."

Ellen nodded, although she could hardly imagine it. Everything truly was changing.

"Will you take the position in New York?" Rose asked.

"I—I don't know. When I left New York, I didn't think I was going to. I wanted to come home. I thought I'd be able to make up my mind better here."

"And have you?"

Ellen shook her head. She still had so much to think about, to decide, to risk. Her mind and heart were both spinning. "I'm just not sure," she said. "But I understand that this is the right thing for you to do, Aunt Rose. Of course I do. I'll miss Jasper Lane, so much, but I understand why you feel you must sell it. Truly."

Rose smiled, tears sparkling in her eyes as she reached for Ellen's hand. "You're a good lass, Ellen Copley."

Yet the ache of loss remained fresh as Ellen walked over to the Lymans' farm three days later. Autumn was truly on the wing, the copse between the properties a blaze of russet and gold.

Yesterday, Ellen had visited Caro and seen her with her fiancé and newfound family, and any fears she'd had that Caro might be rushing headlong into something unwise had been put firmly to rest. She'd never seen her cousin so happy, and Jack positively beamed, a man hardly able to believe the kindness Providence had shown him. They already had plans to expand the Wilson homestead, and Caro couldn't wait to spruce up the little farmhouse. The children, too, seemed livelier and more settled, although Ellen knew they still had to miss their mother. Even so, the family that had been created from disparate and jumbled pieces looked to be a happy one.

"Mum has given me two of her quilts, and Andrew offered to paint the kitchen. Goodness knows it needs it! I'm going to dig up the garden, as well, so next summer we'll have a full vegetable patch." Impulsively, Caro had clasped Ellen's hand. "I'm so happy, Ellen, happier than I ever dared to dream I'd be."

"I'm so glad," Ellen said, meaning it. There was no twinge of envy for Caro being settled in life while she was not; her cousin had worked too hard and fought too fiercely for those she loved for Ellen not to be truly happy on her account.

Now, as she walked up to the farmhouse, Ellen wondered what reception she would get at the Lymans'—and what reception Louisa had received from her husband upon her return. She'd been giving them space these last few days, but she hoped, for both their sakes, that they had had a joyful reunion.

The answer was clear enough as she came into the farmyard and saw Louisa standing on the front porch, one hand shading her eyes as she looked to see who her visitor was. A moment later, Jed joined her, and slipped his good arm around his wife's waist, the gesture awkward yet heartfelt. Ellen's heart seemed to lift with joy and twist with an old sorrow at the same time.

She smiled and called out her greeting.

"It's good to see you, Ellen," Louisa said, and Jed gave her one of his old, teasing smiles.

"Back from the big city, it seems, and with no fancy airs?"

"None that I can see." Ellen laughed, and that flash of longing flickered away to nothing as she saw how happy her two friends were. The feelings that had been tangled up inside suddenly unknotted, as easily as a string. Her feelings for Jed, Ellen realized, had been nothing but the ghostly remnants of something long in the past. "It's good to see you both," she said meaningfully.

Louisa blushed and Jed nodded. "We had a lot to talk about these last few days, but I think it's finally settled."

"Settled…?"

Jed straightened, his expression turning resolute. "We're leaving the island. Farming's not the best work for me anymore," he explained with a nod to the empty sleeve pinned to his shoulder, "and Louisa's father has a job for me in the bank in Seaton. I aim to take it, and we'll settle outside the town, so we'll still have a little bit of land."

"I'm going to garden," Louisa said with a self-conscious smile. "Do you know, I missed it, when I went back to Seaton?"

"You're going to work in the bank…" Ellen repeated dazedly. For the second time that day, she was stunned. "But…"

"You might not think me much of one for learning, but I did the farm accounts and I think I'll be able to manage well enough. I asked a lot of Louisa coming here," Jed explained stoutly. "It's time I gave just as much, and the truth is, I want to. It's time to move on."

"But what will happen to the farm? Your father can't run it on his own?"

Before Jed spoke, Ellen knew what was coming. "He's selling up," Jed said, and a heaviness settled in her heart. Everyone was leaving her beloved island, just when she'd come back. How could it be so? "To the Glenns."

"You know they're buying Jasper Lane?"

Jed nodded soberly. "Rose told me. They're going to combine the two properties. It's what's happening across all of Canada, and the States, as well. Bigger farms, fewer farmers. It's the way of things now, for better or worse. We've made our peace with it."

And so she would have to, as well. "And Lucas…?" Ellen asked after a moment, doing her best to keep her voice neutral. "He doesn't want to come back here, I suppose, and run things?"

"Lucas belongs in Toronto," Jed said firmly. "He always has. Although we've appreciated his help."

Ellen's startled gaze flew to his. "His help…?"

"Lucas has been helping with the farm," Jed explained gruffly, not quite looking at her. "Sending half his paycheck home, at least, sometimes more. We couldn't have managed without it, I'm ashamed to say, even though I'm grateful. Powerfully grateful."

Ellen fell silent at this news. In the past, she'd as good as accused Lucas of shirking his duty to his family's farm. It shamed her to realize he hadn't been. *Of course he hadn't been.* If she knew him at all, she should have known that, absolutely. In that moment, she realized something else; Lucas had to have been the anonymous donor who paid for Peter's treatment. How could she have ever doubted him for so much as a second? How could she have not realized, when he had always been so unfailingly generous with his time, his attention, his care?

"So he will stay in Toronto, then?" she asked.

"As far as I know. He's coming back to the island, though, to see Louisa and help settle things with the farm. In fact, he should be here by tomorrow."

"Tomorrow," Ellen repeated slowly. "It will be good to see him."

Louisa's eyes narrowed in an all too familiar way, as a small smile curved her lips. "Will it?" she said, and Ellen chose not to reply.

CHAPTER TWENTY-SEVEN

Ellen walked slowly back to Jasper Lane, savoring the autumnal sunshine even as her heart felt both heavy and light, dragging from the sorrowful weight of all the news she'd heard, and at the same time cut from its moorings, free at last, able to soar... if only she could finally dare to spread her wings.

What would her life look like without her beloved island in it? Where would she go? She had come back to the island—to the place she felt she belonged—thinking she would stay here, or at least hoping she would, or perhaps just hoping she would know what her next steps should be.

She knew now they couldn't be on the island, and even as she mourned that loss, she accepted its rightness. Amherst Island had been her safe harbor when she'd needed it, but she had always known, on some level, that she couldn't stay there forever. So where would she go?

Return to Glasgow, where her little house waited for her, along with her friends Ruby and Dougie? She could make a life for herself there, perhaps offer private art lessons, earn enough to get by if she managed the dwindling remains of her savings. Perhaps she'd still be able to take up the offered position at the Glasgow School of Art. Or she could move to New York, and take up the life there that seemed so dazzling and new. She already had friends—the Framptons, *Will...* would he stay in New York, if she returned? And yet she knew she didn't want him to. Just as she knew New York was not the place for her, despite its allure, and neither was Glasgow.

Neither place gave her that soul-deep satisfaction she craved, the true and utter sense of belonging she'd once thought the island gave her but now knew would not, and never could.

So where was it? More importantly, *who* was it? She'd begun to realize, if only dimly, that belonging didn't have to be a place, but could be a person. The only person.

Ellen paused by the pond where she'd spent so many happy childhood days, playing and sketching. The trees drooping over it were yellow-leaved, and a few had already fallen onto the surface of the pond, which was murky after the summer's rains. The season was turning once again, as those winds of change blew without mercy or warning. Where would she go? Where would she finally *stay?* She had hope at last, the weariness of war shed for something newer and deeper—if only she could dare. *Dream.*

"Hello, Ellen."

Ellen stilled and then slowly turned as a wonderfully familiar figure emerged from the woods on the far side of the pond that served as the boundary between the Lyman and McCafferty farms, almost as if she'd conjured him from her own imagination, the secret longings of her own heart.

"*Lucas.*" His name sprang to her lips, surprise and delight audible in her voice as he walked towards her. "Jed and Louisa said you weren't coming until tomorrow."

"I decided to come a day early. There's so much work to be done. I stopped by Jasper Lane, and Rose told me you'd gone to see Jed and Louisa. I thought I'd find you here. How are they?"

"They're doing well. They're going to move to Seaton. But you must know that already—"

"Yes, Jed told me, when he wrote. I'm glad for them both." He crossed the clearing to stand in front of her, his hat in his hands, an easy smile on his dear, familiar face. How well she knew it—the glinting blue eyes, the sandy hair, the whimsical smile, the wry yet serious look, the affection she'd taken for granted and yet depended on. Utterly.

Lucas had been her best friend and stalwart companion for so much of her life. It was in this very spot where she'd first shown him her sketches, and he'd encouraged her to follow her dreams. The trouble was, she'd always been so scared to, just as he'd said.

And now?

"You know about Jasper Lane?" she asked and Lucas nodded. "Rose wrote Peter, who told me."

"And you must know about your place as well…?"

"Yes, I'm helping with the contract of sale." Lucas smiled sadly. "Dad was ready to leave, in the end."

"Jed told me that you'd been helping with things," Ellen said stiltedly. "Sending money. Why didn't you tell me?"

Lucas smiled ruefully. "It felt like boasting, to say as much, and the truth was, Ellen, I wanted you to believe the best of me. I always have."

"Oh, Lucas…" She bit her lip. "I should have done. I realized that as soon as Jed told me. I should have known all along… and Peter, as well. You paid for his treatment, didn't you?"

He nodded, and she shook her head in regret.

"I'm sorry for doubting you, even for a moment. I never should have."

He shook his head, a smile still in his eyes. "It's in the past now. We don't need to revisit old hurts."

But that was exactly what Ellen wanted to do… and bind them up again. The certainty of her conviction left her nearly breathless, and yet also wanting to smile, to laugh, with the sureness of her own feelings. After years of pretending otherwise, of denying the truth of her own heart, she finally realized what she should have known all along. She loved him. Perhaps she'd always loved him. But what if Lucas didn't feel the same way? After all these years…

Lucas cocked his head, his gaze sweeping over her. "Will you return to New York, to take up the position at the girls' school?"

"You know about everything, it seems!" Ellen returned with a smile.

"Rose mentioned you'd been offered a position teaching art. It sounds perfect. I'm so happy for you, Ellen."

Ellen nodded, her mouth drying. Her heart hammering. She knew Lucas meant what he said, and yet… Now was the time to speak. To dare. So much of her life had been dictated by fear—fear of failure, of being hurt, of being alone. She'd hung back, quiet and scared, the determined wallflower, just as Will had said, rather than risk her heart—whether it had been as a tangle-haired orphan in Vermont, or a shy, dreaming artist in Scotland. But now, finally, she wanted to risk her heart, risk everything, in the biggest and best way possible. She needed to… for her sake, as well as for Lucas's.

"I've thought about taking the position in New York," she admitted, her voice little more than a thready rasp. "It does seem perfect, and in truth I didn't know why I was resisting so much. I decided to return to the island. I felt I could think more clearly here."

"And can you?"

"Yes—of course, it's helped that Rose has told me about selling Jasper Lane. That makes thing easier, in a way." As much as she wanted to declare her heart, fear kept her skirting the issue, even now.

"So you will take the position." For a second, Lucas's warm smile faltered, the sparkle in his eyes dimming, and that was enough to embolden Ellen further.

"No, I won't. That is, I don't want to."

Lucas frowned. "Why not?"

"Because there's one thing holding me back." Ellen's heart was hammering, a tremble in her voice as she looked at him. "Or rather, I should say, one person."

"One person?" Lucas's gaze swept her face, looking for answers, even as he did his best to keep his expression neutral. "Who might that be?"

"You."

The look of astonishment on his face was almost laughable, except she was so very nervous. Risking things—this much—was *hard*.

"Ellen, I've always encouraged you to follow your—"

"No, I don't mean that." Ellen took a deep breath, and then a step closer to him. "Although maybe I do. I am following my dreams, Lucas, and my dreams are here with you. Do you remember, all those years ago, back at Queen's, when you asked me if I could... care for you... in time?"

Lucas went completely still, his expression of astonishment turning to one of wary, focused alertness. "Yes," he said quietly. "I remember it very well."

"And then, during the war... when you saw me at Royaumont... you said you still cared for me then."

"I did."

"I've come to realize..." Ellen paused, her face fiery, her heart beating like a drum, "over the last few weeks and months... that I do care for you. That I've always cared for you, even if I didn't realize it. Even if I took your feelings for granted, while I didn't recognize my own."

"But I thought..." He lapsed into silence, and Ellen knew what he was thinking. *Jed*.

She shook her head. "I've been so tangled in my own thoughts," she confessed. "And I didn't know my own heart. But who was it who was always there for me, Lucas? Who did I share my drawings, my secret self with, and who was always patient and kind and listening?"

"Yes, but..." Lucas swallowed. "Those are the actions of a friend, Ellen, and that's what I've been to you. You told me so yourself. Just a friend." A note of old bitterness crept into his voice and he shook his head as if to dismiss it, offering her a rueful smile of apology.

"I was young and childish when I said as much," Ellen told him. "I confused love with infatuation, I can admit that. I'm old and wise enough, I hope, to know the difference now." She licked dry lips as she continued with painful uncertainty, knowing her own heart but not that of the man she knew she loved. "That is, if you still feel the same way after all this time. I wouldn't blame you if you didn't…"

"The same way?" Lucas repeated in disbelief, and Ellen looked at him, full of doubt. Then he let out a laugh of pure joy, ringing clearly as a bell through the still wood. "Ellen Copley, I've never changed, not even for a moment. Not for a *second*. I didn't want to distress you with that knowledge, so I never said anything, but it's the truth. I love you. I've always loved you, from the first moment I saw you, I think. It's only grown deeper with time, and I know I'll never stop."

"And I love you," Ellen said simply, meaning it with every fiber of her being, every ounce of her heart. She loved him. She'd always loved him, even if she hadn't realized it. Even if she hadn't let herself realize it. Saying it out loud was wonderfully freeing, bringing both joy and wonder.

Lucas let out another laugh of incredulous happiness as he shook his head in amazement. "I never thought that this would happen. I never dreamed that you would care for me the way I care for you…"

"You've been such a good friend to me, Lucas. I feel I don't deserve your love, after—"

"Don't say it," Lucas hushed her, his face suffused with tenderness. "I've been a good friend, and now I have the privilege to be so much more." Gently, he took her in his arms, pausing to look down into her eyes as Ellen tilted her face upward, offering her heart, her whole self.

As Lucas softly kissed her, Ellen knew that this, not her beloved island, not dear Jasper Lane, was home. Finally, sweetly, she'd found the place where she would always belong, always be understood and accepted, and it was far more wonderful than she could have ever imagined. Whatever the future held—Toronto, New York, or an even more distant and unknown horizon, she knew she would face it with Lucas, the man she loved, the man she'd always loved, even if her stubborn and contrary heart had insisted otherwise. She was finally home, and it was the sweetest place on earth. Home here, with Lucas, as hand in hand they walked back to Jasper Lane.

A LETTER FROM KATE

I want to say a huge thank you for choosing to read *Return to the Island*. If you did enjoy it, and want to keep up to date with all my latest releases, just sign up at the following link. Your email address will never be shared and you can unsubscribe at any time.

www.bookouture.com/kate-hewitt

Ellen's story has been with me a long time—nearly thirty years—and it's such a joy and privilege to be able to share its final chapter with you. I spent much of my childhood near Amherst Island, in Ontario, and I've always considered it my true heart's home.

I hope you loved *Return to the Island* and if you did, I would be very grateful if you could write a review. I'd love to hear what you think, and it makes such a difference helping new readers to discover one of my books for the first time.

I love hearing from my readers—you can get in touch on my Facebook page, through Goodreads, Twitter, or my website.

Thanks and happy reading,
Kate

f katehewittauthor

💻 www.kate-hewitt.com

🐦 @author_kate

ACKNOWLEDGEMENTS

It's been such a thrill to share this story, which is so dear to my heart, with a new audience. As ever, I am indebted to the wonderful team at Bookouture who work so tirelessly on behalf of all the authors. Thanks go especially to my editor Isobel, who patiently dealt with me working on several books at the same time and occasionally getting a bit confused between them all!! Also many thanks to my copy-editor Jade, who had a particular challenge in dealing with a trilogy that had seen several incarnations and was sometimes caught between the versions. I don't know how you managed to keep track of all the ages of everyone, but thank you!! Thanks also to everyone else at Bookouture who works on my books, in marketing, audio, foreign translations, and in more ways than I even know. You're all amazing!

Thank you also to my Aunt Sally and Uncle Ross, whose cottage on Amherst Island inspired the setting of this story, and to Andrea Cross and the other residents of the island who arranged a lovely visit for me there, and also provided me with archives from their historical society. I am indebted!

I also must give thanks to Becky Wendling, the original Ellen fan (don't hate me for the big change I made to the story!), and to LM Montgomery, whose wonderful heroine Anne Shirley (and Gilbert Blythe!) have given me so much joy and first inspired me to write my own stories.

And lastly, thank you to Cliff, my wonderful husband, and my very own Gilbert! I love you!

Made in the USA
Monee, IL
22 July 2023

39701530R00149